ENEMY
OF THE
RAJ

Alec Marsh was born in Essex in 1975. He graduated from Newcastle University with a first class degree in history. Beginning his career on the *Western Morning News* in Cornwall, he went on to write for titles including the *Daily Telegraph*, *Daily Mail*, *The Times* and *London Evening Standard*. In 2008 he was named an editor of the year by the *British Society of Magazine Editors*. He is now the editor of *Spear's Magazine*, a title focused on luxury lifestyle.

He is married and lives with his family in west London.

Also by Alec Marsh and published by Headline Accent

Rule Britannia

ENEMY
OF THE
RAJ

ALEC MARSH

ACCENT

First published in Great Britain in 2020 by
HEADLINE ACCENT
An imprint of HEADLINE PUBLISHING GROUP

1

Cataloguing in Publication Data is available from the British Library

ISBN 978 1 7861 5804 8

Typeset in 10.5/13pt Bembo Std by Jouve (UK), Milton Keynes

Printed and bound in Great Britain by Clays Ltd, Elcograf S.p.A.

Headline's policy is to use papers that are natural, renewable and recyclable
products and made from wood grown in well-managed forests and other
controlled sources. The logging and manufacturing processes are expected
to conform to the environmental regulations of the country of origin.

HEADLINE PUBLISHING GROUP
An Hachette UK Company
Carmelite House
50 Victoria Embankment
London EC4Y 0DZ

www.headline.co.uk
www.hachette.co.uk

To Herbert and Douglas

Chapter One

The jungle outside New Delhi, March 1937

For some time now Sir Percival Harris had been turning green. It had come on shortly after dawn as they made the walk of a mile or so from their camp into the jungle. At first in the early light his face exhibited a certain pasty gloss, rather like he'd got a case of sea-sickness going on – despite being five hundred miles from the coast. He hadn't lost his cheer, however. That disappeared when their hunting guides, the *shikaris*, led them through the dense forest to the tiny clearing by a *nullah* or dry river bed, where the afternoon before they had left a goat tethered to a stick, inviting attack by the tiger – and they saw it gone. The blood on the ground and large pug marks indicated a large tiger, as did the signs of the body being dragged away by a powerful creature. That's when Harris's bluster vanished. Then in the improving light Ernest Drabble, his old friend, saw the tinges of green appear beneath the rim of Harris's pith helmet.

Back at the camp, while men were secured from the four surrounding villages to act as beaters, Harris hardly touched his breakfast. Instead he drank three cups of black coffee, and checked his ammunition sockets five or six times, before retiring to his tent to lie on his bunk and stare up at the fabric above his head. Now the poor bastard's face was the colour of gangrene – one that is likely to take off its victim within hours.

Harris was, Drabble mused silently, a man transformed. When

1

just 36 hours before he had been indignantly booming, 'I won't be the first Harris in two centuries not to shoot a tiger!', he now looked like he was going to retreat into a coma of fear. Perhaps it was fair enough.

After a week of nothing – four goats had been left out nightly at various locations across the nearby jungles, which the shikaris and Harris (now armed with A. E. Stewart's *Tiger and Other Game* he considered himself an expert) judged to be perfect for enticing 'Old Stripes' to show himself – suddenly the heavens had opened.

For the tiger prowling the nearby forests was not just any top feline predator; no. As of three days previous it qualified as a man-eater, thanks to some poor, half-lame buffalo-*wallah* who was snatched in broad daylight from the edges of a local village. His partially-eaten remains and mangled crutch were found several hours later. The hysterical witness described the tiger as being very pale – almost ghostlike – and very, *very* large. A thirteen-footer, they said.

What therefore had begun as a private shooting expedition by Harris – a flight of fancy which he somehow regarded as a rite of passage owing to various ancestral shooting trips – was now transformed into a public act. It oughtn't have come as a surprise to him therefore – but it evidently did – when shortly after eleven o'clock, he was roused from his tent and his tortured solitude.

Pulling back the oily canvas flap of his tent, he froze – before him stood a veritable army of volunteers, drawn from the local four villages. They were armed with sticks, clubs, hoes, and axes.

'One hundred and eighty-two beaters, *sahib*,' beamed the local headman. 'Very good.' They stood in a vast circle around the camp, gazing at him like an imperialist hero, delivered of them by Vishnu to rid them of their new scourge.

If they'd fallen prostrate before him, Harris would not have been more surprised. Drabble stifled a grin. To be fair to him, Harris did a passable job of taking it on the chin.

Affecting a military bearing, and accompanied by the shikari, he did a lap inspecting the assemblage, rather like a judge at a village show or a visiting dignitary reviewing the honour guard. He sent the youngest boys and a couple of the more elderly looking men, including one who was clearly lame, home. They would not do as beaters. And then, smartly taking up his rifle, he gave orders for the shikaris, beaters, and assorted other members of the entourage to fall in behind him, and set off purposefully. In the right direction.

For Drabble this was all rather interesting: it permitted Harris to live out various fantasies that underpinned his world view – something they had argued over many times, namely the rights and wrongs of Britain's imperialist policy. But it also trapped him into an even more exposed and more pressurised situation. If he failed to kill the tiger now – or worse, if he winged it and the angry beast careened off and went on a wild killing spree taking out various locals – then Harris's failure wouldn't just be personal, bad enough that that would be with several hundred natives watching. His failure would be letting down the whole imperialist shooting match. Drabble knew that that would be weighing on his friend's shoulders too, as he strode out in front of his volunteer army of helpers. That Harris was by his own admission a hopeless shot, born as he was with two left eyes, didn't help. In this respect the fact that this man-eater was said to be a thirteen-footer was to be welcomed: the bigger the target the better. The truth was that the tiger would need to be the size of an elephant to make a meaningful difference to Harris.

So, with all that going on, it was small wonder that Harris was turning green. As far as Harris was concerned he had the weight of the British Empire on his shoulders – as well as the immediate safety of about two hundred souls in his hands. It was now midday and the shoot was set. Any moment around a hundred of the beaters, who were formed up some six hundred yards off, would start shouting. They would then approach, thrashing at the trees and undergrowth with their sticks in order to wake up the tiger which would be expected to be sleeping in the middle of the day after its feed. It would – so the plan goes – move away from the oncoming noise, and follow the path of least resistance straight into the 'kill-zone', directly in front of the sights of Harris's double-barrelled hunting rifle. If the tiger went in a different direction, either to the left or right, then the remaining seventy men had been arranged safely up trees, in a vast V-formation. Their job was to cough or clap if they saw the tiger coming their way: that was enough usually to make the tiger turn and change course. Eventually, the tiger would be funnelled into the firing zone before Harris's gun.

That was the plan, at least. And a strict instruction was that on the first shot being fired, all beaters must climb trees immediately – in case the tiger was not killed outright and charged in their direction. All things considered, man-eater or not, it would be best if Harris missed the animal altogether, thus sparing them the dangers of having to deal with an injured tiger. The golden rule? Never follow an injured tiger: not unless you wanted to commit suicide.

The day was heating up nicely, too. Drabble, now up a banyan tree, looked over at his friend; Harris lay with his rifle at the ready on a small platform tied about fifteen feet from the ground. The sweat poured from his face and his hands trembled. He wiped them again on his sleeves to dry them. Every now and then Harris pivoted from side to side, staring intently down the sights of his rifle – in the way that his instruction manual had told him. He was imaging the tiger rushing from the jungle. Drabble caught his eye and shot him a thumbs up; Harris nodded in reply and forced a smile.

They waited.

Until the moment it started everyone was under very strict orders to stay absolutely silent – for fear of rousing the tiger prematurely. A breeze rustled the leaves in the trees around him, but the overwhelming sound was the monotonous tonk-tonk of a copperbird somewhere in a tree close by, joined intermittently by the tap-tap-tap of a golden-backed woodpecker. Harris

4

changed position on the wooden shooting platform, which creaked gently beneath his weight, and proceeded to clean his spectacles. Drabble heard several crows cry and there was a brief loud chatter of monkeys. Harris had replaced his glasses and picked up his rifle, cocking the first barrel. He swallowed hard and gave Drabble an assertive nod.

Drabble put his hand to his hip, where his Webley revolver was holstered; he hoped he wouldn't have to use to it, but instinct had told him not to come on this venture unarmed. Not that he would like to be staring at a tiger armed only with his Webley. But it was better than nothing if it came to it.

In the distance the beaters started shouting. Their words were muffled by the dense jungle but the noise was unmistakable – and loud. So too was the snap and snatch of their sticks as they thrashed their way through the undergrowth. Drabble knew that the next two minutes were vital. To his left, some ten yards on, he could just make out the turban of the next in the human chain of watchers whose job it was to cough or clap if they saw the tiger trying to leave the shooting zone. Drabble took one last glance at Harris, now lining up his eye on his sights again; and then focused on the ground before him – watching for any sign of movement on the jungle floor. The shouts of the beaters and the drone of their sticks was getting louder. Any moment now the tiger would be here . . .

Drabble heard a loud cough. He saw Harris's body jerk on the platform, swivelling right towards the direction of the cough. Suddenly Drabble heard footsteps. He looked down and saw stripes on a whitish-brown background, moving silkily like fish in the shallows. He clapped loudly and the tiger turned lithely on a sixpence; Drabble glimpsed the swish of its tail. In that moment, Drabble turned to see Harris. He saw Harris squeeze his left eye shut, his face pressed against the stock.

'BOOM!'

A tongue of fire flared from the muzzle and smoke billowed into the void.

The tiger roared. It was deafening and protracted and then he heard it charge – back in the direction of the line of beaters, breaking through the branches and undergrowth.

'I hit it,' exclaimed Harris, as he urgently reloaded. And now, thought Drabble, we have an even more dangerous man-eater on our hands. But there was no time to think: a stag came crashing across the jungle floor, followed by a doe and her young. Next, monkeys bounded through the trees all around them. The jungle was running for its life. A family of mongooses and wild pigs charged by below, squealing in fear.

Amid the pandemonium there was a distinct human howl. O Lord . . . He turned to Harris. Where was Harris? He looked down and glimpsed Harris running along the jungle floor, reloading, in the direction of the tiger. Christ.

For Harris that was suicide. If he came face to face with the tiger he'd have to be very sure of his shot and confident in his abilities to down it before it downed him, and Drabble knew that was not the case. Harris was not the man for a sure and confident shot under those circumstances. Bloody fool. Drabble slipped down from the tree – landing hard but recovering before falling flat on his face – and charged after Harris. He raced along the path of broken branches and hauled out his Webley on the run.

'Harris!'

The jungle path widened abruptly, opening up along the nullah. Straight ahead Drabble saw Harris, kneeling, rifle shouldered, taking aim. Perhaps a hundred yards further on was the tiger, clawing up at the feet of a fat beater who hung from one of the sprawling branches of a vast banyan tree. Drabble saw the barrel of Harris's rifle wavering. It was a dangerous shot but he had no choice. Harris fired. The shot boomed out –

The tiger roared and spun around, now looking at Harris. Its eyes were large, yellow, and luminous, and somehow intoxicating. Out in the daylight Drabble saw just how pale it was; and its size – the long body running back from the broad, powerful shoulders and that large head. It was breathing heavily, and there was a decided nick in its left ear – an injury of some standing; its red tongue curled up beneath the silvery bristles of its muzzle. Drabble heard it grunt and start towards Harris. Quick as a flash, Harris was up and stumbling backwards, his arms jerking fearfully. He had one shot left, and if that missed he was toast.

The tiger strode coolly towards him; he had the measure of the man before him and was determined to make him suffer for it. Harris retreated faster, breaking into a rearwards trot, and raised his rifle for that last shot. Suddenly he tripped, his arms flailing, and crashed down on his back. He fired as he hit the ground, a cloud of smoke and flame enveloping his foot.

The stalking tiger's powerful shoulders and hind parts compressed – and then it pounced towards him.

A shot rang through the air; higher in pitch than the dense boom of Harris's rifle. Its aim was surer. The tiger landed in a heap, barely a yard from where Harris lay, and rolled over on its side. Drabble lowered his Webley revolver; he then took two steps quickly towards his right, aimed again, this time just below the tiger's throat, and fired. The creature jolted at the impact of the round but was otherwise motionless. He took another step towards the animal and fired again, this time at its shoulder.

Many is the tiger, he had been told, will spring back into life having had a bullet put into it. Drabble could not make a mistake. Next, he picked up a rock and threw it at the stationary beast. It bounced off the broad, striped side and rolled away. There was no movement from the tiger.

'Well, Harris sahib,' he sighed. 'This man-eater won't be troubling anyone else.'

Drabble cocked the Webley and went over the tiger. He immediately spotted a wound from one of Harris's shots at its hind parts. That probably explained why it hadn't immediately charged Harris.

Drabble gave the tiger's mighty paw – it was silvery and the size of a small dinner plate – a decided kick. It moved lifelessly. He took in the length of the body, marvelling at the size of the thing, and then noticed it; the bullet hole from his first shot – right between the bugger's eyes. He couldn't have done that better if he'd tried.

At that moment the shikaris and cheering beaters started rushing into the scene, shaking their sticks and spears in jubilation and talking excitedly. Drabble turned to Harris.

'Harris?'

Harris had fainted. The right lens of his spectacles was cracked, and fresh blood was collecting in a steadily expanding pool around his outstretched right foot, the toe of which was scorched black from the muzzle-flash and partly disintegrated. You stupid sod, thought Drabble.

'Stretcher!'

Chapter Two

'Now, the one thing everyone knows about being in the Tropics is that it's imperative to drink gins and tonic — *constantly,*' waxed Harris cheerfully, as the turbaned waiter placed two drinks before them. Harris seized the glass. 'In this searing heat your life absolutely depends on it. Otherwise one will die of dehydration — or worse, malaria.' His heavily bandaged right foot was propped on a stool placed before his rattan chair, so to the casual observer it might resemble a nasty case of gout. In all other regards his turnout was impeccable: cream cotton double-breasted suit, paisley handkerchief, pale blue shirt, starched white collar and Granville club tie. His spectacles had been repaired and his blond hair had been parted so that in many respects — with the lightest of tans — he looked as well as he had at any time in the twenty-one years that his friend Drabble had known him. And he was, except that he was now one toe lighter on his right foot. The doctor said he was lucky only to have lost the one, and fortunate that it wasn't the big toe. Rather important, big toes, apparently.

'How's the foot?' asked Drabble.

Harris waved the enquiry away; it was a sore subject.

'Cheers,' he said instead, raising his glass. They clinked.

'Is it painful?'

'A touch itchy, that's all,' he frowned. 'Nothing that the gin and tonic can't cope with.'

A savagely hot breeze gushed in from the open window,

which looked out over the Imperial Hotel's stunning green, spreading lawns. The hotel was an oversized art deco monstrosity with an unremitting geometry that taxed the eye, but the gardens *were* beautiful. A fan turned decoratively above, rather too far away to be any use.

Harris sighed.

'We should have stayed at the club.'

'It's meant to be rather nice,' replied Drabble. And a good deal less expensive, he might have added.

It was a week since the shooting of the tiger; it had taken a full day to get Harris to hospital on the back of a two-wheeled cart, and they had arrived back in Delhi by train after the second night. Despite his injury Harris has fussed inordinately about ensuring that the tiger skin was properly preserved and a particular taxidermist had been engaged – the best in New Delhi, apparently. 'The way things are going here, it might be the last tiger the family gets,' Harris had pronounced gloomily.

Drabble smiled at the recollection and took in the scene. The hotel's lobby bar offered a broad cross-section of the ruling class: there were British Indian Army officers in the main in khaki; English women in pale starched dresses; men of business – *box-wallahs* as they were known dismissively by the local hierarchy – sweating into three-piece suits of cream and white. The principal difference between a similar crowd in, say, the Ritz or Savoy in London was the sheer acreage of facial hair on display. All the men, with the exception of Drabble and Harris, wore deep moustaches or broad mutton chops; it felt like being in a Victorian painting. As for the ladies, there was a certain Edwardian formality to the quantity of their dress and their hair. As was often remarked, British India was twenty years behind the times. These European men and women were being attended to by an army of finely uniformed and impeccably mannered Indian waiters. At the far end of the bar, beyond the lobby and down the stairs, a corridor led to a vast swimming pool, perfect for the conditions. It was really rather nice, Drabble had to admit. Though he officially despised it, of course. But it would do as a resting place while Harris convalesced from the accident, before the real purpose of their trip to India could begin.

There was a polite cough and he looked up to see a smallish man, one – right on cue – sporting a deep moustache, the sort you imagined shouted 'Fire!' under a pith helmet at Omdurman. He was probably in his mid-fifties.

'Sir Percival?' asked the man, proffering his card to Harris. His voice had dried quality to it, like it had been left out in the sun for too long, but his lean face was curiously unlined and spoke of a life lived in the shade of a topee. 'My name is Arbuthnot. I'm from the GOI – may I sit down?'

He didn't quite wait for a response before drawing up a chair. 'GOI' stood for 'Government of India' and this was a text-book example of how people seemed to speak out here; there was no time expended explaining any of it to the newcomer. His taking of the seat gave Drabble the chance to observe the top of his head: he nudged Harris's elbow. Originating at the left-hand side of the man's head, a weave of silvery-brown hair, probably a foot long, curled around the crown. It made for what was quite possibly the most ornate comb-over in the hirsute history of mankind.

Arbuthnot pulled at his starched cuffs from under his black morning coat and began:

'If, gentlemen,' he offered Drabble a meaningful look, 'Professor – if you are prepared to tolerate a brief interruption, it is my sincere pleasure to welcome you to these shores on behalf of the government of India and to express our great relief that you were not injured further with your recent feline encounter.' He paused for Harris to acknowledge this sentiment, and continued, but not before offering a small bow of recognition to a passing guest in the lobby bar. He turned away and lowered his voice, discreetly. 'What brings me here, Sir Percival, is a delicate matter, which if you'll permit me, I'll come straight to – what, may I ask, is the precise nature of your interest in His Highness Sir Ganga Singh, the Maharaja of Bikaner?'

If Harris was the least taken aback by Arbuthnot's knowledge of him or his undertaking, he did not evince it. He lowered his gin and tonic. 'I think it speaks for itself,' he asserted. 'The Maharaja is a staunch friend of the Empire, a great patriot, a leading member of the Chamber of Princes here in India, and a great supporter of the government's federation plans – he's progressive and forward-looking. He's therefore of great legitimate interest to my readers, and, of course, he's got his golden jubilee this year. And he likes shooting tigers – so all in all, he's a thoroughly good egg and makes for excellent copy.'

'I see,' replied Arbuthnot, after a moment's reflection. He adjusted the knot of his tie, which was patterned with Masonic symbols and distracted Drabble's attention. 'I suppose from our office's perspective, we wondered if he was a tad old hat – we do have quite a few other maharajas on the books who are a good deal younger and even more progressive than Ganga Singh, much as we like him. I confess we wondered if you would you be open to the idea of considering one of those instead for your interview – assuming you only want the *one* maharaja?' He raised his eyebrows quizzically before continuing: 'The Maharaja of Bandahan, for instance, is a sensational shot and, I gather, has a collection of one hundred Rolls-Royces.'

Harris looked over at Drabble doubtfully. He did not like being pressed on such matters. Harris asked:

'Is there something *wrong* with the Maharaja of Bikaner?'

'Oh no, heaven forbid. No, he's entirely on side. It's just a question of *nuance*.' Arbuthnot smiled. 'We simply thought that Bandahan might be more to your taste. I dare say you know of him? His new fiancée is a Hollywood actress, and she is very nice *indeed*. All in all, he's rather hot property at the moment.' Arbuthnot cleared this throat, 'I could get it all fixed up for you in a jiffy.'

Harris frowned.

'But Bikaner has granted me the interview; it's all fixed for Thursday – he's unveiling a statue and so on. It's all arranged.'

'Oh,' Arbuthnot swatted this obstacle away with his lean hand, like a fly in his face. 'We can have it unarranged without any indelicacy or inconvenience for you. The Maharaja will understand.' He offered Harris a firm smile that seemed to imply that the matter was settled.

But Harris wasn't moved. He looked over at Drabble, his brows furrowed. 'I would need to clear this with my editor,' he began. 'After all, the *Evening Express* has sent me all the way to meet Bikaner . . .'

'Of course, of course,' soothed Arbuthnot. 'We wouldn't want to upset the order of play at your end, and if your editor insisted I know it could be accommodated, in due course.'

The moustache widened over the stretched-out lips of Arbuthnot's tight smile. Drabble realised that the absurd comb-over belied a steely nature that should not be underestimated.

'Perhaps,' continued the official as he rose from the chair, 'you might like to let me know once you've telegraphed your editor and had the switch confirmed? You can telegraph or telephone me, as you wish. I assure you, you won't be disappointed by the Maharaja of Bandahan, or his delightful fiancée.' He cleared his throat in a manner that might have bordered on the lascivious — Drabble wasn't sure — but was at odds with the impression of stolid Victoriana that he otherwise emitted. 'Of course, from an official perspective, it's not quite cricket, but, strictly off the record, they *do* make a lovely couple.' Perhaps not everything about British India was twenty years behind the times. Arbuthnot went to go.

'But . . . surely,' stammered Harris. His mouth was opening and shutting like a man suddenly deprived of his trousers. 'Surely, you-um-you're not suggesting that I *can't* interview the Maharaja of Bikaner?'

Arbuthnot turned back.

'Oh, heaven forbid. No, of course not.' He spoke in apparent horror — as though the very thought of it were beyond human comprehension. 'You can interview whomsoever you wish. I can't stop you – and I wouldn't dream of such a thing. It's a free country, after all. *Well,* so long as you're not Indian.' With that Arbuthnot gave a cold smile. 'Let me know what your editor decides,' he added. He walked smartly away. Drabble watched him shrink into the distance as he crossed the immaculate black and white marble floor.

'Christ alive,' hissed Harris, turning to Drabble. 'Where on earth do they find them?'

Drabble set down his drink. 'I'm not sure I know. But I tell you this, they clearly don't want you going anywhere near Bikaner.'

'Which means we have to go.'

'Can they stop us?'

Harris pursed his lips:

'I don't actually know. I shouldn't think so.' He drained glass, and braced his hands on the arms of his chair. 'But I don't think we should dally any longer in case they decide can. We are, after all, in a foreign land.' He picked up his walking stick. 'You know, Ernest old man, I think it would be unwise to underestimate these Imperialist johnnies – absurd hair-do or no absurd hair-do.'

'Yes,' Drabble agreed. 'You have to take yourself extremely seriously to have hair like that.'

'Quite,' declared Harris.

They moved towards the stairs. 'Memory serves,' noted Harris, 'there's a train in the morning that will get us into Bikaner tomorrow night –'

Harris halted, his gaze fixed across the lobby. A young woman walked straight towards him. She was a good-looking blonde of middle height and wore a figure-hugging summer-weight tweed suit that finished just below the knee. The neckline was heavy on the pearls but the ensemble showed off the essential lumps, bumps, and narrowings of life – in short, she was right up his street.

Better still, she was flashing him a bright smile.

'Pardon me,' she said, her voice a low breathless tenor offset

14

with just enough girlishness to make it beguiling. 'Might you be Sir Percival Harris, the tiger-shooting correspondent of the *London* —?'

Harris made a genteel bow and then took her hand, which hadn't quite been offered but was within polite grasping distance.

'Heinz,' she stated. 'D.M. Heinz of the *Calcutta Enquirer*.'

'*The* D. M. Heinz?' repeated Harris with delight. 'I've been enjoying your syndicated reports for months; I had no idea that you were a wom —'

Drabble stepped back — unnoticed by either interlocutor — and slipped away. Chances were, Bikaner might have to wait a little longer. But just in case they did leave Delhi in the morning, Drabble was determined to see a little more of it first.

Also, if Drabble was going to spend the greater part of twelve hours on a stiflingly hot train with Harris, then he would need something else to read. This dovetailed nicely with the rising frustration at his own sheer ignorance of the country and the culture surrounding him. This was an ignorance made all the more vexing for him by its familiarity: he had spent most of the first five years of his life in India, at Ramgarh Cantonment, where his father was stationed in the Indian Army.

Yet all he now remembered of his Indian childhood were the stories that had been repeated enough times in family circles to stick. There was the time a python found its way into his bedroom: the alarm had been raised and his father had arrived and shot it. Aziz, his father's bearer, removed the offending reptile, carrying it out pinioned between two sticks: no other snake made the same mistake. (To Drabble's knowledge, this was the only time that his father had fired his revolver in anger throughout his long service in India.) The other family story was half true, like the best ones. Drabble, here aged five, had apparently run away from the cantonment after being reprimanded for some small error in the nursery. That last part was true: he had been scolded by his mother, and didn't like it. But it wasn't escape he sought, rather it was adventure. So he want for a walk, got utterly lost – Drabble remembered that sensation of fearful dislocation more than a quarter of a century later – and then the sun went down. He was in the forest, of which there was plenty in the area, and it was very dark indeed. In the end he saw a rocky outcrop, which he climbed: it wasn't for pleasure, he hadn't learned it was fun at that point. Rather it was motivated by an urge he later recognised as survival. From the top he could see the military cantonment and the way home. He strolled in, covered in dirt but otherwise unharmed, just as the bugle was calling the Retreat and the flag was coming down. After that he was packed off to school in England, and he had never been back.

Exiting the hotel, he took one of the waiting motor-taxis and instructed the driver to take him to the Red Fort – via Viceroy's House. The drive took them south first, down onto Kingsway, a vast mile-long ceremonial road, straight from the imperial rule book. Alexander, Nero, Napoleon to Mussolini, they would know this for what it was immediately. It was the stuff of their dreams. And frankly, it made their efforts at it look amateurish. Above the traffic and motorbuses, above the low-lying cloud of soot and smog and smell of wood-smoke, was the vast dome of Viceroy's House, from which flew a Union flag which must accordingly have been of preposterous proportions.

As they approached in the evening sunshine, the lower parts of the massive colonnaded structure emerged from the gloom; it was vast, larger than the palace of Versailles – so the popular press said – and fabricated from something like a billion bricks. Up close it was a seemingly never-ending sequence of columns with tiers upon tiers of windows, arches, and levels, like an enormous rust-coloured wedding cake to tyranny. Before it was arranged a neat line of Indian Army soldiers in full dress uniform, and behind them a broad series of steps the length of a football pitch led up to the august interior. Drabble told the driver to pull over and he got out of the cab briefly to try and capture its grotesque magnificence. It was immense, and so new you could almost smell the paint. He gazed along its length, taking it all in. Christ alive. You had to hand it to them. It *was* bloody impressive. What a shame that it stood for just about everything he hated most about the country of his birth.

Drabble got back in the taxi. They looped around and headed back down the other way. In the distance was the elephantine All-India War Memorial – 140-odd feet of tawny red brick bathed in the golden sun of the Delhi evening. They passed between two identical and similarly oversized official government buildings, set back from the broad highway and bedecked with Union flags. They took the next left, and sped northwards up along Connaught Place, and then left the imperial heart of New Delhi. Crossing the railway lines, they passed into the old city of the Mughals. The sun was setting, promptly as it does in the Tropics, when they reached the Red Fort. Swathes of its ornate edifice were lost to the encroaching dusk. A native policeman directed traffic at the crossroads. Bullock carts, bicycles, rickshaws, pedestrians and tongas vied for advantage in the gridlock.

Drabble paid off the taxi driver and set off on foot. All around was the architecture of the Mughals – designed to convey the authority and prestige of an old, derelict order.

He had given himself the task of locating a bookshop selling English texts, and been told that such a shop could be found near the Red Fort. The scale of the structure, however, meant that finding it might very well not prove feasible, particularly given the time available.

He set off along a main thoroughfare running perpendicular to the proudest section of the fort, along which were shops and hotels in and buildings in elaborate Mughal style: pointed Persian arches and trellises vanished into the night. Hoardings advertised the wares of the shopkeepers, and the road was thronged with pedestrians, European and Indian, some of the latter laden with tall baskets atop their heads. They merged with the pell-mell traffic of motor-cars and horse-drawn carriages, hand-carts and camel trains – the cries of beasts and drone of internal combustion engines, along with the smells of petroleum, dung, and spice, overlaid with the repetitive cries of the vendors: *chai-chai-chai* . . . And then, all of a sudden, through half-shuttered windows, Drabble saw a dimly-lit book lined room.

An Indian shopkeeper sat at the high desk swept off his spectacles and got to his feet as Drabble entered. 'Sahib,' he exclaimed warmly. Drabble saw scores of leather-bound tomes with flying Persian script. 'We have books in English and European languages over here, sahib,' said the shopkeeper, leading Drabble further inside. 'In particular, we have an impeccable selection of Shakespeare and Kipling.'

Drabble emerged with a book on Hinduism and a copy of Tod's *Annals of Rajasthan*, which though two hundred years old, he knew was still regarded as an official primer on the region. That told you something about official attitudes to the subcontinent.

He walked on until the human traffic ahead became almost too congested to continue: the wheeled traffic in the road had increased too, but over the din he could hear occasional cheers and shouts. Evidently the road ahead was closed. Quite a few pedestrians were now turning back to continue their journeys by other routes. A camel drawing a cart was being indecorously hauled around by its owner – the camel protesting every step of the way. Curiosity gripped him; Drabble pushed his way through the crowd until he reached the roadblock.

A cordon of Indian policemen linking arms enclosed a protest on the far side. There must have five hundred or more Indians; men and women, old and young, some well to do, others dressed more poorly. Interspersed across the crowd were banners, proclaiming 'Swaraj' or 'self-rule' and 'Swadeshi', 'home rule' in English. Others read, 'English go home'. Standing in the middle of the front row of protesters – formed of people standing arm-in-arm, was a man of perhaps thirty. Dressed in a brown *sherwani* – a traditional long Indian coat with standing collar – he was shouting slogans – Drabble recognised the word Swaraj.

Every now and then crowd would erupt, shaking their fists in anger. And the object of their protest? The anonymous-looking building to the right, which Drabble now noticed had a brace of armed Indian policemen flanking the front door, over which hung several flags, including the Union Jack. It was a police station. The antagonist's words – poetic, soaring, poised – filled their closed road, captivating the crowd of protesters.

Just then, the door of the police station opened: the sound of the lock being unbolted audible even, and out stepped a British police officer, followed by an Indian non-commissioned officer, a turbaned *subadar,* armed with a rifle. Standing well over six foot but taller under the pith helmet, the Englishman wore brown leather riding boots, breeches, and a khaki tunic underneath his leather Sam Browne belt. A pistol was holstered at his hip and he carried a pair of brown leather gloves behind his back in his linked hands, A leather riding crop was pinned under his arm. He walked straight towards the speaker, and stopped about two yards in front of him.

'Now look here,' he bellowed, like a headmaster addressing chapel. 'You've made your point,' he drawled. 'But it's getting late now, and it's jolly well time for you all to go home to your wives, your husbands, and children. Understood?' he added.

The crowd, hitherto impassive, now erupted. The officer meanwhile, still with his hands calmly together behind his back, impassively turned and nodded to the subadar. He in turn gave an order and in that moment a dozen or so policemen emerged from side alleys and doorways, beetling forcefully into the crowd, and yanked away the banners, hauling their owners with them. The poetic rhetoric of the antagonist started up again; his fist was raised and the crowd began to cry 'Swaraj' amid other words that Drabble could not understand. The British officer turned to the subadar and this time made a swish of the air with his hand: the two policeman at the door of the station marched smartly forward and seized the speaker, whose voice only raised in pitch and ferocity as he was dragged away towards the door, which opened and shut immediately behind him. The officer pulled on his gloves in a gesture of finality and clutched the riding crop behind him.

He squared up to the crowd:

'Now listen to me,' he shouted. 'You've been told to go; I've been very clear. I respect your right to protest, but now you have to go home.'

He paused. No one moved.

'Go on –' he bellowed, glaring at the men and women in the front row. 'Go on!'

It was like watching a farmer shouting at his cattle. Either the man was exceptionally brave, or he was utterly deluded. Even in the presence of armed policemen it was hard to see them firing upon a peaceful crowd. But there was no way that this mass of humanity could simply be dispersed by the force of one man's larynx.

Still no one moved.

The officer sighed, and cleared his throat. He stepped up to the front row of crowd and immediately struck the face of the man before him. The blow was a sideways hit with a closed fist and the man's head went with it. Before he could recover the officer hit him a second time, striking downwards at the top of his head so that he fell almost to knees. A third blow did just that. The officer turned to the next man along and clouted him hard on the side of his head. A second and third blow followed. No one dared to lay a finger on the British officer. Drabble felt rage well up inside him – the native policeman braced himself against his advance. The British officer turned towards a third victim.

And then it began to happen. A young woman in a *sari*, wrapped her hands protectively around his head and shoulders of the man beaten first, and, crouching, took him away. Then others began to peel off. It was over.

As the third man to be assaulted by the officer collapsed bleeding to the ground, the crowd was no more. What had been a mass was now a series of countless fragments; the police cordon was dropped and the pedestrians began to flow back and forth along the road, just as the traffic resumed. The British officer nodded to the subadar and removed his gloves. They both walked smartly into the station smiling to one another. Job done.

Drabble glanced over at the woman who had been standing next to him throughout this. She was Indian, perhaps thirty, and had a baby in sling on her chest. Their eyes happened to meet. She abruptly lowered her gaze, her face fearful, and hurried away into the dispersing crowd.

Drabble started off in the direction he had come from, towards the junction of the Red Fort, the ramparts of which were now lost in darkness. But after a few paces he turned back. In the distance the Union flag hung limply above the door of the police station.

He could not let this pass.

His knock at the door of the police station was answered promptly. He told the constable that he wanted to see the 'Superintendent, sahib', and was requested politely to wait in a small, stifling room, which was cooled by a barred window jammed ajar and a small wire-caged fan in the corner. Large flies buzzed around the lonely electric light bulb hanging from a cable from a crack in the middle of the ceiling.

Presently the door opened and a different constable, a tall Indian of around twenty-five, asked him to follow. They passed through the busy station office where about a dozen khaki-uniformed police officers filled out paperwork or pressed stamps onto documents, at various desks. Before these sat handcuffed and manacled men patiently waiting for the bureaucracy of their cases to be processed. Among them was the antagonist in the long jacket who had just been dragged inside. He sat, his hands cuffed, hunched forward looking down at the floor, his lightly bearded face drawn.

At the back of the room an elderly Indian man swept the floor.

They arrived at a door marked 'Superintendent H. Goodlad' in chipped white paint. The constable knocked and showed Drabble in on the voice of command. The British officer whom Drabble had seen in the road minutes before looked up from the desk where he was filling out, in a long flowing hand, a blue paper form, marked 'incident report'. On one side of the desk stood his pith helmet, and on the other was a tumbler of what looked like whisky, and several piles of files. The door shut behind him.

Goodlad, still writing, blinked up at Drabble's momentarily, just for long enough for Drabble to see that he was plainly exhausted. Then he returned his gaze to his document. On the wall behind him was a framed print of the King in coronation crown and ermine robes. In the corner stood a tall cabinet heaped with more disordered brown files. Goodlad completed whatever it was he was writing, slotted the pen in the inkwell and took up his whisky – actions interspersed with an infinitesimal nod in the direction of the chair for Drabble's benefit.

Drabble chose to remain standing, a point that did not go unobserved.

Goodlad set down his drink, his features hardening.

'What can I do for you?' he asked. His tone did not sound helpful.

Drabble stared down at him and said, 'I just saw what you did out there.'

'And?'

'I was disgusted by it.' Drabble found anger coming to his voice and the words shot out, 'Arresting innocently and peacefully protesting men; shamefully beating three unarmed men. You're a disgrace.'

Goodlad raised his eyebrows at that in mock surprise. He leaned down behind the desk and pulled out a drawer. He stood a bottle of whisky on the desk before him and followed this up with a glass. A small nod said, there you go.

Drabble made no move towards the malt. Goodlad appeared to weigh him up.

'How long have you been in India?' he asked. 'A week or so? A month, perhaps?' He fished a cigarette out of the metal box and struck a pungent match. 'Why don't you take a seat?'

Clouds of smoke tumbled towards Drabble.

'No, thank you,' he said, as he looked through the cloud at Goodlad's complacent expression; at the crooked English teeth, yellowed by the tropical diet of tea, whisky, and nicotine; at the spare square-jawed arrogance under its neatly parted hair flicked with grey that could have belonged to a country parson. Drabble clenched his fist.

'You treated those protesters like animals,' he said. '*Worse* than animals.'

Goodlad's eyes hardened.

'Well, what did you expect?' he roared. 'This isn't bloody Dorking, you know.' He lowered his voice, presumably so that it would not carry past the door or the thin partition walls into the busy office beyond. 'We treat them like that – I wouldn't care to use your word myself – *precisely* to keep them in their place. How else do you expect a hundred thousand Britons to control three hundred million Indians across an area the size of the Continent?'

Drabble started to reply; Goodlad cut in, his voice a hoarse whisper:

'It's done through little more than force of personality – our personality. And yes, therefore it's a bluff; a vast bloody continental bluff based upon one important notion in particular – one you'll come to understand soon enough: that in India, whether you like it or not, *we* are the master race. And if we weren't, then there's no way in God's green earth that we would be able to keep this show on the road. Now the good news is that because no one – or at least very few people – ever dares call this bluff, we continue it and, quite frankly, we'll keep going until the long-distant day comes when we are forced out, something which I personally have no intention of ever allowing happen. I'm certainly not giving up the ghost on my watch.

23

'And nor, Professor, should you will its end, because who do you think pays for the upkeep of your ivory tower, eh, but the British empire? And what is India, if she's not the gleaming bloody star of that empire. Now you might hate everything that the empire stands for, but just remember who pays for your exalted position of judgement in the first place.' He drew sourly on his cigarette. 'So do me a kindness. Be good enough to take your Marxist pretensions and bourgeois predilections – and *fuck off* of out of my station.'

With that he pulled out a brown folder, spun it round and flipped it open – stabbing his finger at the photograph – of Drabble – paper-clipped to a cover sheet. Below was his name under a header marked 'confidential'. The picture looked about two years old – Drabble could not place its being taken. He met the cold brown eyes of the imperialist across the table.

'So what will happen to him?' he asked, indicating the man outside.

'Who? Oh, him? Who cares? The man is a known Communist sympathiser. I dare say I'll let him out in a few days, once he's calmed down a bit.'

'He looked pretty calm out there just now.'

'To the untrained eye, that might be the case.' Goodlad stubbed out his cigarette and unhooked the telephone handset. 'Now, it's not your concern, Professor.' He began to dial. 'So if you don't mind . . .'

Chapter Three

But Drabble did mind, and he still minded the next morning as he and Harris took a motor-taxi to the New Delhi station. It was not early: Harris did not like to do early, but it was early enough for the mist to be rising from the Yumani, and the sky of the old city to be filled with the smoke of thousands of fires – brewing chai and cooking up a breakfast for the imperial capital.

Like everything else in this city, the station was immense and new – seemingly regardless of the surroundings or what had preceded it. They alighted and with the help of at least two more porters than was strictly necessary, they and their baggage were conveyed to the appropriate platform – past ordered lines of soldiers and their kit, past British and European travellers, and children with notices tied to them; past governesses with their charges, and their memsahibs. A string of boys watched a cross-legged, turbaned snake charmer play his pipe to the occupants of several baskets arranged before him on the floor. Upon a tinkle of rupees landing on the corner of his cloth robe, his tune sped up, and a hissing head ascended into view. The boys squealed or retreated, just as Drabble and Harris passed by, their baggage following in stately procession of porters.

They boarded the 9.05 for Jodhpur in good time, and had a small compartment to themselves – or rather they shared it with Harris's baggage, which took up an inordinate amount of space. A *chai-wallah* came by and they had tea. Then Harris bought three different English language newspapers from the vendor passing by on the platform.

The train left the station punctually, a fact Drabble commented on.

'Well, they don't have unions out here, do they,' remarked Harris, as he lit his pipe. Though he himself was a member of a union – one particular to his profession – he considered all others to be inferior and solely the preserve of Leninist-Marxist anarchists bent on the destruction of Christian Western society.

The smoke cleared as they left the station – the brick ramparts familiar to rail passengers in London were not present here, however. Instead the line seemed to be raised somewhat and overlooked roofs by the hundred, dwarfed by the gleaming domes of great mosques and the rectangular mass of the Red Fort. Men and women were gathered in open-sided dwellings around fires, their livestock or beasts of burden tethered beside them or roaming free. Small children in rags ran and played in the paths waving and shouting out, to each other or to the passing carriages, Drabble did not know.

'Christ alive,' exclaimed Harris with stinging venom, from behind the paper wall of the *Calcutta Enquirer*. He flexed the newspaper: 'Can you believe it?' he asked, clearing his throat and reading: 'The leading mountaineer and historian Professor Ernest Drabble, currently touring India on a vacation, has been hailed as hero after slaying a vicious, injured man-eating tiger at point blank range armed only with a revolver, it has emerged.'

Harris briefly lowered the newspaper, his face puce with indignation. He read on, his voice rising in pitch: 'Shooting with a hunting companion – *unnamed!* – Professor Drabble, a leading mountaineer who narrowly escaped death after falling during an heroic attempt on the North Face of the Eiger last year, saved his companion and several hundred villagers with a perfectly aimed shot between the man-eating tiger's eyes – shot coolly at the range of just six yards. Villagers have appealed to the District Officer for him to receive a special commendation from the Viceroy –'

Harris roared and crushed the newspaper into a disordered mass before rolling it into a vast ball. Simultaneously he surged to his feet and bundled the offending item from the window, which he then slammed shut in protest. He plonked back down into his seat.

'What a minx!' he roared. 'What an absolute minx – doesn't she know who I am? I'm ruddy well Sir Percival Harris, a knight of the bloody realm.' He tore up the next newspaper, the *New Delhi Herald*.

Drabble grinned.

'Am I to understand that Miss Heinz's reporting does not meet your exalted standards?'

Harris lowered the *Herald*, glaring. 'Did you put her up to this?'

'Oh, now that *is* ridiculous!'

Harris brought the newspaper back up.

'I wouldn't put it past you sometimes, you know.'

He lapsed into silence, and resumed reading. After a few minutes he turned a page.

Drabble contemplated opening the window which Harris had closed, before returning his attention to his book. They both continued like this in silence for a short while; the only noise was the sound of the train clattering along the rails.

'What are you reading?' asked Harris at length. He laid aside his newspaper and starting patting at his various pockets.

'A book on Hinduism,' replied Drabble absently.

'Any good?' Harris brought his pipe out of his jacket pocket.

'So far, very informative.'

'Good,' said Harris, his teeth gritted on the stem of his pipe. He began filling the bowl with tobacco from his leather pouch.

'Are you going to open the window before we suffocate in here? It's stuffy enough as it is in here, without that fug of yours.'

Harris cast Drabble a baleful glance. He got up and yanked open the window. He then completed the task of preparing his pipe with due ostentation.

'What bothers me most,' he announced after a few minutes more of silent brooding, 'is that I thought she *liked* me; I really did.' He inhaled on the pipe, smoke tearing from his mouth in the breeze from the window. 'But it seems she spent the evening just buttering me up to get a story. In short, she was being disingenuous – and I fell for it.'

'And you've never done that?'

Harris shrugged, 'Not quite like *that*, old man.' He frowned down gloomily at the bowl of his pipe. 'Never,' he added, this time with greater insistence. 'I'm mean, for goodness' sake, there's a line you don't cross.'

Drabble slipped a book mark into his place, and set the absorbing introduction to Hinduism to one side.

'Is there something else you need to tell me?'

Harris glared. 'Are you sure you didn't put her up to this? You do seem to be enjoying it, rather.'

'Nonsense, I was simply interested in knowing what your "line" was, that's all.' He smiled. 'As a matter of fact, I never knew you had one!'

Harris growled and returned to his newspaper, which he clasped before him with white-knuckled fury. Drabble knew there was no way that his friend was actually *reading*.

He watched smoke rise from behind the wall of newsprint, then cleared his throat:

'If you want my honest opinion, I expect she was offering you the professional courtesy of anonymity. Take it from me, this sort of publicity can be pretty boring – I should know,' he added pointedly. At the time of the Eiger fall, Harris had gone to town on Drabble's endeavours. He still wore 'the bouncing don' moniker, like it or not. Mainly not.

Harris lowered this newspaper but said nothing. He drew on his pipe and looked disapprovingly at it. Perhaps it wasn't drawing correctly.

'I think I'm about ready for another cup of tea,' he announced.

At that moment, the door clunked and drew ajar. Drabble

looked over, half expecting to see the conductor or ticket inspector. Instead –

'Miss Heinz!' boomed Harris with glee. Any misgivings about her reporting talents had evaporated and Harris jumped to his feet and all but dragged her into the compartment. Snatching up her small leather and canvas suitcase, he racked it for her – meanwhile assailing her with questions about her unexpected appearance.

Drabble thought he noticed Miss Heinz blush at little at the strength of Harris's welcome, probably with due justification, and she glanced over uncomfortably as Harris bundled her into the seat opposite Drabble and sat at her side.

She was dressed in a pale khaki safari trouser suit, along with a blancoed cork topee which all might normally have been regarded as masculine attire but which she carried off with aplomb.

She had a buckled handbag like an attaché case. A particular stone – an emerald – formed the centrepiece of a large brooch set in silver on her left lapel.

'Now what a pleasant surprise,' Harris asserted, as they settled in their seats. Miss Heinz smiled at them both and took out a silver cigarette case from her hip pocket.

'Do you mind if I smoke,' she asked, in the husky yet somehow girlish voice of hers.

'That's quite all right,' cooed Harris, rifling his pockets and striking a match almost before the poor girl could get the cigarette to her lips.

Outside the highlands of Rajputana sped by at a stately forty miles per hour. Drabble (who always sat rear-facing when he travelled with Harris, because of the latter's acute travel-sickness) glimpsed aft sections of the long train curling around a steep hillside. To the right the lowlands stretched away, green, dramatic unspoiled jungles with just the occasional roof to tell you humans had arrived. It permitted you to contemplate the existence of the world before mankind . . .

Miss Heinz was speaking. 'I have to confess that it's not really a surprise at all,' she stated, as smoke snaked from her delicate nostrils. Harris beamed at her, and somehow the beam intensified. She broke free from his intense gaze and focused her attention on Drabble, momentarily. 'When you said you were coming to interview the Maharaja of Bikaner, I knew I had to join you,' she said. 'I–I–I've wanted to meet him for years . . .' She looked back at Harris, her large brown eyes visibly softening in what was most clearly a very winning fashion. 'I give you my word I won't hamper your interview,' she said meekly. 'You've come a long way for it, but–but–'

'But you knew you had to come with us –'

Far from being appalled at the prospect of any professional intrusion, Harris merely glowed in the glorious light of her attention. Drabble had not seen anything like it in a long time. From behind his friend's gold-rimmed spectacles, the eyes were transfixed on Heinz's oval face: 'It will be a pleasure to have you join us –' he shared a glance with Drabble, thereby including him in the response. 'Your presence will only *enrich* the experience in Bikaner, I'm sure.'

Drabble concurred politely, as Miss Heinz smiled with all her white, even teeth at Harris. But as she did so she peeped from the corners of her eyes at Drabble, and he caught a look of decided calculation.

Harris, naturally enough, was blind to it. Instead he brought out his hip flask and toasted the success of their outing, before sharing it around.

'I can only imagine that His Highness Sir Ganga Singh will be enchanted to make your acquaintance,' he declared. 'The man, after all, is a living legend – and known to be a superlative judge of character.'

Unlike Harris, thought Drabble.

Sir Ganga Singh, the Maharaja of Bikaner, was undoubtedly something of an international celebrity: of the six hundred or so Indian princes – men who between them ruled around a third of the geographical landmass of the Indian Subcontinent as junior partners to British – he was easily the most conspicuous to the world at large. Not only had led his famous Bikaner Camel Corps in battle in the service of the British Empire – against the Boxer rebellion in China – but he had also taken them to Flanders and then to Egypt during the Great War, where he was also a member of the Imperial War Cabinet. The Maharaja then capped that by being one of just two Indians joining the British Empire delegation at the Paris Peace Conference after the war, and he was then a signatory of the Treaty of Versailles proper. Finally, Sir Ganga had also addressed the League of Nations and counted himself a friend of the late King.

Which was some going, when you considered what he had started with: prior to his rule, Bikaner was known for nothing more than producing camels – and devastating famines, which had led many of its people to abandon its barren desert landscape for the more verdant promise of neighbouring states, almost all of which were more prosperous in comparison. Indeed, notable princely states included the nearby Udaipur, or Hyderabad and Mysore in the south.

Yet Sir Ganga Singh had turned Bikaner around. His ambitious canal scheme brought water to around a thousand square miles, eradicating the periodic fear of famine for ever, and he built a railway (and it was *his* railway and *his* land) across his kingdom, which had also changed the experience of life there for good, in both senses of the expression. He was, therefore, an outstanding example of the enlightened monarch, so enlightened in fact that he had even instituted a legislative assembly in Bikaner with free elections – keeping pace with changes across the border in British India in the 1920.

And so loyal was he to the King-Emperor George VI and Mother England, that the government had seen fit to grant him his own ex-RAF De Havilland bomber which he used to police the Thar desert, a vast expanse of territory which ran northwards all the way to the border of the Punjab. Therefore, for

31

patriotic, empire-loving readers of Harris's newspaper, there could be no greater nor more appropriate Indian celebrity for him to interview.

Which made Sir Ganga Singh's golden jubilee, falling in September 1937, a particular gift for Harris, not least because he also wanted to bag his own tiger – before either the tigers or the Raj ran out. And tigers were something that the Maharaja of Bikaner knew about, too: he had personally been responsible for dispatching some two hundred of them in his time. And had shot with King George V and Clemenceau. So whatever else, Drabble was expecting to see an awful lot of tiger rugs over the next few days as the Maharaja's guest.

But it was not only Harris who was interested in meeting the Maharaja: Drabble, too, knew that this would be a rare experience. Few opportunities were likely to come his way where he could get so close to such an intriguing figure. And that was partly why he had come along for the ride. Only partly. Drabble also wanted to return to India for his own reasons. He hadn't set foot on Indian soil since he was five, and he was curious to renew his acquaintance.

'You know he's very, *very* keen on federation, don't you,' said Miss Heinz.

'And so is Linlithgow,' added Harris glumly. Lord Linlithgow was the new Viceroy, who had arrived the previous April, and now called the monstrous Viceregal palace in New Delhi home. For the myopic readers of Harris's newspaper Linlithgow was not an appealing figure – on the contrary, he had been architect of a 1935 Act of Parliament which gave greater local and provincial self-government to Indians, something they opposed bitterly.

Drabble asked,

'And federation means precisely what?'

'In a nutshell,' replied Heinz, 'It's a unified India – so that's British India proper and 565 Indian or Native States officially brought together under one roof for the first time. In return the princes get to sit or choose someone to sit for them in the proposed future Indian upper house alongside a mathematically built-in majority of placemen appointed by the British government. That will act like a House of Lords, sitting above and moderating the decisions of a democratically elected lower house.'

'Is this happening?'

'Not likely,' stated Heinz. 'But Ganga Singh is the most vocal supporter of it by far – he drove forward and effectively ran a body called the Chamber of Princes, which the government was rather lukewarm about at first.'

'Now they like it, though,' intervened Harris, brightening. 'And the good news is that the princes – if they fall into line behind Singh – can help us by being a bulwark against rising populism and effectively undermine calls for home rule in other parts of India.'

'And that's a good thing?'

Harris and Heinz exchanged a glance.

'Of course,' boomed Harris. 'It's in everyone's best interests if the Raj endures – albeit with gradual steps towards eventual self-government for Indians.'

'I see, and how long will that take? Twenty years?'

Harris brightened further. 'Well, if we can hang on till then, that would be super, wouldn't it?'

Heinz nodded.

'We estimate that with the appropriate policies we can stave off independence until 1984,' she stated dryly. 'If we play our cards right.'

Drabble shook his head. Imperialists. They did not change. In the final analysis, everything was calibrated to simply clinging on.

'We'll see,' he said. 'As the historian of the party, it's my duty to tell you this for nothing: you lot are on the wrong side of history – no matter how many miles of railway you lay; no matter how many children's hospitals and schools you build, you're basically going to go down as the bad guys. John Stuart Mill had it right: self-rule is the best rule. Imperialism is morally bankrupt and the sooner we settle up and clear off, the better.'

Harris frowned hard at him with a pained expression – almost like he was witnessing the euthanizing of a beloved family pet. Miss Heinz, however, wore a half-smile on her pretty face, an expression reminiscent of Superintendent Goodlad's at the police station the night before. She thought, no doubt, *this chap doesn't know the half of it.* Well, thought Drabble, I probably don't, but that's fine by me. 'And you know what,' he added. 'I'll be keen to ask His Highness Sir Ganga Singh about that if I get the chance. I know he's got some strong opinions –'

'Easy now, Ernest,' soothed Harris.

'Tell me this, Harris –' Drabble's blood was up now. 'Just how far are *you* prepared to go to maintain British rule here? Are you prepared to shoot protesters? Would you pull the trigger?'

He could see Harris was grinning now – squirming because he knew he had no answer for this – and shaking his head.

'Oh, it won't come to that, Ernest . . .' he was imploring. Of course there was no way on God's green earth that he would agree to such barbarity; he had too much humanity in him. But Miss Heinz might; she was a different kettle of fish, and looked at Drabble like a cornered cobra.

'The fantasy of the pink-coloured quarter of the world is just that,' Drabble pressed on. 'For a while, you might have been able to make the case for some form of paternalistic motivation for imperial intervention, but ultimately there needs to be consent – and without it the whole shooting match just doesn't add up.' He looked at Harris, 'It's time you faced up to it, pal – and you too, Miss Heinz. We've run out of pink paint.'

Harris rolled his eyes, cooed, 'Oh, Drabble!'

Miss Heinz, shaking her head, reached for the wall-mounted ashtray and extinguished her cigarette with a sharp stabbing action.

'Well, there we are,' declared Harris with excessive cheer. He got to his feet and stepped carefully over to the window, through which a huge landscape of jade-green jungle-coated hills could be seen. 'Either way, we'd better make the most of it while we can. Who's for a gin and tonic, or perhaps –' he extracted a slim pewter flask from his pocket – 'a *chota peg*?'

Chapter Four

They stepped down onto the empty railway platform at Bikaner Junction station shortly after 9pm. It was hot – an order of magnitude hotter than Delhi – and this intensified the cloying mass of coal smoke in the air and the intensity of the spice in the air. The station buildings – looking very new – were in partial darkness, lit only by a string of electric lights which ran like bunting along the entire length of the station's overhanging roof. These dainty bulbs led the eye along the train, through the soot and the steam, to the spot several carriages further along, where another group of passengers were alighting; here several porters buzzed about handling a mass of baggage. A silver Rolls-Royce, its long angular bonnet gleaming in the electric light, waited, its engine running, just a short step or two from the carriage, and a turbaned servant stood waiting. A pair of flags hung from the apex of the twin running boards above each front wheel. In the darkness Drabble could not make out their design.

'Ah,' declared Harris, pointing his stick in the direction of the Rolls. 'That must be our car. The Maharaja is expecting us, after all.' He set off in its direction; Drabble and Miss Heinz exchanged a puzzled glance. Neither of them, it would appear, had reached the same conclusion. Drabble called out -

'Now look here,' barked Harris, using that slightly boorish, officer-class tone that Drabble noticed he had added to his repertoire of voices since arriving in India. 'There's clearly been some sort of mix-up – I think you'll find that this is –'

The porters melted away, leaving Harris addressing a distinguished-looking Indian gentleman of about sixty who was clearly the prime individual of this party. He was a small, bespectacled man swathed in a white shawl clutched around his neck, reaching his knees. Drabble recognised the slight figure immediately. And so did Harris.

'Er, um, yes. Well, umm, gosh,' he removed his pith helmet. 'Privileged to meet you, Mr Gandhi,' he declared, the boorish tone gone. The lights from the car caught on Gandhi's round gold-rimmed glasses as he regarded Harris. He said something – and then nimbly stepped up into the waiting Rolls, which purred away into the night.

Harris come bounding back over.

'Did you bally well see who *that* was?' he puffed. 'Blimey,' he said, noting their expressions, 'I had no idea he was *that* small.' He gazed out after the car which turned the corner and vanished. 'Practically a leprechaun,' he grinned. 'Now we know why Arbuthnot wanted us away: something's clearly afoot in Bikaner.'

Miss Heinz frowned at him – presumably irritated by his apparent enthusiasm for a person that she held with such displeasure. 'What exactly did he say to you?' she asked.

'Absolutely nothing at all,' beamed Harris. 'But he had this incredibly inscrutable expression, and actually this rather peculiar way . . .' He sighed. 'What a charismatic little fellow.'

Drabble smiled.

'That,' pronounced Miss Heinz, 'is exactly what we're up against.'

They rescued the luggage, and emerged from the temple-like structure, expected to be assailed as they had been in New Delhi, but arrived instead to find a large, dark empty square. In the distance the lights of the city of Bikaner twinkled. Reputed among the native states for its early adoption of electric lighting, this cityscape was dotted with bright illuminations, but elsewhere darkness was draped across the world like a vast cloak. In the distance was the outline of the fort – but there were countless roofs with smoking chimneys and dark masses of public buildings long-since shuttered for the night. A warm breeze came at them from the west, blowing hot from the great desert that lay beyond the city and ran all the way to the Punjab a hundred miles away in the north-west. Drabble inhaled the dry desert air.

The headlamps of a large motor-car flared into life from their right, bleaching them with light. It stopped abruptly in front of them, and through the glare they saw a large, booted figure climbed out: the silhouette of a pith helmet was visible, as were the outline of breeches and his broad middle. If the figure of Gandhi could have an opposite, this was it.

'The name's Pagefield,' the man-mountain announced blithely as though the effort of speech was almost too much for him. 'I'd be obliged if you chaps hopped in. There's plenty of space in the back —'

Drabble and Harris exchanged a glance; the tone made it clear that this was not an invitation they were accorded the choice of rejecting. Drabble called out, 'Who are you?'

'Me?' the speaker paused. 'I'm the British Resident of Bikaner, which means, Professor Drabble, that you are cordially obliged to do precisely what I ask.'

'You lot are meant to be here tomorrow evening,' noted Pagefield drily, as the car drove through the broad boulevards of Bikaner's princely centre, past darken grassy lawns and neatly planted trees. 'And you,' he said, turning partway towards Miss Heinz, 'are not meant to be here at all — who are you, in fact?' His heavy eyelids narrowed as he regarded Harris then Drabble, as if trying to work out who was responsible for the appearance of the unexpected female, one who was clearly not unappealing.

The tone of Miss Heinz's reply betrayed her disapproval at being regarded as an adjunct of either Drabble or Harris. 'The *Calcutta Enquirer*?' replied Pagefield in a tone of exasperation, as though he didn't quite approve of the newspaper or of the city. 'You're rather a long way from home, aren't you, miss?' He waved his hand dismissively from the front passenger seat, which his mass occupied almost entirely, saving for a narrow space for his driver. 'I'm sure it will all "check out", as they say in detective stories.' He cleared his throat. 'We just like to know who we've got from Mother Albion jogging about the place. Ah –' the 4.0-litre Crossley swept through a pair of open gates and up a small incline, 'here we are. Home sweet home.'

They pulled up in front of a statuesque stone mansion that could have been snatched up from Hampshire: a couple of decorative cannon and two sets of tall windows flanked a pillared porte-cochere, above which flew the Union flag. Elsewhere there were pots of geraniums parked with regimental precision. A pair of *sepoys*, Indian Army sentries, came to attention as they alighted. Pagefield saluted perfunctorily and lumbered up a short flight of stone steps to the double front doors, over which a Royal coat of arms was positioned. He stripped off his gloves and pith helmet and handed them with his swagger stick to a waiting Indian servant in white.

'I'm absolutely parched, Abdul,' he declared, addressing a second Indian attendant, this one dressed in a dark morning coat. 'We'll need five gins and tonic, please, *chop-chop*, and do send someone up to fetch Captain Dundonald, will you?'

The man withdrew, and Pagefield led the party through along the corridor to the rear of the property and into a commodious salon. This was arranged in club style with various wicker armchairs, chairs, sofas, and tables dotted about. The windows were open, fans turned, and the temperature was tolerable. It was only now that Drabble really became aware of Pagefield's extreme bulk, which combined with his height – he was a head taller than six foot – probably tipped the scales in excess of twenty stone. The belt around his waist would easily have encircled Drabble, Harris, and Miss Heinz, and perspiration beaded on the fatty flanks of his face. The outstanding feature of his face was a mole which was an adjunct of the right fleshy part of his nose, giving the impression of a third nostril.

'Gins and tonic, everyone?' Pagefield asked placidly. The Indian barman could be heard already mixing the drinks at double time.

Pagefield invited them to sit down and planted himself at the centre of a sofa meant for two, which he filled easily, receding into the mass of silk cushions, like a pasha on the verge of decadence. He brushed aside his mop of grey hair and smiled genially at them all, like a kindly prep school master scoping out a boy for the science field trip. He reached for the first of two glasses placed before him.

'Good health,' he said to one and all, raising his gin and tonic, which looked dainty in his large, heavy hand. 'Allow me to offer you a warm welcome to Bikaner from the Rajputana Agency.' At this he took a great gulp of his drink which left barely half of the vessel's fluid behind. 'Now,' he smiled, allowing his large heavy face to relax around his fleshy mouth. 'I've got good news for you and bad news: the bad news is that none of you is allowed to leave the Residency until further notice – not without my permission. The good news is that as well as fine gin and tonic, I have the best wine cellar in Bikaner outside of the Maharaja's palace and we have a swimming pool, which is just about the only thing that stops us going stark-raving mad in the summer.'

Harris attempted to protest but Pagefield spoke over him.

'Don't fret, Sir Percival,' he bulldozed emolliently. He moved on to his second gin and tonic. 'You shan't miss the grand unveiling on Thursday morning and you will get your interview, that I promise. The Maharaja is very, *very* keen to fulfil that commitment. That I can guarantee!' Pagefield grinned. 'In order to keep you occupied I have a packed programme of Bikaneri immersion for you tomorrow – a grand tour of the state in other words – which I trust you will enjoy. There is nothing to worry about –'

Harris finally cut in: 'But what about His Highness?' he demanded. 'He telegraphed me last night. He's expecting us this evening.'

'Calm yourself, Sir Percival,' said Pagefield. 'It's all been settled. In point of fact the Maharaja is not expecting you this evening, and in any event he is indisposed.'

'Indisposed with the most dangerous man in British India, presumably?' asked Miss Heinz.

Pagefield frowned over at her, squishing his face as though he was trying to read small text on the back of a bottle. 'I'm afraid that as the British Resident I'm not privy to all of the Maharaja's engagements, private or public.' He spoke with apparent sincerity. 'Perhaps Sir Percival can ask him, if he has the chance on Thursday?' He cleared his throat. 'Which reminds me, one small matter I would draw to all your attention, should you forget: we are not in fact in British India. Bikaner is an independent sovereign state, nominally anyway. And of all people the Maharaja would likely be a little bit touchy about that one.'

Pagefield smiled at each of them and put down his second glass, which was already empty. 'Now, honoured guests, shall we have some supper? I don't know about you but I'm famished.' He heaved himself up from the settee and inspected his wristwatch. 'Is twenty minutes enough time to change?' he ventured. A glance at the party offered no opposition. He turned his large face towards the opening leading to the hallway and bellowed, 'Abdul!'

'What in God's name is this place?' asked Drabble as he looked out of the open windows of the second floor of the British Residency. Before him, beyond the lawns and herbaceous borders of the Home Counties-grounds and the eight-foot high perimeter wall, the lights of the city of Bikaner and the royal palace, the Junagarh Fort, glowed invitingly. 'Christ alive,' he growled under his breath. Shards of glass twinkled on the pinnacle of the perimeter wall.

'What do we do?' asked Harris somewhat abjectly. He looked down at his bandaged foot: there wasn't much he could do. Drabble gazed back out at the city beyond: somewhere out there was Mahatma Gandhi, one of the world's most compelling

41

figures and the man who would, notwithstanding the machinations of diehards like Superintendent Goodlad or Miss Heinz, someday quite possibly lead India to freedom. That he was out there, and likely as not meeting the Maharaja of Bikaner, made it very interesting. Next, the simple fact that the GOI – Drabble swore, he was doing it now; he corrected his pattern of thought, the fact that the *Government of India* had actually made the effort to prevent Harris's presence in Bikaner at this time, and had now effectively taken them prisoner without any grounds whatsoever in order to prevent whatever it was that they thought they might do, meant that something was going on. And the fact that Pagefield had known his identity, too, rankled with him; just as it had with Superintendent Goodlad – indeed, Pagefield could be forgiven for knowing who was travelling with Harris, but Goodlad had no good reason to know about him. For whatever reason, the Government of India had decided that Professor Ernest Drabble, a relatively unknown historian from Sidney Sussex College, Cambridge, was an enemy of the Raj, one that required some official observation.

Christ knows why, thought Drabble – though his minor public profile following the climbing accident the year before and his anti-imperialist views might be enough to excite paranoid officialdom. In any event, being an enemy was certainly better than being a friend of the Raj. He gazed out at the silhouette of the royal fort: it was something like a thousand yards long, with steep red sandstone walls picked out in the electric light of the city making it hard to avoid. He looked at the high bastions. Something was afoot. Something important. The powers that be didn't go to so much trouble in order to conceal nothing. And this was before he had even given consideration to the presence of Miss Heinz: she hadn't just come along for the ride by chance or because of Harris's charms. He simply wasn't that charming.

Drabble leaned out of the window, and looked down at the ground – a potted geranium stood about twenty feet below, on the fringe of the gravel drive. Beyond it was the turf, and then flower beds and the high, shard-tipped wall. That all offered no great obstacle. Next he reviewed the Junagarh Fort. Getting there would not be hard, but getting *in* to find out what was going on was not going to be easy. Nor would be explaining himself if and when he was discovered. But there was nothing insurmountable about any of it. And that made it tempting. It was a little bit like a mountain. Why would you climb one? Because it's there, as Mallory said.

'I think,' said Drabble, as Harris pulled out his dress shirt from his suitcase, 'I'll skip supper.'

'Really?'

'Yes,' he stared out at the mass of the fort. 'I feel like a walk.'

'W-what are you going to do?

Drabble peered down over the windowsill.

'I'm still deciding.'

The first challenge would be to exit the British Residency unobserved. Since Pagefield had made it very clear that they were his forced guests – prisoners was the real word for it – for another day at least, and given that it was the seat of British influence in the region, one would imagine that it was a relatively secure environment. There were two armed sentries at the door for a start and at least one or two more doing the rounds. And there he was: turning the corner, a turbaned soldier, just yards below, Lee-Enfield rifle slung over his shoulder, doing his utmost for the British Empire. Good man.

Drabble checked his watch and then went to his bags: he never went anywhere without a twenty-five-yard length of climbing rope and a compass, and Rajasthan was no different.

Harris, who was now dressed in his dinner suit, lit his pipe, 'I'll tell Pagefield that you've got a bit of a dicky tummy or that you've retired. I can lock the door behind me when I go down, though I daresay they'll have a spare.'

'Let's cross that bridge if we come to it,' said Drabble.

Ten minutes later they were ready: the lights were out, and Drabble had a crude map of the city drawn on a piece of Residency notepaper in his pocket. He gripped his hemp climbing rope – the far end of which was knotted around the legs of the cast iron bath – and leaned backwards out of the second floor window.

'Be careful!' hissed Harris.

From a cord at his waist hung a deer-skin rug borrowed from the room. They had waited for the sentry to pass, giving them now approximately six minutes before he was back again.

'Good luck, Ernest old man!' Harris waved. 'I'll keep watch for you. If you get a really good scoop I'll share the byline with you!'

Drabble stepped out, the line became taut, and he began to reverse his way down the exterior of the building. He carefully sidestepped the windows of the lower ground floor, and nimbly landed to one side of the potted geranium, looked up, and waved at Harris, who was already snatching the rope back up.

Drabble made a low dash towards the wall, which was taller than the eight feet he had estimated from the window. There was nothing to get hold of on the wall, so he scaled one of the bordering trees and, having thrown the rug over its glass shard-embedded top, half jumped onto it; feeling the glass press against the pelt, he got his leg up and was over.

He dropped down onto the hard dusty ground outside the wall and walked smartly away from the compound – away from the entrance where a guard might spot him, across the broad thoroughfare and towards the dark streets of Bikaner. Several dozen camels, under blankets and tightly corralled against the walls of the bazaar, filled a large part of the opening. Various robed figures moved around among them, casting shadows into the night. On the left a dozen carriages were lined up, their lean horses still tethered to them, heads deep in feeding sacks. Their drivers slept, wrapped in their robes, on the leather seats of their carriages.

From here the fort dominated the cityscape. It was directly

due east and Drabble knew that so long as he kept in that direction, broadly speaking, then he couldn't miss it. The narrow pathway through the bazaar – with dozens of stalls either dormant or still being packed up for the night along either side, many framed under the strings of electric lights – zig-zagged this way and that. Then, abruptly, Drabble was out of the bazaar, and the space opened up into a square. Beggars, loiterers, off-duty shopkeepers, and camel-men all gathered around low fires. There were prouder buildings beyond – two to four storeys high, stronger-looking, and with twinkling light seeping from the lattices and shutters of upper floors, and smoking chimneys above. These were the homes and havelis and offices of Bikaner. Jutting into the sky above them was the fort – powerful, and faintly malevolent.

Drabble kept moving. To pause for too long would only draw attention to himself. That said, a lonely sahib walking around Bikaner at this time of night unattended was probably conspicuous enough. Drabble headed towards a break in the larger buildings before him, where he saw a road running approximately in the direction he desired. He forced his way through a pack of beggars and hawkers, and was soon among ornate dwellings, in quieter and more handsome streets. A covered carriage clattered by and all around were the unfamiliar smells and sounds of an alien culture, one that he half-recognised but only subconsciously.

As he closed on the city centre, these buildings, by stages, became bigger and more spaced out. They also changed purpose: soon they were for government functions or municipal departments, with flags flying from their roofs. Drabble reached a vast layout of boulevards and parks and wide roads running this way and that. He saw statues and fountains, and ornamental copses by lakes, and then straight ahead was a gate set in the high walls of the Junagarh Fort, an imperious pile that filled the eye. Most of it was in darkness but in occasional lights and burning braziers he glimpsed high bastions connected by lower walls capped with rounded Oriental crenulations. Here and there were pretty balconies with domed roofs that appeared to be standing on stilts. It was enchanting. Lights shone from within the guardhouse outside the gate, where a profusion of soldiers was gathered.

Drabble checked his watch: he had abseiled from the window of the British Residency thirty minutes ago; assuming all was well, Pagefield and his ilk would still be in the dark about his departure. Quite possibly.

He straightened his college tie and walked directly to the most lavishly turned-out soldier he could see at the front gate. He was armed with an ornate spear – it was even garlanded with an orange bow – and wore a splendid moustache.

He listened respectfully as Drabble introduced himself as Harris, produced his business card, and asked permission to enter the palace in order to wait upon his highness the Maharaja, with whom he had an appointment – which he further evidenced with the telegram that Harris had received from the maharaja's office the day before.

Minutes later he was in, and sitting in a visitors' parlour, waiting to be conveyed by whoever had been nominated to handle this late-arriving guest.

'Sir Percival sahib?'

Drabble looked up to see a young Indian in white uniform, broad sash at his waist. 'I shall take you to Mr Panikkar now, if you please.' He led Drabble along marbled corridors; at first doorways led off to the left, and arches to the right opened up to a great courtyard with ornate gardens beyond which was an architecturally significant doorway, once again flanked by guards, leading to what Drabble supposed was the heart of the palace: and where he needed to be. They turned away from the courtyard behind, passing the grand offices of the senior figures of the state: here the walls to either side were decorated with great gilded mirrors as well a mighty paintings of hunting scenes; here was the Maharaja firing upon rampant tigers from the relative safety of a *howdah*; there was a hippopotamus being dispatched by a hunter.

Drabble did not know how much further he was going to get before arriving at the office of Mr Panikkar, whoever he was, but he knew that when he did it wouldn't take long for his deception to be discovered: indeed Panikkar himself might already be alert to the fact that the British Resident had decided to temporarily detain Harris regardless of the Maharaja's invitation and therefore be somewhat surprised to see him. He might also have immediately telephoned to Pagefield to check – meaning that Drabble was walking towards immediate arrest. Finally, it was possible that Panikkar knew what either Harris or Drabble looked like, at which point he would be exposed, and likely as not detained.

Drabble's clever ruse to gain entry to the fort no longer looked very clever at all: it certainly did not seem to offer an outcome that led to him discovering the true nature of Gandhi's presence in Bikaner or the reason for their detention. Indeed, his best bet might be to get out of here as soon as he could. He had been impetuous. At best. He had allowed his indignation over their treatment and his curiosity to get the better of his judgement. At the next available junction – with corridors leading off in both directions – as the footman walked on, Drabble silently peeled away to the right. The corridor ahead was clear. He broke into a sprint – as light-footed as he could manage.

He had to get as much space as he could between himself and his chaperone, and there was no knowing how many seconds it would be before his disappearance was noticed but that would be all he needed. With every step he expected a cry or shout – but no siren or alarm was raised.

At the next corner he slowed to an officious pace and started to get himself back towards the courtyard: once inside the principal building he knew he would be able to find his way out. A double file of soldiers headed his way along the corridor: he spurred right, ascending a broad staircase to the first floor. Here he knocked at the first door, which he reckoned led to a room fronting onto the courtyard, and entered: it was an unoccupied office in darkness but for the light from the courtyard seeping in through the shutters from the courtyard. He shut the door behind him and sank back against it. His heart was beating fast. He had been a fool.

Drabble checked his wristwatch: it was 10.05 pm If it hadn't happened already then any minute now Pagefield would be receiving a phone call telling him that a missing Briton was on the loose in the fort. That's if he hadn't already called to warn the palace first to expect him. He opened the window and discreetly drew the shutter back to get a view into the courtyard. As he hoped, the windows were all but next to the first floor balcony of the central building. He scanned the courtyard – it was virtually empty, save for the two sentries guarding the entrance to the main palace building, and climbed out of the window. His toes found convenient purchase on a narrow decorative stone ledge which protruded about a yard below the windowsill: he edged along the wall, clinging to the stonework of the window, and from there leapt the yard and a half to the balustrade of the balcony. He got his foot up and a second later was over the barrier and crouching on the far side; out of sight and inside the main palace, his heart pounding.

Drabble drew a deep breath and took stock. There were open arches at window height running the length from the end of the balcony to a ceremonial centre where they were extended to full length. Drabble crawled along to the doorway and peered in. Inside was a broad gallery, which he expected looked down upon the entrance hall of the structure. No one was in sight, so he went inside to get a better look. From this vantage point he saw two more uniformed guards at a grand doorway leading to the next chamber on the floor below: ahead, on this storey, a pair of doors, somewhat more domestic in size, led off in each corner.

Carefully drawing open the left hand of these, Drabble was finally rewarded for his efforts: and he permitted himself a smile. It led into a small private gallery, with screen doors at either end, overlooking a vast state room, adorned with illuminated panels of Rajput warriors and ornate reliefs crisply realised in red Rajputana sandstone. Below, looking past a vast chandelier of a thousand pieces of crystal glass, he saw a horseshoe arrangement of chairs, occupied by dozens of princes in their finery; turbans of silver and gold, adorned with pearls and gems; the room glittered and glistened. At the lucky end of the horseshoe were two prime figures: the Maharaja of Bikaner, dressed in white uniform, long coat with a yellow cross-sash and thatch of medals and decorations on his breast, and his bejewelled, plumed turban. Next to him was a crouched figure dressed simply in a hand-woven white cotton *dhoti* wrapped from his shoulders. His head appeared shaved and he wore a greying moustache beneath his generous nose which supported a small pair of gold-rimmed spectacles: Mahatma Gandhi sat seemingly motionless, looking ahead at the gathered princes. You had to wonder what he made of this richly adorned caste: not much, in all likelihood. He had been telling them to throw off their jewels for decades.

'Why should we give up our sovereign rights and property,' croaked an elderly voice in heavily accented Indian English from below – the back rows of the horseshoe were obscured by the ledge and balcony. 'Many of our states have been around longer than half the nation states of Europe – some longer even than England.' The room echoed to 'hear-hears' and the Maharaja glanced over anxiously to Mr Gandhi. Another figure stood to speak and the room fell to silence: he was an imposing mass enveloped in orange silk robes topped with a golden turban.

'My forefathers have ruled Mysore since 1399,' he declared acidly. 'I can tell you all right now that I have no intention of supporting this motion: whatever happens to British rule, *we* can and *we* will endure.' His powerful, heavily ringed hand shot in the air. 'You may regard the comparison as trite or unworthy,' he said, jabbing his finger in the direction of Sir Ganga Singh and Mr Gandhi, 'but Mysore is significantly larger than several European countries combined; we are prosperous, we are outward-looking – we can and we will adapt and survive and continue to flourish regardless of whatever happens to British India. At this present time I can see no need to amalgamate ourselves with British India or its successors – such as by grace of God, our King-Emperor, may permit. I can see no benefit to be accrued from discarding seven centuries of tradition and continuity: it will not make my people richer, any happier, or improve their conditions. On the contrary, the only benefits I see accruing from this are to whatever successor arrangement takes shape ruled from Delhi. We have made our pacts with the British – some good, some less so. But let us now keep our powder dry and see what comes next, and make new arrangements if and when necessary. I do not support this initiative and I urge the chamber to throw it out.' He plumped down into his seat, amid a ripple of applause.

Sir Ganga Singh got to his feet. 'Thank you, Your Highness, for that contribution,' he stated. 'I now invite Mr Gandhi to offer a few words in response to the Princely contribution. Mr Gandhi –'

Leaning on the arms of the chair, the wizened figure pushed himself up and stood. In so doing he was partially obscured from Drabble's view by the bottom of the low-hanging chandelier. Drabble saw that by moving into the next gallery along – connected by a small connecting screen door – that he should see him clearly. He moved silently through to the next compartment and got a better view: Gandhi was not quite smiling. He looked to the left and then the right. He had still not said a word. The room was dead silent. Then he began, his voice barely audible.

'Your Highnesses –'

Just then, Drabble heard the sound of something metal and heavy being dropped – the decided *clunk* of it landing hard on the floor – and then rolling. There was a scuffle and slight scramble, the squeal of rubber soles sliding on a polished floor, Drabble guessed amid panic and recovery by whoever had dropped the original item. The noise came from the adjoining gallery. Drabble slid over.

Through the screen he saw of an Indian man – jet black hair and the partial profile showing a light beard, dressed in a long brown traditional coat or *sherwani*. He crouched, bent forward, straining to retrieve something lodged beneath the wooden balustrade. Something about his desperation was unsettling, as was the sweat pouring generously down his face. He knelt forward to reach further . . .

Drabble silently opened the screen door and got behind the man just as he started righting himself from his full stretch and was getting back up. His right hand was balled around a black object which Drabble recognised immediately; the ring-pull dangled over his knuckle and he was about to snatch it out – but then he evidently realised someone was behind. He turned to look.

Drabble recognised the unshaven face that confronted him immediately. It belonged to the agitator he had seen the night before in Delhi, awaiting his fate: the man who had led the protest and been beaten in the street. There was the same pinched frown at the bridge of the nose and the heavy eyebrows that met in the middle. The side of his face was heavily bruised – doubtless from Superintendent Goodlad or one of his officers. Now, though, the expression was one of wide-eyed determination.

Drabble lunged for the hand grenade. The force of his effort sent them both over – Drabble, whose hands were clamped around the hand that held the bomb, landing mostly on top of the would-be bomber. He came down heavily, hoping it would wind him and it did. The bomber grunted painfully but was fighting, using his free hand to strike at Drabble's face and kicking up his knees and scrambling to get free. In the background Drabble was suddenly aware of shouts from below. They crabbed along the floor of the gallery, sandwiched between the fixed wooden benches and the balustrade, Drabble clinging on for dear life to the hand that held the grenade. The bomber scrambled back fast, giving his legs clearance to kick Drabble in the head: he grinned as his heel landed hard. Drabble leaned into the blows and surged forward, breaking the space and headbutting the bomber in the groin as hard as he could. Now it was his turn to smile.

The man cried out – and Drabble was atop him; looking down into the whiskery face, smelling the stale odour of ghee and garlic on his breath and seeing defiance. The bomber suddenly let go of his right hand, releasing the grenade, but held on to the pin with his left. It whipped free as Drabble and the Mills Bomb tumbled backwards. Still holding it, Drabble doubled over and then charged towards the far screen door on his knees and elbows. The bomber flew after him, leaping towards him and landing on his back, crushing him to the floor: in that moment the small pineapple-shaped grenade spun from Drabble's grip and out through the open doorway.

He heard the hand lever spring free.

He whirled around as the bomber sought to scamper over him to get the grenade: but Drabble held him. *One thousand*. He wrestled to free himself – but Drabble held firm. *Two thousand*. Suddenly Drabble let go – but the man did not now scamper towards the bomb – instead he darted for far door, in the other direction. *Three thousand*.

Drabble snatched up the grenade, and ran back out towards the open balcony and the large courtyard beyond. *Four thousand*. His heart thumped in his chest. He reached the balustrade to see the courtyard thronged with princes and their attendants feeling the main chamber –

'Take cover!' he shouted, and slung the grenade through the window of the empty office that he had come from. *Six thousand*. Drabble turned away from the balcony and hurled himself towards the interior.

The explosion was deafening. There was a sudden rush of air. The noise hit – and the flash lit the whole courtyard, casting shadows on the walls that Drabble glimpsed as he landed. The six windows and shutters that lined the office blasted out and smoke poured from the dark scarred opening left behind. Broken glass, splinters, and fragments of masonry pelted the floor and his back and continued to rain down for several seconds.

Drabble rolled over, looked out at the doorway, the balcony and billowing dust, his chest heaving. He shut his eyes and let his head fall back with relief, feeling the crunch of glass and grit under it. Disaster averted. He took a deep breath. Thank you God. Then remembered the bomber.

He scrambled to his feet – every muscle in his body ached. Just then a sharp pain knifed through his brain, causing his head to spin. Christ alive. He swallowed and took a deep breath. Thank the Lord for the adrenalin that had saved him from feeling it sooner. He rubbed his head groggily . . .

'Don't move a muscle,' commanded a voice in crisp King's English. He looked over. Through the dust, in the darkness, Drabble saw a dozen or so turbaned soldiers kneeling in line with rifles aimed at him and a British officer standing behind them, his revolver raised.

Chapter Five

Drabble was cuffed, led to a police van, and then driven a short way to the police station, a modern building with the red and saffron flags of Bikaner flying from it at regular intervals. There, after giving a statement, he was left, still handcuffed, to stew over his crimes in a cell – declarations of innocence ignored until further notice. He eventually slept a little on the skinny bunk, but the dawn woke him early.

Laying on the bunk, gazing up at the fresh light from the window, Drabble felt confident of a swift vindication – one which would draw his incarceration to a rapid close. It was the only reasonable course, after all, just as it was fairly reasonable that he would initially be presumed guilty given the presentation of the circumstances.

The precise timing of the bombing – apparently just as Mr Gandhi was speaking – made it appear like an attack aimed at *him*, but the simple fact of the device meant many of occupants of the room would be injured regardless. What he couldn't square, then, was who would want to attack both Mr Gandhi and his senior cohort of Indian princes. It might be reasonable to find those interested in attacking one of them – plenty of people hated either the princes or Mr Gandhi, but not necessarily both. That said, Gandhi's position against armed struggle, in favour of peaceful means, did put him at odds with the most extreme nationalists. But the princes? Why bring them into it? They would have to be sufficiently nationalist to regard the princes as

54

collaborators of the British, that might be sufficient. Either way, he thought, we were clearly dealing with an individual with very extreme views; one who had the ability to penetrate the royal palace, too.

Shortly after eight o'clock Colonel Pagefield arrived, his immense bulk immediately making the cell feel even smaller and more claustrophobic. He looked down at the bunk, which rather looked like it would collapse under him, and having noted the smell from the bucket and that Drabble occupied the only chair, called back out to the guard.

A few minutes later, they were seated in an interview room that was a little larger but did not suffer the same smell and had three or four suitable chairs. Pagefield ordered tea from the guard, a stubbly, stooped fellow evidently possessed of a disposition for pleasing his fellow man. He walked away saying he would do his best. Pagefield took out a meerschaum pipe, which he proceeded to fill with tobacco and beamed at Drabble.

'Well, *this* is a fine to-do,' he remarked in an avuncular fashion. 'Fancy yourself as a modern day Captain Blood, do you?' Pagefield grinned, and lit the pipe, the bowl flaming as he puffed at it. 'In a moment, a certain Colonel Stewart is going to arrive. Colonel Stewart, whom you met last night but weren't formerly introduced to, is the Maharaja's chief of police and head of security. He's obviously having a challenging day.' Pagefield paused and offered a flat smile. 'My suggestion to you, my learned Professor, is that when he arrives you keep the obfuscation to a minimum and tell him exactly what happened. Otherwise Colonel Stewart is liable to become rather agitated. That's if you want to keep your head.' He puffed elaborately on the stem of his meerschaum. 'That's how they roll here,' he added with a delicious smirk. 'A swift sword stroke.' To illustrate the point, he made sharp slicing gestures with his hand.

The interview room door was unbolted and opened to reveal a spare, military man north of fifty. It was Colonel Stewart, and Drabble recognised him as the officer who had arrested him the night before. He wore the khaki uniform with red collar flashes of a full British Army colonel – and the look of a man who had not slept. He was followed into the room by a Bikaneri officer kitted out in a similar uniform, but with the insignia of a police inspector. They both sat down. The inspector passed Stewart a dossier from his leather briefcase.

'Ernest Drabble,' he said firmly. 'I am holding you on suspicion of the attempted murder of his High Highness, Sir Ganga Singh, the Maharaja of Bikaner, in addition to the attempted murder of His Exalted Highness the Nizam of Hyderabad, as well as Their Highnesses the Princes of Mysore, Udaipur, Jaipur . . .'

By the time Colonel Stewart reached Gandhi's name, Page-field had finished his pipe and was gently emptying its contents against the heel of his boot. Stewart laid down the paper and looked over at Drabble.

'This is a palpable nonsense,' he declared. 'There must be witnesses who saw me fighting with the bomber – the man you should actually be hunting? The fight is, after all, what sounded the alarm. Without my intervention, the men you just mentioned would all have been blown to smithereens – or not far off it.'

They let his statement stand a moment.

'You entered the palace under false pretences,' continued Stewart. 'To what end?'

Drabble eyed Pagefield, who was observing him closely.

'To find out the truth, and escape a bogus imprisonment.'

'Bogus –' Pagefield spat the word with surprise. 'How dare you. You had clear instructions and you ignored them; not only that, but you effectively broke in to a top secret diplomatic conference. It's unconscionable conduct for a British subject and in flagrant opposition to official instructions.'

'Yes,' agreed Stewart. 'What *were* you planning to do with this "truth" when you found it?' The man's voice was dry, as though a lifetime in the tropics had baked his larynx, and there were liver spots in the hairline of his neat grey hair.

Drabble considered his response.

'In all honestly, Colonel, I don't know. The simple fact is that I disapprove of illegal confinement —' he scowled at Pagefield, 'and as I said, we had seen Mr Gandhi at the station, and I wanted to know what was afoot, not least because it seemed strangely coincidental with our imprisonment. We knew something was up and simply wanted to find out what.' The logic seemed feeble in the cold light of day, but there it was.

Stewart nodded.

'If that's as you say, why was it that you threw a Mills bomb into a crowded courtyard full of some of the most important men in India? I don't see how that helps you find the truth?'

'I've told you before,' insisted Drabble. 'I wrestled the Mills bomb from the real would-be bomber and saved the lives of everyone on your charge sheet, and a good few others besides, I dare say, by throwing it *across* the courtyard into an empty office.' Drabble's temper got the better of him and he shook at his handcuffs. 'This is preposterous. How many terrorists shout "take cover" when they throw their bloody bombs?'

'We have only your word for that,' replied Stewart tartly. 'Rather more importantly, since we have tried and failed to find the second man who you allege was involved in this outrage: then we can only conclude that your fellow conspirator or what have you is a will 'o the wisp —'

'He's not a ruddy will 'o the wisp,' interrupted Drabble. 'Look, I've seen him before in Delhi. If you contact Superintendent Goodlad of the Imperial Police in New Delhi, I will get you a name for him.'

Stewart looked doubtfully at Drabble.

'We have so far been unable to locate Goodlad,' he said, glancing over at the inspector, whose expression was equally implacable. 'But we are still endeavouring.'

He picked up the file that the inspector had produced and opened it on his lap, leafing through several of the pages, until he had seen enough. He closed it and dropped it down on table before him. 'You're a former member of the Communist Party of Great Britain; you continue to consort with known, active Marxists; you've previously taken part in anti-imperialist marches in London; you were even present at a home rule protest in New Delhi two nights ago – interestingly, that *was* confirmed in a security bulletin. As far as I can tell, Professor Drabble, you are a dangerous anarchist, and if there are any more like you teaching our best and brightest young things in England then God help Mother Country.' His face had coloured as he spoke. He cleared his throat. 'Fortunately for us, you are an incompetent anarchist. Your final throw of the Mills bomb was so bad that in the event only one or two persons received cuts and bruises as a result. For that you should be grateful. It might spare your miserable neck when this comes to trial.' Stewart rose from the table and put on his pith helmet. 'As far as I'm concerned, Drabble, you are a disgrace to Britain and the Empire.'

Drabble began to protest, but saw it was pointless.

'I'm innocent!' he exclaimed. 'Damn you!'

The door closed heavily and was bolted, leaving Drabble with Pagefield. The British Resident struck a match and lit his second pipe.

'Well I can't say I entirely disagree with him,' he announced cheerily, tossing his match to the floor.

'There *was* another man there,' insisted Drabble. 'He *was* going to bomb the meeting, killing or mutilating everybody. And I know who he was.'

'Except you don't know his name.'

'Not yet. When he strikes again, I'll be proved right.'

'Proved right isn't the same as innocent –'

'Look here, Pagefield, answer me this; what possible motivation would I have to want to kill these Indian princes or Mr Gandhi for that matter? H'm?'

Pagefield sighed expansively.

'What you're conveniently forgetting, Drabble, is that you were in point of fact an intruder into the palace; you then threw a bomb in front of scores of witnesses, albeit in what turned out to be fairly harmless fashion, but it could quite easily have killed or injured rather a lot of important people – quite apart from unimportant people. In that sort of circumstance, your "motivation" is rather after the event.' Pagefield offered a sardonic smile, 'Dare I say it? If only you'd been a good boy, done what you were told, and stayed for a curry supper, then all of this would have been avoided.'

Pagefield got to his feet and moved to the door.

'But they'd still be picking pieces of half the royal houses of India out of the panelling of the Junagarh Fort.'

'And Mr Gandhi too,' sighed Pagefield. He rapped on the door with his swagger stick, and waited for it to be unlocked. 'Unfortunately, as it stands, the authorities only have your word for it.'

Drabble threw up his arms:

'Pagefield, what's going to happen to me?'

The British Resident contemplated him for a moment in the doorway.

'Lord knows,' he said. He gave a lopsided smirk, 'Let me say this, whatever it is, you've probably got it coming.' He sighed wearily. 'If I had a penny for every well-intended do-gooder from mother country, I'd be a . . .' the conclusion of the sentence failed him and he shook his head. 'Drabble, you know, the problem with people like you is you don't know when you're not wanted. I'll do my best to get you out of here, so you know, but then I want you to jolly well go home. Is that understood?'

Right now, being sent straight home was a damned sight more attractive option than spending any length of time in a Bikaner prison.

'What about this bomber you've got on the loose, Pagefield?'

'If I were you, I'd focus on your own problems. They are grave enough as it is. Apologise to Sir Ganga Singh – and pray that he takes pity on you. I mean it,' he added.

Chapter Six

Harris was awoken by the heavy curtains of the bedroom being drawn with unceremonious ferocity by Captain Dundonald. Searing sunlight flooded in, and he was suddenly aware of others in the room, opening his luggage and rifling through his belongings.

'Hell's bells,' he wailed, as the noise, light, and unwarranted commotion intensified the pummelling, thumping sensation in his frontal lobes. 'I think I'm having a stroke.' He pulled the covers over his head and whinnied piteously, 'Christ alive. I need water. Water. Ernest, old man, fetch me some water. Please,' he croaked, 'it's an emergency . . .'

Suddenly he remembered: Ernest wasn't there. He hadn't come back last night. Harris had sat up with a bottle of whisky waiting – he remembered that the last thing he had had to do was to stay awake until Ernest had returned, so that he could lower the rope, permitting him to climb back. Oh, Lord. What had he done? 'Ernest,' he cried, snatching back the bedsheets. 'Where's Professor Drabble?' he demanded, scowling at Dundonald, and gripping his forehead. He growled at the various soldiers who busily snatched through Drabble's belongings, and were leafing quickly through their books. 'Get your hands off our things. What right have you got? What the dickens are you looking for?'

One of the privates slung down the poorly coiled rope onto the floor.

'Get dressed,' ordered Dundonald. He nodded at the soldiers. They seized the rope and various other objects on their way out. 'You'll be brought down for questioning shortly when Colonel Pagefield returns. Hurry.'

The door slammed shut. Harris tottered to his feet, still clutching his forehead as the pain of the hangover lanced through his brain. 'Holy Hannah,' he wailed as he approached the wash basin and regarded himself in the mirror. His face was the grey pallor of an elephant's gusset. His tongue was stained yellow from turmeric or some other Eastern spice, and his stomach was bloated – and churning. A sudden painful tension welled up in his nether regions, which had only one satisfactory answer. His eyes widened in horror. 'Christ alive –'

He steadied himself against the dresser and broke wind continuously for five or six seconds. Afterwards, sighing, his torso felt less rigid, like a children's helium balloon freed of the burden of quite so much gas. He cursed again under his breath. The face before him was not death warmed up, so much as death out cold. 'I've got to save Ernest,' he realised as he looked into the mirror.

Harris splashed water onto his face, pushing the fluid into his hairline and pores. Next he shaved – badly, cutting himself three times – and proceeded to brush his teeth, taking care to file his tongue to within an inch of its life. After all of that, and combing his hair, he battled his stiff collar and dressed himself. At the end of it, he looked respectable enough.

'I'm still drunk,' he realised, looking into the mirror.

Downstairs, he found Pagefield eating breakfast in the dining room and talking with Dundonald, who broke off and departed when Harris arrived. A vast platter of fruit sat in the middle of the table, which the host was plucking exotica from.

'There's also porridge, if you can stomach it,' Pagefield told him. 'And tea, which I think you might need.'

Harris salted some porridge generously and drank a cup of scaldingly hot tea.

'Where's Drabble?' he managed to croak.

Pagefield raised his eyebrows quizzically. Perhaps he was weighing up precisely what Harris did or didn't know. 'The professor is being detained by the Bikaner police,' he stated at last. 'Drabble was involved in an incident last night. You're bound to hear more soon, but that's all I can say at the moment.'

'An incident? Is he hurt?'

Pagefield considered this before answering. 'Not significantly. A few cuts and bruises.'

'Oh, thank heavens. But why on earth are the police detaining him? What has he done?'

Pagefield quartered a mango with his knife and fork. 'I really can't say at this stage.'

'Why not?'

He sighed and laid down his knife and fork. 'What on earth were you both thinking?'

'What do you mean?'

Pagefield waited for the Indian servant at the end of the table to finish arranging the fresh coffee pot but he took too long. Pagefield erupted, 'Will you get out,' he roared and the servant all but fled. The Colonel turned on Harris, 'Don't play games, Sir Percival. If you don't answer my questions, then you could well end up being charged as an accomplice to attempted multiple murder, not to mention terrorism charges. Do you understand?'

Harris, who had been chewing his porridge slowly, now swallowed hard.

'What on earth are you talking about?'

'The death penalty is well within reason, to be perfectly honest.'

'The-the *death* penalty?' screeched Harris. He glared at Pagefield: 'What on earth has Ernest done? Sodomised the royal guinea fowl?'

'He broke into a royal palace –'

'Oh, a bit of jape – a schoolboy prank –' Harris searched for his words, and found his feet, 'to ruddy well show that we

Englishmen can't be bullied about by some jumped-up, provincial colonial what-nots.'

Pagefield's fat lip curled.

'And how about hurling a hand grenade at twenty of India's most powerful princes?'

Harris lowered his porridge spoon.

'What?'

'It's to go no further —' Pagefield shot Harris a look that told him in no uncertain terms not to entertain the notion of defying him.

'N-now hang on Pagefield,' Harris stammered, 'it's fair to say that Drabble isn't a massive fan of the Empire — nor is he a particular plaudit of the hereditary principle when it comes to government, but I tell you this, Ernest Drabble is *not* and never would be the sort of man to do anything like that. No, no.' Harris scooped up a spoonful of porridge and shovelled it in. 'I'm afraid, Colonel Pagefield,' he broke into a caustic chuckle, 'that the Bikaneri police have fingered the wrong man for this one.' He shook his head, 'And if this sham continues, I will ensure that any miscarriage of justice is exposed for what it is — mark my words.'

As Harris drew breath, Abdul arrived at Pagefield's side and whispered into his ear. Pagefield rose.

'Excellent,' he pronounced. He beamed down at Harris. 'Sir Percival, Colonel Stewart is here to interview you . . .'

After an hour of questioning by Colonel Stewart and the really rather serious Inspector Bhattachardjee, Harris was given his liberty, liberty that was to remain in the grounds of the British Residency, pending further investigations until further notice.

'But how long will that be?' he protested. 'We have passage home booked in a fortnight from Bombay.'

The questioners remained impassive in such a way as to convey their disinterest in Drabble and Harris's prior travel arrangements.

During the preceding interview Harris had admitted his part in drawing up the rope necessary for Drabble's escape from the residency and for lying about his friend's illness to Pagefield in order to explain his absence. But Harris insisted trenchantly that it was entirely Drabble's idea to go off on a madcap traipse across the city to find out what Mr Gandhi was doing there, and that he could have had no idea of quite where that would lead him. Pulling up ropes did not quite make Harris an accomplice to much, so with reluctance, and doubtless motivated by a desire to keep the entire matter as quiet as possible in the British press, the journalist was not to be charged or detained under suspicion, so long as he was prepared to cooperate, which required complete confidentiality. Harris agreed readily.

The interview scheduled for the following day with the Maharaja and the attendance of the official unveiling of the statue were both on hold pending a final decision and a review of security arrangements due to take place that evening.

'I've come a very long way to conduct this interview,' Harris told them importantly. 'My editor will not take kindly to having the paper's valuable time and resources wasted if this does not go ahead.' Neither policeman looked especially irked about their apparent responsibility to Harris's superiors.

'If any word of this attack leaks out to the press, then there will be no interview – ever,' repeated Stewart.

Harris had offered the necessary assurances. Visits to Drabble were forbidden for the time being, added Stewart.

'And when will Ernest be released?'

'That will be in the hands of the judges to decide,' stated Inspector Bhattachardjee coldly.

Harris nodded his acknowledgement of that contribution. He didn't like the cut of Bhattachardjee's jib and didn't mind showing it.

The truth was that Harris wasn't convinced that the judicial systems of princely states should apply to British subjects – certainly not ones who were professors of Cambridge University – but he didn't like to press the legal point.

'You do both at least agree with me that he's not your man? Drabble is telling the truth. You do understand that it's quite simply absurd to think he was actually attempting to do any-thing of what you suggest? In fact it's frankly laughable.'

No one was laughing on the other side of the table: in fact, their expressions conveyed a tedious level of humourlessness.

'You'd be surprised at what people are capable of doing, Sir Percival,' said Bhattachardjee, not unsympathetically. 'You really would.' The inspector exchanged a meaningful glance with Col-onel Stewart, and added, 'At the very least, Professor Drabble will likely be fined for deliberate destruction of official property, with offences related to the wounds inflicted on several members of the Maharaja's household staff by the bomb he threw, by the possession of an illegal weapon, and for illegally entering a royal Bikaner palace. If I were to explain that this last offence alone carries a maximum sentence of five years' imprisonment, you'll appreciate quite the position that Professor Drabble is in.'

'Oh, tosh with knobs on,' fizzed Harris, throwing up his hands, but then clutching his forehead in agony.

'You might think it ridiculous, Sir Percival,' intoned Colonel Stewart, 'but I don't think that your friend will be needing his return ticket to Southampton any time soon.'

That comment sobered Harris up fast. For the first time he considered seriously the possibility of this business going awry. Was it really credible that Ernest would be imprisoned for intruding into the royal palace? I mean, in India. Come off it. This was precisely the sort of thing that got brushed under the carpet in places like this. *Plus*, was it really plausible that Drabble would serve a prison sentence, when in point of fact he must surely have averted a potentially disastrous incident? Harris scoffed and shook his head.

'Well, gentlemen,' he stated sombrely. 'I thank you both for your candour, and wish you a good day.' He reached out – to the astonishment of both Stewart and Bhattachardjee – and shook their hands vigorously. From now on, he decided, these men were to be his friends.

★

Where was Miss Heinz? That was a question, and a question-and-a-half, which Harris considered as he sipped a gin and tonic and looked out over the immaculate sunny, south-facing lawn of the British Residency. And why was it that he had been detained and questioned, but she, a member of their party, was seemingly above suspicion?

The conundrum bothered him, less than the hangover he still carried bothered his head, mind you, but it rankled. Where was she? He looked over to the bar and called out, 'Abdul, have you seen Miss Heinz?'

'Sight-seeing, Sir Percival sahib,' he replied smartly. 'With Captain Dundonald.'

'Captain Dundonald?'

'Yes, sir.'

Bloody cad, thought Harris, as Abdul returned to polishing glasses. That Scottish snake was grousing around his grass. And a damned impertinent one at that, if his conduct that morning was to be counted. Harris fumed and then sipped his gin and tonic. He had to get to see Ernest to assure him that everything would be well – or at least get word to him that Sir Percival Harris was on the case. Yes, he thought, as he took another sip of the gin and tonic. He had to do what he could to get the matter resolved. And he had to act with alacrity. Harris gazed out across the broiling lawns towards the high perimeter walls and sighed. Was alacrity with one L or two . . .

And then he had it. He was forbidden from leaving this dreaded place, but that didn't mean that they could deny *Ernest* visitors, nor communication with the outside world by other means. He checked his pocket watch: it was a little after eleven o'clock.

'Abdul,' he cried. 'I have to send a telegram to London this very instant.'

'London, sir?' replied Abdul coming around to the stand by Harris, a pristine starched white napkin draped over his sleeve.

'That's right. I also urgently need a chocolate cake to cele-
brate an important birthday. Does cook know how to make
chocolate cake?'

'Oh yes, Sir Percival sahib,' beamed Abdul. 'It is Colonel
Pagefield's favourite.'

'Excellent,' declared Harris as he reached for his stick. 'Let
the baking begin!'

Chapter Seven

Drabble stood on the chair and looked through the bars of the cell at the lengthening shadows across the broad, walled compound. Inmates in various states of human dilapidation perambulated around its dusty confines now that the glare of the midday sun had passed. He hadn't been here long enough to discover the daily rituals, nor did he feel up to a walk. In truth, Professor Ernest Drabble, no stranger to the odd tight corner, felt rather deflated. And what was more, he knew it. After the excitement and adrenalin of the fight, it seemed wholly inconceivable that this fate could possibly have befallen him. It was odd; he simply didn't believe that anybody could be quite so obtuse as to think that he was the attacker. More than this, nothing about his situation seemed to offer any respite: there were no loose bars in the windows; no hiding places in the cell from which to spring an attack on his keepers; nor had an unfeasibly large cake arrived from some well-wisher with all the trappings of escape therein concealed. In fact, he had no immediate means of escape on offer; he confronted an obdurate bureaucracy, and the only person that he could appeal to for help was an inept, or corrupt, morbidly obese official in the person of one Colonel Pagefield, who patently despised him. Drabble shut his eyes: there was only one thing he could do – and that was hope that something might happen. Or to fake an illness and hope that he might be transported to some sort of security-light sanatorium from which he could escape this overheated Lilliputian hellhole.

He swore and looked up at the sky, high above the high walls, where not a single cloud interrupted the brownish, blue heavens, and a line of Wilde's *Ballad of Reading Gaol* came to him: 'He walked amongst the trial men/in a suit of shabby grey/A cricket cap was on his head/His step was light and gay/But I never saw a man who looked/So wistfully at the day . . .'

The door to his cell was unbolted and a new guard arrived with a tray. The man, in his forties or fifties, smelled strongly of tobacco and had a dry cough that didn't sound promising. He set down a metal tray, which had a covered bowl of curry, a chapati, and a wooden mug of water, on the narrow table, laying it down with the cautious diligence of a holy offering. The guard even turned his back briefly on Drabble, thus giving him the opportunity to attack, but the man who had come close to scaling the north face of the Eiger, the man who had defeated a notable plot just months before, felt nothing but glum lethargy. The truth was that he'd had enough of schoolboy heroics. His stupid, boyish idea of getting into the palace on Harris's behalf had been utterly foolish, and frankly disrespectful of Bikaner and its ruler. The fact that it led to his so-far unrecognised act of heroism – dare he use such a word – didn't alter it one moment. Pagefield could go to hell, quite frankly, but the Bikaneris – the individuals in the police station – these all seemed to him to be thoroughly decent folk just trying to do nothing more than get through the day. Admirable enough. As if to prove the point, the guard, having deposited the supper, smiled and left the cell briefly, only to reappear with what looked like a large white cardboard cake box. He placed this with some formality on the table and then bowed before backing out of the room like a medieval-titled flunkey at the state opening of Parliament.

Drabble stared down at the box. There was no way on God's green earth that there was a cake inside it. There couldn't be.

He went to look, but couldn't quite allow himself to.

Surely there couldn't be.

He levered open the lid and looked inside: a round chocolate cake with the words 'Happy Birthday' iced across it met his gaze. A card was slotted in beside it. The unruly handwriting was Harris's and he had underlined various letters:

'Dear Drabble,' it said, 'Happy birthday!' Then beneath, he'd added: 'Keep your spirits up! Never mind the flies! Into every life rain must fall! Full steam ahead! Enjoy the cake!'

Drabble slotted the lid of the cake box shut and looked out at the sky through the bars. It didn't take a decoding expert to notice that the starting letter of the five sentences in the note spelt 'knife'. He frowned down at the cake. How had Harris got it through? It's a small marvel that he hadn't added, 'Chocks away!' or something similar just to ram home the point.

Drabble shook his head: bloody fool. But he went back to the cake box, opened it up and gently lifted the cake, which he noticed was circumvented by a generous, rather wide ribbon. It was rather solid, almost loaflike, and heavily dusted generously on top with cocoa powder. Lifting it up, Drabble gave a dry cough as the powder caught the back of his throat. He broke it carefully in half and got his fingers underneath it to its belly: sure enough, there was a metal object, his own penknife no less. Drabble placed the cake back down together neatly, shut the lid, and saw that his hands were stained brown by the chocolate cake. He wiped them, leaving dark brown streaks on his trousers, and then sat down to his curry supper.

So what was Harris's plan? Use the file in the penknife to brake the bolt of his handcuffs; then feign illness in the dead of night, summoning the guards; then overpower the guard using the threat of the knife; then gag the guard with one of his socks, say, and then tie his hands with the cake ribbon; then steal his uniform and black up using the cocoa powder from the cake so that in darkness he might reasonably walk unnoticed straight out the door – so long as no one took too close a look?

Holy mother of God. Drabble clenched his chapati angrily into a ball and threw it with venom against the wall. That was a plan of such insulting stupidity that only Harris could have dreamt it up. And not just Harris. But Harris in the grip of a mighty, prolonged, regret-infused hangover. To think for a moment that a scheme of such profound absurdity, a scheme of such ridiculous, frankly distasteful and racist conception, could possibly work. The fact was that it was nothing better than precisely the sort of prep-school prank that had ruddy well landed him there in the first place. Good grief.

Drabble looked down at his curry and realised that without the chapati he would have to pour it into his mouth. There was nothing for it. The chocolate cake would suffice. And then he would try Harris's appalling plan.

He looked up to the bars and saw that they were now lighter than the background behind them. Night would soon start falling and he didn't intend to spend any more time than he needed to in this cell. He looked down at his shackles; these had already chafed his wrists. He wouldn't miss these either.

Drabble ate the cake and got to work filing one of the metal cuffs with the knife. Progress was slow, but he had nothing else to pass the time with.

Harris, now dressed in black tie for dinner, was sitting in what had become *his* chair, in the drawing room of the British Residency, drinking a cool gin and tonic in the wake of an electric fan. It was better than nothing, even if it was mainly moving more hot air in his direction. Harris thought of Drabble for a moment, then decided not to. The guilt was too much for him. But he did wonder if the cake had reached his dear friend and whether he had deciphered the code. Harris grinned to himself. He was still pleased with his idea; moreover, he knew that if Drabble got the knife then he would get out. Then what? That's the bit he hadn't sorted out, but he knew that they could cross that bridge if and when it came to it. They always had done before. They would flee Bikaner, get to Bombay and escape.

He looked over at the grandfather clock: it was well after six and he had hoped to have heard from Colonel Stewart by now about the interview with the Maharaja. It was scheduled for the following morning, immediately before the unveiling of the new equestrian statue of the self-same man at eleven o'clock.

He had written up thorough notes based upon his conversations early in the day with Pagefield and then Stewart and Bhattachardjee, and was fully prepared to write the whole story on the basis of their testimonies – plus Drabble's of course when he got it – in revenge if they welched on the interview with the Maharaja.

Suddenly he glimpsed Miss Heinz, dressed in a long, flowing cream skirt and blouse, strolling like a dizzy flapper across the lawn with Captain Dundonald, he cutting a fine figure in his white dinner coat. Harris held his stomach in for a moment, but knew it was useless. He pushed up his spectacles and strained his eyes: Miss Heinz looked quite transformed – and what was that? Did their hands casually touch as they paused to admire the pear tree? Rage started to boil up in Harris and he gripped his gin and tonic with fury.

'Ah,' declared Pagefield. He clicked his fingers at the bar and Abdul caught his eye. 'They make rather an attractive couple, don't you think?' he said to Harris, who glowered out towards the lawn.

'H'm,' he said, after registering his guest's mood. 'Well, as far as I'm concerned, it's a ray of sunshine on an otherwise challenging day in paradise.' His tone was morose. 'If Dundonald can bring that one home, it will certainly make table plans a good deal easier to manage, and it should stop him getting into any further difficulties.' Pagefield cleared this throat. 'Which reminds me,' his attention returned to Harris, 'I had a word. Sir Ganga Singh *will* meet you in his office for thirty-five minutes at eight o'clock precisely tomorrow morning. You'll be driven from here promptly at seven fifteen precisely. Then you're to accompany me at the Maharaja's unveiling, and then attend the official lunch afterwards? Satisfactory?'

'Highly.'

'Good.'

Pagefield stood watching Dundonald and Heinz through the

window in the fading light. He emitted a withering sigh but said nothing. 'Christ, I need that gin and tonic.' He looked over at the bar, and snarled, 'Abdul!'

Miss Heinz and Captain Dundonald flirted throughout dinner – through to the trifle and then the most half-hearted cheeseboard Harris had ever seen. The disagreeableness only ended when Pagefield brought the social affair to a close by retiring not long before ten. Harris had had enough of it too by that point. The guests, who included a visiting Anglican priest and a European engineer on the Maharaja's staff, were relatively distracting. But none of them distracted from the looks of mild irritability that he saw Pagefield shooting in Miss Heinz's direction. As he savoured a pipe and one last whisky in his room before turning in – along with a chapter or two of Kipling – Harris could only wonder at the probable cause. Likewise he could only wonder at how Drabble was getting on.

There was a knock at the door, and Pagefield burst in.

'We've received a telegram for you from London,' he announced. He did not disguise his fury. 'It's from the palace.'

They both knew precisely what he meant about that. He proffered it to Harris.

'You've read it?'

'Of course I bloody well have,' he growled as Harris scanned the spare response. 'I don't know what you think you've done to earn royal favour, but they're certainly not interested in helping Drabble.' So they weren't, thought Harris. Pagefield glared. 'Don't try and pull rank like that on me again. After your interview tomorrow, Sir Percival, you're leaving Bikaner and Rajputana – for good. You're nothing but trouble.'

He turned to leave and almost walked straight into Abdul, who he saw was in a state of some excitement.

'Colonel Pagefield sahib,' he declared, getting his breath back. 'There's an important message from the police headquarters. You're to go there *this* instant.'

Chapter Eight

The high and low bolts securing the door of Drabble's cell were drawn and the heavy metal panelled door swung open. Low light streaked in from the corridor, and he was led along the corridor and shown into an interview room, where Colonel Pagefield sat waiting.

The British Resident looked tired and smoked a cigarette, his fat wet lips pecking at it in an agitated fashion. He had removed his homburg and was dressed in a double-breasted black dinner suit that contained enough fabric to shelter a family of Bedouin. 'What in God's name do you want, Drabble?' he roared. 'There's quite enough going on here without histrionics.' He glared at the guards: 'And where's that chai I bloody well asked for?'

The officer with the stoop reversed out muttering apologies like a chastised courtier. He closed and locked the door, leaving a second policeman standing watch in the corner. 'So what in God's name can possibly be so bloody urgent that you call me away from the residency after ten o'clock in the ruddy evening, on the night before the Viceroy visits?'

Pagefield pulled at the cigarette, the cloud of smoke pouring ostentatiously from his nostrils. Drabble didn't like the man, but he had decided that he was trustworthy.

'Do you want a slice of cake?' he asked.

Pagefield accepted. The guard was sent for and the cake retrieved – and a slice produced.

'It's chocolate,' chewed Pagefield, with approval. 'Where did you get that from?' he asked, quite possibly recognising the handiwork. Drabble confirmed his suspicions and invited him to take a slice, one which Drabble had already cut with the penknife, which was now in his sock. He then slipped out the square of newspaper that the cake was sat on, and unfolded it. 'This is,' he said, pushing it towards the masticating Pagefield, 'yesterday's *Calcutta Enquirer*. If you look here, you'll see that the paper's correspondent, MV Heinz, is presently in Rangoon covering a trade conference.'

As this news sank in the door was unbolted and tea for two arrived – two glasses of black tea in saucers, sugar cubes slowly dissolving at the base of each. 'Therefore it's quite impossible for Heinz to be in Bikaner, staying at the British residency and flirting with Sir Percival Harris.'

'She's moved onto Captain Dundonald,' stated Pagefield, his mouth still full of cake.

'Has she now?' Drabble watched the police officer withdraw. 'I presume that Captain Dundonald is intricately appraised of the arrangements for the visit by the Viceroy tomorrow?'

Pagefield nodded gravely, then wiped the corners of his mouth clean with a spotted handkerchief. 'So who do you think she is?'

'And what's she up to?'

'Quite.'

'I've no idea,' replied Drabble. 'But my instinct is that she almost certainly has something to do with the attempted bombing last night – *and* quite possibly with whatever might be to come tomorrow if nothing is done to prevent it. The Viceroy *plus* the Maharaja at a public gathering offers a tremendously tempting target for those so minded.'

Pagefield nodded disagreeably.

'All right, Professor, I may as well tell you that I had my own suspicions confirmed this afternoon by a telegram from the editor of the *Calcutta Enquirer*. Miss Heinz is an impostor. I am yet to present her with the discovery – that was due to wait for the morning.'

'I would seriously consider bringing that forward,' said Drabble. 'And seeing what explanation she can present. It's hard to see how she could possibly be involved, but the timing and fact of her presence is a coincidence too far – if you want my opinion.' Drabble took a sip of the tea: nectar after the water he'd been given that day. 'For what it's worth, Inspector Bhattachardjee told me that they'd searched the gallery above the state room in the royal palace and found no signs of a struggle, less even of my fight with the bomber last night. Now, I distinctly saw the bomber catch his sherwani on the door as he flew through it once he'd thrown the grenade. If nothing else there would have been scuff-marks left on the polished woodwork of the floors or benches. I know the palace was a ruddy mess after the Mills bomb went off, but that area was not touched and if they didn't see that either they're incompetent or –'

Pagefield cut in. 'Someone had got there first and sanitised the scene.' He put his tea down and thoughtfully squeezed the large mole that sat next to his right nostril. 'Sincerely,' he declared in a low, sober tone, 'I don't believe that this lot are corrupt for one second. I never have. They're good people and actually really very loyal. Nor are they incompetent. I also appreciate the pressure that Stewart is under to the deliver a suspect, and that in you he's got someone who ticks quite a few of the boxes – you jolly well stuck two fingers up at these people and they don't take kindly to that. And that's before we come to the fact that two dozen witnesses saw you lobbing a bloody bomb across the main palace courtyard.'

He licked his broad lips and took out another cigarette from a silver case, which he lit, his eyes still focused on Drabble. 'The thing is I believe you,' he added, his nostrils flaring like he'd just caught a foul odour. 'And you know what this blighter looks like – and that makes you an invaluable asset, because if you are telling the truth then he's a serious threat. It's too late to cancel tomorrow's ceremony; Linlithgow would never go along with it, nor would Sir Ganga Singh,' he continued, running his thoughts out loud, 'so having you there is essential. All that said, I unfortunately can't simply release you – would that I could; Bikaner is still technically an independent state. So I'll need to get Stewart to agree or work out how it can be done procedurally to ensure you can get to the unveiling and be in a useful position to help if this blighter shows up. If all else fails I can speak to the Maharaja or the Foreign Secretary direct but that will royally piss off Stewart.'

He took a thoughtful drag of his cigarette, and pressed on, rather looking like Stewart's feelings didn't matter too much: 'Regardless, the first thing I'll get them to do is try to get an artist's impression made up, which can be circulated to the guards. It would be a start. Stewart couldn't disagree with that. In fact, I'm rather surprised that he's not done it already.' Pagefield pondered this, and then got up to leave. 'I'll see Stewart now. Hopefully, for the good of all concerned, you'll be out of here in a jiffy and well in time for the ceremony at ten tomorrow morning. If he refuses then I don't know what to recommend. I certainly couldn't sanction you taking matters into your own hands – not for one moment – so I'd have to leave that one up to you.' He cleared his throat. 'I'll also question Heinz.'

Pagefield replaced his homburg and moved off, then remembered something. 'I read in your file that you turned down a knighthood.'

Drabble offered a bland smile and shrugged.

'I see,' replied Pagefield thoughtfully. 'Bit of a berk, aren't you? Night-night.'

Chapter Nine

The clock above the police station gates chimed six times. Across the courtyard, the tiled roofline and upper storey were silhouetted by the amber dawn. Drabble, lying waiting on his bunk, smelled strongly of chocolate. He had been awake for some time and had prepared himself; no word had come through from Pagefield or Stewart about his release and he knew that if he waited any longer the station would be full of staff and harder to escape than ever. It was now or never. That it would make him persona non grata in Bikaner for the rest of time, well; honestly, he could live with that. Especially if by so doing he saved a life or two. He didn't plan on coming back anyway.

It was time. Easing himself off the bunk, he went to the door and pummelled it with the palm of his hand. He kept going as he heard the guard approach — the chatter of keys at his hip announced it — and only stopped when the hatch snapped open.

Drabble croaked the word 'doctor' and then pressed his fingers deep into his throat. He retched forcibly; vomiting productively on the second go. He went for a third stab as the guard unbolted the door quickly. Light flooded into the dark cell and Drabble pounced: his hand clamped over the guard's mouth and the knife against the man's throat. Drabble pushed pressed a sock into the man's mouth.

'Kneel,' he hissed, pushing him to the floor.

The guard got to his knees. Drabble pulled at the man's long white shirt, or mufti, which he hurriedly removed, and then

78

lowered him onto his side and tied his hands at his wrists behind his back with the stout ribbon from the cake. He pulled on the shirt, stole the keys from his waist, and, in a final nod to verisimilitude, he carefully prized off the man's broad white turban and pressed it imperfectly onto his own head.

Drabble bolted the cell door behind him and headed along the corridor, head bowed low, adopting the stoop of the guard. He passed the door of the interview room, and walked along the dark corridor, noticing the flies dancing around the single electric light fitting.

Ahead a broad streak of pale daylight broke into the corridor from an open doorway on the right, the guardroom, which Drabble had noticed on his way in. A wireless played traditional Indian music from within – a sitar and female soprano were reaching sublime, if mournful, heights. Drabble knew he might be challenged at any moment. He simply kept his head down, looked straight ahead and maintained a steady, inconspicuous pace towards the locked door at the end of the corridor; the one with a small barred window that led to the station proper. He passed through the light and through the dissipating fog of tobacco emanating from the guardroom. He focused on the door, knowing he would have to unlock this without any difficulty, and started to feel each of the iron keys on the thick rings individually to see if any stood out. There was one with string bound around its large bow, a sign, perhaps, of significance or regularity of use. Drabble sank it in the lock and turned it confidently. It jammed – with a clang – and he withdrew as silently as he could and tried the next key. The mournful soprano fell silent:

'Vijay?' called a voice from the guardroom.

The second key failed. Drabble inserted the third.

'Yes?' he replied, speaking in Hindi – he'd used the word a fair amount since arriving in the country a month before and it came out well to his ear.

The guard coughed in the corridor behind him. The third key failed. Drabble unthreaded it and pushed the fourth key in.

'Vijay?' repeated the voice, louder and now a touch insistent. Drabble's interlocutor was standing right behind him.

Drabble turned his head back, keeping it bowed, so that the broad turban kept his face in darkness and found himself looking into a cloud of tobacco smoke: a tall silver teapot was thrust into view.

Drabble nodded and took the pot, still bobbing his head as he tried the key in the lock. It turned – he got through the door and shut it behind him.

He set the teapot and the keys down on a wooden ledge along the wall, and made for the exit. At the front door of the station he nodded a salute of farewell to the guard and walked to freedom. The feeling of the gravel beneath his shoes and the sensation of the fresh air on his face made him smile. He reached the far side of the road, and entered an alleyway of shops and stalls, keeping up his moderate pace and stooped gait. No one paid him the slightest bit of attention. They were too busy setting out their wares in the early morning gloom.

He continued into the warren of byways and shopping lanes – not quite knowing his direction, but building the distance between himself and the station. It would not be long – minutes at most – before Vijay managed to dislodge the sock and raise the alarm, or his tea-thirsty colleague grew impatient for his brew.

He discarded his turban, using it to wipe away the cocoa powder, smearing it from his face. He lodged it behind a box of dates and moved on. A glance over his shoulder told him that he wasn't being followed and he headed on, knowing that soon the interconnected web of narrow shopping routes would come to an end. He passed a tall narrow shop, its frontage, walls, and ceiling filled with silver teapots like the one handed to him in the station, and saw its keeper. He was the custodian of a fine, waxed handlebar moustache, and sat barefoot on the step of his shop contentedly smoking a clay pipe. He raised his hand to present his wares as Drabble passed.

Unkempt camel traders, people who looked like they had

80

spent many days and nights on the road – in the desert – milled about at the end of the market, their occupations soon confirmed by the presence of dozens of the animals, feeding, spitting and bellowing in a roped enclosure. Drabble emerged from this knot and saw a waiting rickshaw; its young driver gave him a gap-toothed smile.

'The British Residency, please,' he said, as he climbed aboard.

Suddenly the deafening roar of an engine filled his ears; he glimpsed a flash of chrome, and was thrown clear of the rickshaw. In a blur he saw the shattered cart and its driver pinioned mid-air from the prow of a saloon which disappeared from sight. Drabble landed hard, skidding painfully on the dirt road, ending up in the mass of protesting camel traders. He saw the car, a Crossley, brake hard – throwing the driver and his rickshaw clear. Then the black saloon began to reverse, and turn slowly, showing the driver covered in blood, and unmoving amid the debris of his shattered rickshaw. Drabble got to his feet, shouting – and began to stride towards the car. Then as the car backed round, Drabble caught sight of the driver: it was Miss Heinz. And she was staring intently at him through the windscreen.

The car roared – its powerful engine sucking in fuel and air – and it gunned towards him. Miss Heinz's face surged closer and he threw himself out of the way of the car. It braked hard, squealing to a halt and reversed wildly, scatting camels and their traders.

Drabble started to run. Run for his life.

Across the broad road were tall wooden warehouses. He aimed for the alleyway between two of these. The Crossley accelerated hard, its engine claiming even the sound of Drabble's own footsteps from his ears. His heart thumped in his chest as he sprinted into the narrow road and turned, charging between timbered blocks. His feet falling and skating on the cratered, litter-strewn dirt road. Then he heard the growl of the Crossley's engine again – and glanced back to see its tall chrome grille and curvaceous running boards careen into the lane. His chest was heaving. A look ahead told him what he knew: this was a bad idea. The lane went on for another fifty yards or so, more than enough distance for the car to catch him . . .

But Drabble had no choice. He sprinted on – searching for a narrow passageway or doorway to deliver him as he ran. He tripped, almost going over with the force of his inertia, but recovered, half limping from pain. Christ, he swore. He noticed his shirt sleeve had been shredded in the fall.

But now the roar of the Crossley – channelled by the high timbered walls of the warehouses – became everything. It denied his ears any other noise. And his chest was in agony. He daren't look behind. The engine grew still louder. Drabble could hear each of its working parts chattering, clattering, growling, and exploding. It got louder and he knew it was but inches behind him.

He suddenly spied a doorway on the right and leapt at it. The Crossley steamed past, barrelling him forwards on a gust of air. He smashed through the door – it yielded – and landed in a heap, his face in the dirt, in the darkness of an unlit storeroom. Outside the Crossley screeched to a halt, and began reversing methodically. Light streaked into the room where Drabble had landed but gave him little information; tea crates marked 'Liverpool' were stacked tidily four or five high, and he could see a way between them vanishing into the void. He saw the profile of the Crossley pass the door and made for the avenue created by the rows of boxes. Soon he had to feel his way, groping along the wall of boxes in the darkness. His heart pounded and soon the only sound he was aware of was that of his laboured breathing. He had to get some distance from Miss Heinz.

He continued into the void, feeling the temperature get cooler, and the rough unsanded texture of the tea crates on his hands. He looked back and saw the edge of the light now looking small in the distance. He sensed his chest rising and falling; and he stopped momentarily to gather his breath. He heard the car engine die and its door slam shut.

He reached the last crate: it must be the end of the row. He wondered if he had reached the end of the building, too. Quite possibly. He glanced back to get a sense of perspective on how far he'd come. Just then the narrow beam of yellow light probed the avenue of tea crates he'd come along. It went left, then right, and then swept along the floor towards him. He stepped past the last box, around the corner, in time to see the beam fill the wall ahead. The spot of light on the wall appeared to intensify – and it somehow bled over the top of the boxes. She was getting closer. Drabble was still breathing hard – a combination of physical exertion, pain and fear, he knew, and adrenalin. The beam of light on the wall continued to shrink and now showed up the grain and nails in the timbered wall, just a yard or two from where Drabble stood. He held his breath. Her soft footsteps were close. The circle of light moved off left and right and then vanished. Drabble heard a metallic click; the sound of a gun being cocked. The ball of light flashed back around and shone again towards the wall, hovering just before him.

Drabble heard the sole of her boot grind against the dusty, sandy floor.

Silently, he reached up to the top crate: it yielded to pressure, toppling immediately. He heard a cry, a rapid scuffle of footsteps and the torch flickered away before falling dark.

Drabble waited, standing in the pitch dark, listening. It was not credible that the box could have knocked her out cold – but she made no sound. Drabble swallowed, his eyes roving around the impenetrable darkness. There was still nothing. He crouched down low, steadying himself with his fingertips against the dusty floor, and then knelt. The only way out of this room, without a torch, was through the door he had come in by, and that he could find easily. If he went deeper into the warehouse, then it would be pot luck whether he could find another way out. He certainly didn't fancy his chances. So back the way he came was the only route. But he was loath to step out. Just in case she was bluffing.

He waited, listening intently. Nothing. He resolved to act.

Drabble crawled out, moving deeper into the building, feeling his way. His fingers located the cold metal corner of a case and another space opened up between the packing cases, and now, rising to his feet, he crept along the wall of crates, doubling back towards the door that he entered.

His hands brushed the boxes and he picked up his pace, confident of his direction. Just then, a light shone past him, throwing his shadow into the darkness.

He dived before the first bullet – it passed close enough to whistle by – and performed a nimble forward roll, leaping up to his feet. A second shot sliced along the box beside him at head height, bursting splinters out into his path. Just then he saw the daylight from the doorway seeping into the gloom and bounded across the aisle as a bullet strayed just behind him. He landed and rolled over the ground, out of the line of fire and into the light streaking in from the door. A moment later he was outside. He took out his penknife and drove it into the rear right and front right tyres, then sprinted for the gap between the far end of the warehouses.

A shot rang out behind him – the bullet raising a cloud of dirt in the track ahead – but he was around the corner before another was fired. He peaked back, seeing Heinz running towards him, revolver in hand. Cantering out into the road, he assessed the scene: a high pink-painted wall, topped by rounded white crenulations, ran for a hundred yards or more. Beyond it there were treetops and the white stone spire of a Hindu temple. He ran towards its entrance – a grand marble archway with ornate Mughal-style carvings.

A bullet ricocheted off the terracotta wall and he ducked into doorway, offering a respectful nod to an old man at the door. Pulling at his shoelaces, and half looking backwards, he ran across the black and white marble forecourt towards the open entrance of the main temple. Turning, he saw Heinz stride in to the compound, calmly holding her revolver in her brown shoulder bag. Her eyes were fixed on him; she was seemingly oblivious of anyone else. She raised her bag – to fire. Drabble ducked and leaped back, careening into three brightly-robed women. Apologising, Drabble backed into an old man and stepped on to a tray of food, scattering its contents and driving dozens of rats scampering into a frenzy.

Without pausing he dodged the rats – darting this way and that – entering a marble shrine, within which a painted woman in scarlet held a trident and a severed head. Before it hundreds of rats feasted at the rims of broad dishes of food arranged on the dais. There would be a way through. Sidestepping several pilgrims, he skirted the shrine, avoiding the rats, and found himself deeper in the structure, looking for a way out.

'Hold it!'

Drabble froze, and slowly turned in the direction of the speaker. Miss Heinz had her handbag trained on him. She cocked the weapon from inside it. He heard the three Indian women in their brightly coloured robes gasp and retreat. If Miss Heinz was hoping for a semblance of discretion by keeping her revolver in her bag, it had failed.

'Professor Drabble,' she hissed. 'Put your hands on your head and walk back to the Crossley. If you attempt to run, I will shoot you dead without hesitation. Do you understand?'

Drabble nodded and placed his hands on the back of his head as instructed. She flicked the nose of the barrel towards the doorway and in that moment they both saw that their path was dotted with rats, including one albino that was washing itself. Drabble took care to avoid the rats, his hands on his head, and picked his way towards the exit. Heinz followed, the pained squeal of a rat telling Drabble – and everyone else within earshot – that she had just trampled on one of their holy inhabitants. Another grunt followed from Heinz.

'Get a move on,' she barked at Drabble. They crossed into the black and white courtyards, and headed towards the outer gateway. Drabble was aware that in the best of possible worlds that a well-timed action by him could surprise her, giving him the moment to disarm her or escape. But he was also aware that the slightest pressure on her trigger finger would bring the hammer of the revolver down at point blank range. Some might risk that – but it was not a percentage call that he was prepared to take. Not unless he had was left without a choice.

But did he have a choice? The doubt crept into his mind as he emerged into the road, and felt the heat of the sun strike the back of his head. By the time his shadow was stretched out before him, he realised that he didn't: Miss Heinz, after all, had done a creditable job of trying to kill him several times already. She had moreover left the rickshaw man for dead without as much as a by your leave. So there was little point in delaying the inevitable by a matter of minutes. Indeed, right now, all he was doing was hastening it.

His pace began to slacken. And if it was her plan to shoot him dead with at least a modicum of discretion – perhaps in a quiet side road by the Crossley – then there was no good sense in helping her in this object. And that could be her only plan.

Drabble stopped. Heinz stabbed the gun into the small of his back. He stumbled forward under the surprising force.

'Keep moving,' she barked. Drabble recovered his footing, and turned to face her, his hands still cradling the back of his head. In his right hand was his penknife; the blade was folded away, but it carried more than enough weight to make it an effective missile. He met her gaze. There was a blank intensity to her eyes; a flatness that told him she knew he was dead already.

'Move it,' she said, jabbing towards him with her bag.

He didn't budge.

'If you're going to kill me, why not just do it here?' he asked.

As Miss Heinz's lips parted to speak, Drabble hurled the penknife at her face with maximum force. In the same action, he lunged at her bag, driving it away. Heinz cried out as the metal object struck her forehead – and she fired: flame and smoke tore through the side of the bag. They landed in the dirt with Drabble on top of her. Heinz growled as his knee ploughed deep into her stomach – he made no effort to break his fall – and he wrenched the bag free. Scurrying back, he pulled the gun from the bag and had it trained on her. The knife had grazed her face and blood ran down from her forehead. She sat up and looked at her blood-soaked hand, then up at him.

'Don't move,' he said.

Heinz's lip curled and she got to her feet.

Drabble gripped the gun threateningly at her.

'You're not going to shoot me,' she spat. She turned away and started striding towards her car.

Drabble called out, 'Don't test me.' She continued regardless. He cursed and fired into the air. But Heinz didn't break step. As she arrived at the corner, Drabble swore again and ran after her. He rounded the corner, arriving into the lane to see her sprint towards the Crossley. He swore and levelled the gun at the running figure, taking aim. But he knew he wouldn't fire. She climbed into the driver's seat.

The four-litre engine of Crossley boomed into life – and the car surged towards him, like a greyhound suddenly released. Drabble raised the gun, aiming at the grille. He fired. The bullet smashed a hole in the metalwork but the car kept coming, the sound of its engine intensifying. He fired again. The bullet appeared to make no difference; the car was closing fast. Through the windscreen he saw pitiless intensity registered in Heinz's maniacal cold focus. He broke the gun – saw he had one bullet left – and raised the barrel and set the blunt sight between the deathly eyes . . .

Just then the tall wheels of the Crossley twitched visibly – and the car snatched violently left. It careened head-on into the side of the building and then flipped with the ease of a playing card, once, then twice. Righting itself, sheer inertia sped it on, smashing into the wall just yards before him. The impact shook the ground. Heinz surged through the windscreen and thumped like she'd been dropped from a passing plane onto the bonnet. As glass tinkled to the ground, and smoke and steam began pouring from the crushed engine, Drabble saw that she was quite dead; her head was entirely perpendicular to her torso.

He pushed the revolver into his belt, and for a moment leant back against the wall, steadying himself, and getting his breath back. He looked back over at Heinz, at her blackened, lifeless, outstretched hand. What on earth had that all been about?

He wouldn't have long to find out. Deciding to avoid the unpleasant task of handling the body and searching her clothing, he returned to the road to gather up her bag, which had been discarded in the fight. This might yield a clue – and even betray her real identity, since he knew full well that she was not MV Heinz. He snatched this up, and held it under his arm like an attaché case, and kept moving, leaving the temple to his right.

Several hundred yards later, he stopped into a discreet shop doorway and searched her bag, finding a purse with local banknotes and some small change. This lot he pocketed, before stowing the revolver in the bag, and carrying it under his arm as before.

He needed to eat, and he needed to change his clothes. For a few rupees he had re-clothed himself in white traditional Indian dress, including a turban, not dissimilar to the one he had walked out of the police station wearing. Next he found a café. Sitting on a stool in the corner of the simple establishment, he drank three of cups of sweet tea and ate a platter of small savoury pastries.

He revisited Miss Heinz's bag. It had been purchased from the Army and Navy stores – Drabble supposed it would have been the branch in Calcutta. As well as the purse, the bag contained a large silver compact containing face powder, and a hairbrush, as well as one or two other small tins of make-up. So far, so little to go on. Then he unzipped the slim compartment at its back, and *bingo*: a British passport. But not exactly; sliding the slim blue booklet out, he saw it was in fact a British *Indian* Passport, issued in the Indian Empire, held in the name of one Millicent Florence Skinner-Chatterjee, whom he saw from the black and white photograph immediately was Heinz. She looked younger, less self-assured, but perhaps happier in the picture, and Drabble noticed something else different about her: her hair. It was dark brown. The handwritten details noted: sex, female; born Bengal, 28th February 1910, making her twenty-seven years old; the document had been issued in Bombay, where she was also domiciled. She was a British subject by birth. The eyes were given as brown, the hair also brown, and the height was five feet seven inches. She had no distinguishing marks. Well, she did now. Lots of them.

But it meant one thing: Miss Heinz was Anglo-Indian, and had seemingly concealed her mixed ancestry with the cautious application of make-up and hair dye. Whether or not that was to support her deception as Miss Heinz in particular or to conceal her Anglo-Indian identity more generally was probably beside the point. Either way – as Drabble was aware from his own upbringing – Eurasians were looked down upon by the Europeans in India, rather as they themselves looked down upon the Indians. It was all part and parcel of the repellent pyramid of racial hierarchy upon which the entire colonial project rested.

Drabble leafed back through the document – notable for its empty pages: a life lived untravelled. He sighed and noticed that, like his own passport, the space on the page set aside for the photograph of spouse was left blank, and she had no children listed. Nor would there be, he thought bitterly. He scanned the document one last time, noting that she gave her profession as *Secretary*, and slipped it back into the bag. That might well have been her normal occupation, but *assassin* was the word that sprang to Drabble's mind. Even if she hadn't been successful, Heinz, or rather Skinner-Chatterjee, showed an astonishing lack of hesitation in going about her task. Indeed, she had undertaken it with decided alacrity and rather a surprising amount of bloodlust, truth be told. Which was rather remarkable for a *secretary*. He drained a fourth cup of sweet tea. She must either be a total fanatic to her cause, or had killed before – and he didn't just have the poor rickshaw man in mind. Moreover, if she had killed before, then she had presumably done it more than once and quite possibly liked it, or had simply become accustomed to it. He sighed.

He retrieved her beige leather purse from the bag and investigated its contents: first, the banknotes – of local Bikaner currency as well as British Indian denomination – as well as the stub for a return ticket to Bombay that Miss Skinner-Chatterjee would no longer be needing. There was a card printed *Col. James Pagefield*, which rather usefully had what he supposed was the telephone number of the British Residence scrawled on the reverse. And that was it: no family photographs or emotive mementos, nothing to betray the individual. Not surprising, perhaps. Hers had not struck him as a sentimental mind given to introspection. Drabble put the purse away and laid the bag aside. He ordered another cup of tea, and noticed a scratch on the side of his arm. Miss Skinner-Chatterjee had not left much to go on. Except, that is, for that rather cumbersome name, and a fair number of cuts and bruises on his person.

His Highness Sir Ganga Singh, the Maharaja of Bikaner, sat at the head of a long, broad, baize-covered table in his office located in the heart of the red sandstone Junagarh Fort. Before him were official papers and manila files running in orderly piles along both sides of this table of state; the apparatus included two gleaming black Imperial typewriters and narrow silver trays dotted along the table containing inkwells, blotters, and fountain pens. The usual army of stenographers and typists and secretaries had been given the morning off so that Sir Percival Harris, intrepid correspondent of the *London Evening Express*, could in privacy draw an appreciation of this great champion of the empire at his work without the encumbrance of their actual presence. The Maharaja, speaking in the clipped English of an Edwardian aristocrat without trace of an Indian accent, sat at the head of the table, where he would normally work, he explained. Oversized pencils in red and blue stood within reach in pots and Harris could readily imagine the Maharaja dabbing and marking at a steady stream of documents and drafts being passed before him for his attention. In the background an ornate longcase clock housed in ebony kept time. It was five minutes past eight. Among the various adornments was a portrait photograph of King George V, a personal friend of the Maharaja's. An enormous tiger skin was stretched across a wall. It was somewhat larger than his own trophy, thought Harris.

A white-uniformed servant poured each of them a cup of tea from a long-spouted silver pot in silence, before withdrawing. The chime of the Maharaja's spoon against the china cup broke the silence, which was otherwise punctured only by the seconds of the clock. Harris was uneasy: it was the unease of an interview about to take place.

He stirred his tea and cleared his throat. Beneath the table, his right foot ached: more precisely, his now missing second toe tensed painfully, but it was a phantom pain that was a new companion in life's journey. He met the waiting gaze of Sir Ganga Singh, who was dressed immaculately in a charcoal morning coat, wing collar, tie and waistcoat. The Maharaja broke the ice.

'Twelve feet, eleven inches,' he declared, throwing a glance at the tiger skin on the wall. 'From nostrils to the tip of the tail.'

'Goodness,' replied Harris grinning. He wrote that number down. 'What a monster, sir.'

The Maharaja smiled. 'My biggest.' He took a sip of tea and replaced the cup in the saucer. 'I got him cleanly with a shot through the shoulder: if only they all happen that easily.' He paused reflectively. 'I gather that you are also a hunter, Sir Percival? Your tigress, may I ask, what size was she?'

'Twelve feet two inches pegged out, sir.'

The Maharaja nodded with satisfaction. 'A man-eater, too, wasn't she? A challenging kill?'

'Positively ferocious, sir,' replied Harris. 'My first tiger.'

'Ah,' the Maharaja smiled. 'A memory to cherish. You were sure to brush plenty of turpentine onto the skin? It's essential for keeping the colour, just so.'

Harris assured him that they had positively deluged the fur in turps.

'Out of interest, sir, how many tigers have you shot?

Ganga Singh contemplated the question for a moment. 'A hundred and eighty-eight.'

'Goodness –' Harris jotted that down. 'And how old were you when you shot your very first, sir?'

Before the Maharaja answered there was a gentle knock at the ivory-inlaid double doors that led to the anteroom; one opened and a secretary entered, carrying a note on a silver salver. The Maharaja politely nodded to Harris, thereby excusing himself, and took up a pair of pince-nez. He frowned down at the note, momentarily, then folded it back up, and dismissed the secretary. He cleared his throat and spread his hands to push himself up from the table. The interview, Harris realised, was over.

'Your friend Professor Drabble,' the Maharaja declared, he turned his head towards the ceiling and fluttered his eyelids, communicating exasperation, 'has escaped!'

Chapter Ten

It was starting to get warm. Even sitting in the shaded bank of seating arranged for VIP attendees, it was heading fast to stifling. The ladies present fanned themselves and the menfolk tolerated it, sourly. There was a low level of conversation but on the whole people seemed determined to do as little as possible. Most of this elevated crowd were local dignitaries – Harris recognised an earnest Indian sweating into a black morning coat, spongebag trousers, and wing-collared shirt, as Panikkar, the foreign secretary. He bobbed about, smoothing over any issues of seating and seniority, like a maitre d' at a smart London restaurant. The tented zone was filled mainly with Indians – Junior Rajput princes and Bikaneri aristocracy, Thakurs in their native finery, gleaming, bejewelled turbans and wives in bright robes. Dotted among these were the European servants of the Maharaja; Harris spotted Colonel Stewart, who looked anxious but was impeccably dressed in his number one ceremonial kit – brilliant white tunic and trousers, pith helmet and gloves, chest glittering like a kleptocratic magpie's nest. A large woman of senior years with a big, important face sat with him, grimly bearing the heat. Harris reckoned she must be Mrs Colonel Stewart. Then there were various others – Harris guessed these to be engineering advisers and so forth, as Ganga Singh was a great builder of canals, railways and public buildings and had many well-remunerated Europeans in his entourage. The further back, the more junior the ranking of the officials or landowners.

Their clothing glittered less and there were fewer fan-wavers attending to them.

Harris had been parked near the front – far in excess of his status – on account of the Maharaja's effusive solicitude. So he was told. In fact, Harris suspected that they wanted him just where they could see him. Which made sense. Drabble had given them enough trouble after all. The seat next to him had been reserved for Miss Heinz, but she had unaccountably vanished and next to her was the seat set aside for Captain Dundonald from the Residency.

There was no sign of him either, and Harris could not but admit to a vexed sense of jealousy at the ease with which their relations had advanced. Dundonald had one of those honest, kind faces that women tended to flock to: it was manly without being downright bovine, and he was also a good listener. Harris had seen it; he actually *listened*, and attentively, too. Even down to recalling details later . . . Harris shook his head. How could a chap compete with coves like that?

He sighed and looked down at Miss Heinz's empty seat. It was probably best not to think about it.

He turned his attention to the statue – the purpose of today's jamboree. It was large, but not so enormous as to be in bad taste, like the sort of thing thrown up at any given opportunity in Central Europe or South America. It was a little larger than life, however, presumably to aid viewing, since it stood on a large red sandstone plinth, and presently it was swathed in a grey cotton sheet. The moment of truth was not far off now.

Beyond the shrouded statue a semicircle of serious-looking policemen bordered a vast throng of locals, who were all enduring the near-midday heat and sunshine for this moment of national celebration. Men, women, and children stood under umbrellas and broad turbans, or gathered under the various trees, waiting patiently to get sight of their prince. There must have been a thousand of them, thought Harris, who noted that down accordingly. Then again, golden jubilees didn't come along that often.

Harris took off his topee and fanned himself with it. They were now waiting for the Maharaja and his party to arrive; then the Viceroy, Lord Linlithgow, would arrive as guest of honour, and there would be speeches, and all the stuff you would expect before heading to the fort for a knees-up afterwards. Movement caught his eye, and he noticed the bulk of Colonel Pagefield appear on the left hand end of the VIP marquee. He was escorted by Dundonald and about two dozen men. He paused, issued an instruction to Dundonald, and then began to file along the row, approaching Harris's position. His size meant that everybody in his path had to stand and lean back. Meanwhile, Harris saw the soldiers, each armed with a rifle, take up positions along the front of the seated area, which naturally included the raised tented island upon which the Prince and Viceroy were due to sit.

Pagefield was out of breath as he sat down on Miss Heinz's chair. 'Don't worry,' he said to Harris. 'She won't be needing it.'

Harris did not quite understand the final note to Pagefield's tone of voice but made no reply.

The groaning and growling of camels seized his attention, and rows upon rows of the Maharaja's Bikaner Camel Corps trotted into view: the grunting of the camels was joined by the crack and jingle of kit and saddlery, and their charges' broad feet throwing up dust. The troopers' white uniforms gleamed, set off against immaculate scarlet piping and their flowing red and saffron turbans, with matching pennants, giving the whole seamless mass the semblance of a vast Chinese dragon. Harris could see Pagefield's eyes flitting around the perimeter – checking that his men were in correct positions. He perspired heavily and smelled strongly of sour body odour. Pagefield glanced over just in time to catch the expression on Harris's face.

'Welcome to Rajputana, old man,' he declared. 'Not much one can do about it apart from bathing every twenty minutes, which becomes impracticable.' He was still checking the locations of his men, then turned to Harris. 'Your friend has escaped from the prison – I know you know that much – but there's been an incident involving Miss Heinz, I'm afraid.' He waited for Harris to register the tone of his voice. 'She's dead. Killed in a car accident about two hours ago.'

Pagefield checked his watch and reviewed the crowd, like a man looking for trouble. Dead, thought Harris. *Dead?*

Pagefield was continuing: 'It's not quite that simple, of course. Witnesses reported her driving the car erratically *at* a European man, one who was dressed in native clothes.' A sideways glance towards Harris confirmed that it was Drabble he was talking about. 'And I should say, it was *my* car that she was driving. Which,' he added dryly, 'is probably beyond repair. Still, that's the least of it . . .'

The Bikaner Camel Corps had completed its march by and was forming up into columns to the right of the stand, before the high red sandstone walls of the Junagarh Fort. They were a glorious sight and every bit as impressive as the Blues and Royals. The crowd of onlookers turned their attention from the camel corps towards an unseen arrival. Then they began to cheer; a black Rolls-Royce – its prow furnished with a scarlet-and-saffron pendant of Bikaner, and a small royal coat of arms mounted above the windscreen – drove into view. From inside, the Maharaja and Maharani waved. Everyone got to their feet.

Pagefield raised his voice to be heard, and continued to address Harris with his gaze firmly on the scene before them. 'The European man in question escaped injury, but his location is presently unknown. Miss Heinz, however, managed to kill a local rickshaw man during her attempts, and gunfire was heard.' The limousine stopped and various equerries leaped out and doors swept and out poured the royal family.

'Miss Heinz tried to shoot him?'

Pagefield nodded. 'Hard as it might seem to believe . . . Oh by the way, Heinz was an alias; her real name was Millicent Skinner-Chatterjee. She was,' he paused for dramatic effect, 'Eurasian.'

'Eurasian –' Harris gasped. 'Only just, surely.' His many unspoken thoughts and feelings for Miss Heinz flashed before him. 'It can't be,' he declared. 'She's white, for God's sake. And what about her hair . . .'

Even as he said it he lost confidence in the assertion and his sentence expired under its own evident pointlessness. These things could be adjusted convincingly. Of course they could. 'But-but . . . she was . . .' Beautiful. That was the word for it, but his words failed him – silenced by a curious blanket of awkwardness. She was Eurasian – and that meant she was beyond the pale, so to speak.

Pagefield patted his shoulder.

'Come, come, Harris,' he said. 'There's no shame in it. The longer you spend out here, the more you realise that.'

Harris's window of response was closed firmly by the arrival of two more Rolls-Royces, which drove into view in stately procession. The first was adorned with two Union flags over the front wheels. Three men in black morning coats and bowler hats strode alongside it – men of the Viceroy's bodyguard. From within emerged Lord Linlithgow dressed in ceremonial uniform of navy blue coat, with golden embroidery and stand collar, and white breeches. A veteran of the trenches on the Western Front during the Great War before going into politics, Linlithgow looked the part. He had the military bearing required to carry off the job of Viceroy – he was straight-backed, tall, and had a thoroughly plausible head – for which Harris was grateful. There was nothing worse for national prestige than having some fidgeting, paunchy cretin swathed in robes of state. Forget critical thinking or analytical prowess: in jobs like this, it all came down to looking the part and knowing when to keep your mouth shut.

The crowd cheered the Viceroy as he stepped down from the car; hats were removed and polite bows and curtseys performed. Harris and Pagefield followed suit smartly – the latter somewhat awkwardly in the space available. Linlithgow, still looking regal despite wearing more clothing than an entire Indian village, acknowledged the gesture with a wave. In particular, his long ermine-lined cape must have been a nightmare in this heat, yet he carried it off as if it were nothing. Two turbaned servants helped ease the Viceroy's train from the car, which pulled away. The bowler-hatted bodyguards formed up at regular intervals around the dais, and the cars moved off. The crowd of VIPs sat, as the Viceroy and his wife were greeted by the Maharaja and being led to their thrones on the raised dais.

Harris felt hot and adjusted his shoulders, an act which temporarily released his sweat-covered back from the embrace of his shirt. Heinz was just someone completely different, but she had also tried to kill Drabble. She tried to kill Drabble, he repeated in his mind. This was incredible. It really was. To conceal her mixed race ancestry; well, that was one thing. It made him suddenly feel strange to think of it again; but he had found her very attractive – he really had. He swallowed hard and cast his eyes towards the mass of Indians standing beyond the ropes, watching the ceremony in the stark sunshine. But she was one of them. That wasn't what the English did. We kept ourselves to our ourselves, because that was the deal. 'Don't fraternise with the natives, old man,' was the unwritten rule. 'They aren't welcome in our clubs. And you aren't welcome in theirs.' And you certainly didn't . . . nor did you want to . . . but Harris was no longer quite sure. It wasn't that simple.

He looked over at Pagefield, whose gaze roved across the crowd with the intensity of a wicket keeper at Lord's. It was frankly very hard to believe. He leaned over.

'What do you think's going on,' he asked in a half-whisper. Pagefield's fleshy lugubrious face projected a sullen quality, like a man unjustly denied his gin and tonics by an overbearing wife. Perhaps he had toothache.

'The only conclusion I can come to is that Heinz was somehow involved in Tuesday night's bombing plot at the fort – and suddenly found that when Drabble escaped from the prison, she had to stop him at all costs from attending today.'

'B-but . . . *why*?' pleaded Harris. He knew instantly that he was being thick but he also knew there wasn't time to work it out. And then, just as Pagefield started to speak, it came to him: 'Because Drabble would be able to identify the bomber . . .'

Pagefield nodded.

'So what does this johnny look like?'

Pagefield glanced over at him and then returned his gaze to the red-carpeted dais, where the Viceroy was now getting to his feet. 'In his wisdom, Colonel Stewart refused to get the artist's illustration done: so all we know is what Drabble told us. The bomber is male, Indian, about thirty years of age, of medium height with a slim build, unshaven, and has a whopping great bruise on the left side of his face.'

The two of them looked out at the crowd of the thousand Indians beyond the ropes, manned by the two dozen turbaned Bikaneri policemen.

The brass band struck up with 'God Save the King' – everyone shuffled again to their feet, many still fanning themselves vigorously. A solid if not full-throated rendition commenced. It was undoubtedly a smidge too slow, which had the effect of taking what was already a rather sedate score into somnambulant territory. Pagefield, chin held up, arms smartly to his side, and his stance braced, sang for five, holding the dirgeful notes long and hard. Untended beads of sweat traced down the side of his large head. Harris found himself fidgeting. Time passed so slowly that he eventually succumbed to checking his pocket watch. The seconds ticked by sluggishly. The band strolled through the interlude into the second verse . . . Harris's gaze went back to the scores of Indian faces he could see on the far side of the ropes.

Where *was* Drabble?

Harris saw the Viceroy unfold his speech and get to his feet during the last, expiring bars of the anthem. Linlithgow smiled over at the Maharaja, and then placed himself sideways to Ganga Singh, so that he could address the entire gathering more easily.

Harris leaned over again. 'Where the dickens is Drabble?'

Pagefield shook his head and said nothing, his narrowed eyes scanning the front rows of Indians at the ropes. Harris saw an old man, with a crutch and white beard; he saw women with infants, he saw prosperous merchants . . . At that moment the chattering from the crowd vanished and the strong voice of the Viceroy could be heard:

'Nothing could possibly give me more pleasure than to join with Your Highness' loyal subjects in the State of Bikaner,' began Linlithgow, 'to pay my tribute of affection and admiration to their ruler by taking the principal part in this ceremony for which we are all gathered together today . . .'

Harris saw Pagefield glance over at Dundonald, standing at the front of the shaded area and discreetly checking it for anybody who looked suspicious. Dundonald shook his head. A gentle refreshing breeze, which had started up a short while before, began to ruffle the white ostrich feathers protruding from his cocked hat. They fluttered in the wind like the keys on a self-playing piano. 'His great services to the British Empire through the years of the Great War and as a signatory of the Treaty of Versailles, his labours at meetings of the Imperial Conference and League of Nations . . .'

The sweat ran down the flanks of Pagefield's meaty face; his head twitched from side to side as he vigilantly surveyed the scene. Harris noted down the Viceroy's speech hurriedly in his notebook.

'I am reminded of an old saying – "Si monumentum requires, circumspice", which in English reads: "If you seek a monument, look around."' There was a ripple of laughter to this, and the Viceroy continued, 'Let us therefore turn away from this veiled statue, and allow our eyes to dwell upon all we see around us of a man's handiwork . . .'

The Viceroy set about praising the Maharaja's many civic improvements – the building of schools and hospitals, the widespread electrification of the capital, the great canal system to bring water to formerly barren tracts of land. 'The spirit that lives in that Fort must surely know that His Highness Sir Ganga

Singh of Bikaner has not betrayed his ancestors, nor the glories of the great traditions of bygone years . . .'

The address continued: culminating in a dramatic cheer from the crowd and clamorous applause from sheltered notables. The Maharaja stood during the clapping and shook hands heartily with the Viceroy. Pagefield exhaled.

The moment now came for the actual unveiling: the Viceroy stepped down from the dais and approached the statue, where-upon he was handed a red cord to pull. It disappeared into the cloth of the shroud. Harris suddenly had a dreadful premonition.

Pagefield leaned in: 'Don't worry. We've checked that. Twice.'

Linlithgow looked over at the Maharaja, his hand held up holding the end of the red rope, and then he nodded sombrely – and yanked it hard.

The veil parted, falling to the ground, and there was a raptur-ous applause and cheering. Orange and scarlet-turbaned flunkies rushed forward to draw away the cotton sheet. It was immedi-ately obvious that the statue bore a fair likeness to the man himself. Harris couldn't speak for the horse, but it looked a touch overdone on the musculature, as indeed did the prince, but such was the way of things. The artist's eye tended to flatter with portraits – and as Disraeli was apt to say of Queen Victoria – when it came to royalty they laid the flattery on with a trowel. Sir Ganga Singh could not be disappointed by his equestrian facsimile. Sitting erect with perfect posture in the saddle, the bronze maharaja's chest was festooned with orders and deco-rations and puffed out. His chin, meanwhile, was held up, just like his ample whiskers, and he gazed forward importantly under those distinctive, arched heavy eyebrows. He was, in short, immortalised as a soldierly visionary. Beneath the lifted fore hoof of the stallion, on the front of the rectangular plinth was a bronze relief of the royal arms of Bikaner. The Viceroy and Maharaja now stood here while an official photographer and his assistant set up a heavy looking camera and tripod. The pho-tographer was under the generous black cloth.

Linlithgow and Ganga Singh talked, both standing with a certain forced formality, prisoners as they were of their garbs of office. The Maharaja steadied the hilt of his sword at his hip. They then made final adjustments to their poses and remained still. The photographer's arm emerged from the folds, and went up; he gripped the rubber bulb between his thumb and first finger lifted high above it.

Pagefield gasped, his large eyes suddenly transfixed on the scene.

'That's not a camera,' he hissed, panic coming in his features. 'It's a GUN!'

Pagefield surged to his feet . . .

Drabble saw Pagefield before he heard him: he glimpsed his blurry uniformed bulk leap up and break through the seated guests and sensed it tumbling and crashing into the row below. 'GUUUU . . .'

But Drabble was already moving. He burst through the cordon and sprang towards the tripod, arms outstretched. He saw the photographer's hand clamp shut around the rubber bulb. He heard the crowd roar, like at a bullfight when it goes badly for the matador. His hands connected with the side of the camera, pushing it. A tongue of fire spat from the lens – smoke engulfed the space before it. Drabble landed hard with camera, crashing down to the ground and finding himself entangled with the legs and cloth. He got up just in time to see the photographer pull out a revolver and fire wildly into the smoke. He had a crazed look on his face and – presumably seeing his intended victims gone – turned the gun on Drabble. Through the smoke Drabble met his eyes: he saw cruelty and fear, and cried out,

'Don't –'

The photographer's forehead exploded like a confetti cannon, showering him in blood and bone. The arm holding the gun dropped and then the body collapsed from the knees, slumping into the dirt. As the smoke cleared Drabble saw Captain

Dundonald, his face set in an grimace. He lowered his smoking Webley service revolver.

The photographer's assistant had been wrestled to the ground and was being restrained with over-zealous force – Drabble averted his eyes as a blow landed on his face. The bowler-hatted security men had deluged the Viceroy, who was being bundled into his Rolls, the engine already revving. The Maharaja, ringed by soldiers, approached Drabble.

'Professor Drabble, I presume?' he said without grandeur. He smiled beneath the lavish moustache. 'It appears that as well as my sincere thanks, I also owe you an apology.' He slipped off his glove and held out his hand.

Drabble shook it and offered the Maharaja his best bow, what he would describe later to Harris as the lowest bow that a good, lapsed Marxist can provide.

The Viceroy's Rolls-Royce drove away.

Colonel Stewart appeared at the Maharaja's side, came to attention, and saluted punctiliously.

'Your Highness, the scene has been secured. In the interests of security, may I suggest we follow the Viceroy's cue?'

Sir Ganga Singh nodded thoughtfully, and pulled his glove back on.

'Thank you, Colonel,' he said, almost with distaste. 'To co-opt Oscar Wilde, one assassination attempt might be regarded as a misfortune, but two looks like carelessness.' He cleared his throat. Stewart's dry, soldierly face was rigid. And so it should be, thought Drabble. 'I'd like your report on this matter for the morning. In the meantime we shall return to the palace, but on foot.' The Maharaja glanced over and gestured with his hand, 'Professor?'

Chapter Eleven

The palace – located inside the vast interior of the Junagarh Fort – was theoretically but minutes away. However Sir Ganga Singh walked in the opposite direction, the heels of his shining black leather boots stabbing the russet gravel. An escort of policemen and courtiers fell in behind as he led Drabble away from the equestrian statue, and the tented seating around with its crowd of onlookers, at a rapid pace. The Maharaja's route was straight into the mass of loyal subjects, who parted respectfully like the Red Sea before Moses. They lowered their eyes from the gaze of the royal personage, some dropped to their knees, their hands held up almost as if in prayer. Drabble had never seen anything like it.

Sir Ganga Singh nodded solicitously at these displays, or gently waved a hand in acknowledgement of the veneration. He slowed his pace, left hand steadying his sword, turning his head to the left and right to ensure that those who had made the effort to see him and had endured the midday sun without shade, were given his attention in equal measure.

'I've read a little about you, Professor,' the Maharaja said, addressing Drabble from the corner of his mouth. He waved. 'The north face of the Eiger –' Ganga Singh flashed him a smile, 'and your work on Cromwell – a dreadfully effective man. But quite awful.'

'As a historian I would observe that he was principally a man of his times. I am happy to leave the morality of his conduct to ethicists.'

'Most prudent of you, Professor.' The Maharaja paused to pat a small boy on the head, then looked back. 'However, you appear to be less inhibited about passing judgement on conduct in our present times.' They moved on. 'I gather, for instance, that you're opposed to British rule in India.'

'Aren't you?'

The Maharaja chuckled.

'That, sir, is an impertinent question.' He shot Drabble a tight smile. 'I am an advocate of greater autonomy for India, culminating in home rule – but with certain conditions – and within the embrace of the British Empire. That is rather different from the typical position of those who call for "home rule" or "independence" for India.'

'It would be a good start, though.'

'Would it? We'll see, shan't we?' replied Ganga Singh. The heavy eyebrows knitted in the middle for the second time as he inspected Drabble. 'I think you have rather a dry way about you, Professor.'

They reached the end of the field of subjects and arrived at the centre of a park: thoroughfares lined with box hedges and tall palm trees criss-crossed a flat, rectangular space, one that was clearly ambitious in scale, cutting rusty brown geometric paths through green lawns. At the centre was a three-tiered fountain like a wedding cake, with luxurious waters splashing down from one level to the next. They paused before it, the breeze fresh and damp, and the Maharaja turned and Drabble followed suit, seeing the whole mass of the Junagarh Fort come into view: its sheer immensity took his breath away.

Walls topped with countless rounded castellations stretched away before the eye, interrupted by towering cylindrical bastions whose high balconies jutted out like letter boxes. In its dusty, almost peachy sandstone, this oriental stronghold was a world away from the flinty medieval fortresses left behind by the Normans and their feudal successors.

'The Junagarh Fort was built by the sixth ruler of Bikaner during the latter half of the sixteenth century – while your

Queen Elizabeth the First was confronting the might of Catholic Spain, we had the Mughals to contend with.' He smiled and then his bright, optimistic eyes gazed towards the walls. His face flushed with pride.

'It's magnificent,' agreed Drabble. The irregular walls stretched far into the distance, resembling the undulating back of a giant terracotta crocodile lying on its side.

'The sandstone comes from the mines of Delmura, just twenty miles away,' Ganga Singh continued. 'It's just as well that the quarries are close by since we needed a great deal of it. It took the best part of thirty years to complete.'

Ganga Singh smiled, showing his teeth, and set off towards the fort, taking fast, long strides. The coterie of followers were taken by surprise, and struggled to keep up, breaking into a trot to draw level.

The Maharaja marched on, his right hand clutching his white dress gloves. His medals and the bejewelled trinket – curved like the end of a small hockey stick – poking from the back of his ornate turban, clinked as he walked.

'You may be interested to hear that I have this morning received a telegram from Chartwell vouching for you,' the Maharaja volunteered. 'Mr Churchill heaped praise upon you in fact.'

Drabble said nothing.

Ganga Singh caught something in his expression and laughed. 'I know, Winston isn't everyone's cup of tea: he's not very popular here among certain communities –' his eyebrows bobbed expressively, 'as you can well imagine. But he's a good man.'

'Not *dreadfully effective*?'

The Maharaja shot Drabble a smile, a ghost beneath the overhang of the elegantly waxed moustache. 'I think we ought to let the historians of the future be the judge of that, don't you?'

The Maharaja quickened his pace, leaning forward into each step in a stance like a Lowry stick figure. His boots crunched into the gravel.

'If I may speak plainly, Professor, do you have any idea about what's been going on here?' He glanced over. Drabble's expression told him the answer and then the Maharaja paused to smile and wave at a throng of his subjects. They returned his greeting with deep, submissive bows. 'I was afraid that might be the case,' he added, addressing Drabble.

They moved on. 'It's a bad business, Professor. We will keep this quiet – out of the newspapers and so forth – but the fact is it has happened.' He shook his head. 'This is precisely the sort of thing that spooks Delhi and before you know it they will want to start interfering in matters of no concern to them whatsoever. Not,' he added, stressing the word, 'without certain justification.' He cleared his throat. 'Has it occurred to you that it's an uncommon individual who regards Mr Gandhi, the Viceroy, and *me* as the reasonable objects of an assassination? One or other of us I can understand, but *not* all three. It is nonsensical.'

Drabble had done, and said as much.

'Mind you –' his mind turned to the protest he had witnessed in the Chandi Chowk in old Delhi. 'The chap is a known Marxist-Leninist – an agitator. There are enough hard-liners out there who oppose what they see as Gandhi's softly-softly approach – and they won't have much truck with you or the Viceroy either.'

Singh regarded him and shook his head with something approaching dismay. 'I would not have called Mr Gandhi's approach soft.'

Neither man said anything for a moment. Then the Maharaja added.

'There is also the question of the Anglo-Indian woman. Miss Skinner-Chatterjee, lately of Bombay, I gather. She killed one of my subjects this morning – ran him down like a dog in the road.' He shook his head. 'Professor, do you ever wonder quite where the world is going?'

They left the question hanging in the air as they approached the outer wall of the fort; their footsteps kicking up red dust. Two sentries brought their pikes smartly upright to attention. Drabble's mind raced with images of his encounter with 'Miss Heinz' that morning, and then the bombing at the fort two nights before. There was a lot to think about. And then there was the protest in Chandi Chowk to consider. In his mind's eye he saw Goodlad, sitting morosely at his desk in his dark office before a portrait of the King, surrounded by heaps of paper – reaching for a lonely glass of Scotch – and offering himself up as the personification of hatred.

They crossed the courtyard. Drabble said, 'I've not had any inspiration about Miss Skinner-Chatterjee. Not *yet* anyway. But the assassin . . . I'm certain I can find out more about him. As I told Colonel Stewart after the bombing, I actually saw the very man on Monday night in Delhi. If I retrace my steps I can definitely identify him – and that should help provide some answers.'

Sir Ganga Singh turned and settled his gaze on Drabble's face. Those deep grey eyes searched his – and for the first time Drabble saw the years written into the Maharaja's face. He had been on the *khadi* for forty years – and in that moment the strain of rule, though it had been more than equalled by the man, showed through. The Maharaja nodded.

'I have a Tiger Moth standing by at the aerodrome –' he raised his hand and a car approached and drew up alongside. A uniformed footman stepped out, and held the door open. 'If I could oblige you to journey to Delhi, to find out what you can, Professor, then I assure you – you will for ever be a friend of Bikaner.' The Maharaja smiled, 'Even more than you already are.' A secretary dressed in black morning coat and striped grey trousers approached with an envelope: which he passed to the Maharaja with a dutiful bow.

'I shall be in New Delhi on the day after tomorrow. Come to my residence – Bikaner House – and inform me as to any progress you have been able to make.'

At the British Residence Drabble was admitted by Abdul, who barely registered his dishevelled native dress or alarming appearance, presumably mistaking them for a species of English eccentricity, to which he was no stranger. Drabble washed – in the mirror he resembled an extra from a theatrical production of *The Man Who Would be King* – and changed quickly into a cream poplin suit and college tie, meaning he now conformed with the sartorial expectations of the British establishment in the Tropics. This might serve his purpose. He packed some essential items to take, and wrote a note for Harris, leaving it propped against his bottle of Glenmorangie whisky – where he was sure to find it but where others might not immediately look. He explained that he would be staying at the Clive Club in New Delhi, and how best to reach him.

Then he went to Miss Skinner-Chatterjee's room. Easing the handle, he found the door unlocked, and slipped inside. The room was spotlessly tidy, the bed made neatly and all personal items put away out of sight. What little she had brought with her, including the small leather and canvas suitcase itself, he found arranged in the rattan wardrobe. The case was empty and apart from a pair of lonely-looking brown leather sandals, standing side-by-side, there were just two blouses and some assorted underwear, besides her suit; the one she had worn when she met them on the train. This was hung up, and its pockets contained nothing to excite interest. He was beginning to feel disappointed when he noticed something that had been there all along. On the lapel of the jacket was a small enamelled brooch of a red rose framed with exotic green foliage. He had half-noticed it before but the actual design had not quite registered.

Now he looked again. It lacked the decorative panache or inherent value one might expect of a piece of jewellery. Drabble unclipped it from the lapel, and took it over to the window to examine it more closely. Its reverse was plain – just the bronze colour of the metal used to fabricate it. He turned it over: and stared down at the rose, crudely drawn with enamelled petals, surrounded by the barbed green foliage. It was not a piece of jewellery. It was a badge of some sort. He decided that it was important and slipped the brooch into his pocket.

'Drabble–' Dundonald's voice cut through the silence like a

summons. It caused Drabble to withdraw his hand guiltily from his pocket. 'What are you doing?'

Drabble brought the two doors of wardrobe together and then turned to Dundonald, who commanded the doorway in a posture communicating recalcitrant opposition. Drabble couldn't help but notice that his revolver, the one he had used with such timeliness at the unveiling, was holstered at his side. 'I was hoping to see if I could find a clue to explain Miss Skinner-Chatterjee's peculiar actions,' Drabble stated. Dundonald regarded him coldly. 'No luck as yet.'

Dundonald watched Drabble go to the desk and begin to pull open the drawers. The first was empty. 'I've already swept the room thoroughly, there's nothing here,' he stated pointedly. 'She was very careful.' Something caught in Dundonald's throat and he added, 'Very carefully indeed, I would say.'

The desk was empty, as was the cabinet by the bed, which Drabble then checked, sweeping his arm under the mattress. He looked around the room one last time, ignoring Dundonald who continued to regard his actions with hostility. Nothing. Skinner-Chatterjee had quite literally left *nothing* behind – unless Dundonald had found it first. That remained a possibility. Drabble stroked the bedclothes back into the neat formation that he had found them in, and then wondered why he had bothered. He gathered up his Gladstone and looked over at the man who watched him.

'I don't suppose she said anything to you all?'

Dundonald's expression hardened.

'The two of you had been spending some time together – I assumed you talked.'

Some of the puff vanished from Dundonald's chest.

'I was in the dark as much as anyone else,' he said, with feeling.

Drabble approached the doorway, which Dundonald continued to occupy. Finally, the man stepped out of his way.

In the corridor Drabble halted, and pulled an envelope from his pocket.

'Would you see that Pagefield gets this for me?' He handed it over. 'I'm sorry about Miss Heinz,' he added.

Dundonald nodded, and Drabble moved off.

As he strode towards the stairs he regretted giving Dundonald the note. Abdul without doubt would have been a more trustworthy messenger.

Outside, the evening sun hit with a punch that you never felt in England. As the car approached, he looked back at the residence, at the two sentries in their khaki fatigues and turbans, their neatly wound puttees, and Lee-Enfield rifles at ease. He saw along the side of the building, at the tidy rows of geraniums and the sprawling bougainvilleas – gleaming scarlet and mauve against the lawns, which were the brown of the wicket at Lord's in high August.

The Maharaja's Rolls-Royce Silver Ghost halted, and the driver was out before he could get to the door, opening it neatly. Drabble took once last look up at the shield over the doors bearing the Royal Arms, and then at the sun-bleached Union jack. He knew he wouldn't be coming back.

Harris was sweating prodigiously into his stiffly starched wing collar and morning coat. He attempted to grin through it but the pain showed in the fragile corners of his eyes. He noted a similar look on the faces of the other Europeans in the ballroom. They chatted cheerfully in the hard voices that they saved for when the servants were in the room, but he could see through the false jollity. It was as though they were playing along in a game called 'master race'. Bugger, he thought, now I'm beginning to sound like Ernest. He ran his finger along the side of his collar and gazed over the head of a small fat diplomat's wife – one who appeared to be wearing most, if not all, of the plumage of a nest of birds of paradise as a fascinator – across the room at a trio of open windows. He had stopped listening to her for several minutes now, not because he meant to be rude but simply because it was too hot for his ears to hear. He noticed the

111

feathers bobbing towards him and replied to the pause in her sentence with the word, 'Fascinating'. She continued.

He smiled at the diplomat's wife and endeavoured to tune in to what she was saying but instead was just aware of her jaw moving and the growing sensation to escape. It wasn't his fault. He wasn't acclimatised yet. It might be best to get some air, even if it's hot air, he thought. What would the temperature be in here, he wondered? Over a hundred degrees. It must be. He fought the urge to run a finger along the lip of his collar.

Acclimatisation. It was a word he had heard muttered by Europeans like a quiet mantra ever since his arrival but no one was quite clear on how long it took to occur. Longer, at any rate. He looked around the room at the other Europeans – each sweating into their own collars and orders and decorations. They didn't appear to be exactly acclimatised either, and most of *them* had been here for decades. Not if the beads of sweat and glistening of their flesh were anything to go by. God's teeth. The Raj wasn't an imperial endeavour, it was a vast exercise in repressed, concerted thermo-masochism.

Harris made a impressed 'Fancy that!' noise when the women paused for breath – and immediately excused himself and headed over to the windows. As well as sweltering breeze, they offered a decent view of the proceedings: a vast ballroom about the size of a rugby-football pitch, with plenty of gold thrown at the ceiling and no shortage of it laid on the walls. Vast chandeliers ran along the centre of the room, gleaming like planets in the full glare of the sun. The overwhelming colour scheme was orange, the national hue of Bikaner.

Yes, it was safe to say that Ganga Singh, or actually rather more likely his great-great grandfather, had spared no effort to create a salon of splendour. The lines of the ceilings stretched for such a whopping distance that Harris couldn't make out the vanishing point. Perhaps, he wondered, it had been the intention to build a room vast enough to accommodate the entire population of Bikaner? It certainly looked like most of them were here.

Dotted among the sea of ornately turbaned heads, he saw the pates of Europeans – servants of the Maharaja's, and the diplomatic corps. There was Colonel Stewart in his sparkling white ceremonial uniform along with his monstrous wife – monstrous because of her gargantuan bossiness and astonishing hauteur. In India, Harris had discovered, women such as Mrs Stewart did not have first names. His eye fell on her with a sudden surge of loathing; she appeared to have an entire ostrich taped to her head, and was burdened by a length of pearls adequate to garrotte a bull elephant. He imagined pulling at the dangling strands and the pearls digging into the rolls of her neck . . .

Pagefield, evidently a bachelor, had changed and now wore the blue and gold braid tunic of the diplomatic class. It looked tortuously thick and he was perspiring copiously – and making no effort to conceal it, not that he could. He was attended to by Captain Dundonald, who had been noticeably distracted since his arrival.

Somewhere at the centre of the melee was the Maharaja himself, and Harris knew that he ought to find him – he really should – but he was aware that the heat in the room was rising cruelly and that the closer he got to the centre would only magnify that. Oh, it was all too much. He took a steep tilt of his gin and tonic, which was warming fast, like everything else in this place, and felt a great weight upon his shoulders. On top of all this his wretched tiger toe ached phantomly within his leather dress shoe. Blast. The phantom toe was probably sweating too.

He was, he realised, on the verge of mild depression. He sighed. India, perhaps, was too much for him. He had overstretched himself. Yes, that was it. He was suffering a specific form of imperial overstretch. He smiled at that. And then he finished his gin and tonic and looked about for a waiter. It was all a question of rehydration, after all. Must drink more gin and tonic . . .

Suddenly he saw her. Beyond the bobbing, glistening pates of a pair of Englishmen in the grip of male pattern baldness, a young Indian woman glided into view. Quite what she was doing in the party, apparently unattended, he could not say – most of the Maharaja's female family observed a species of purdah and were unseen. But here this young woman was. Unless of course, the heat had finally started to warp his mind, and like the some blighter stranded in the desert, he was hallucinating. No, she was *certainly* alone. And you know what else? thought Harris, the hallucination was remarkably striking. Her face was turned just slightly to one side, revealing the contour of her nose, and the swell of her full, shapely lips and a certain jinx-like playfulness apparent in her large, almond-shaped eyes. Goodness, thought Harris, as he found himself approaching, his feet seemingly under the command of a greater being. He needed to get a closer look.

Goodness.

A richly embroidered silk headscarf of cool fuchsia just about framed her luscious black hair, which tumbled over an inch of bare shoulder with risqué abandon. The silken locks also met a dress of abundant opulence matching the scarf in hue. Emeralds glistened at her ears and her slim, smooth throat and a beautiful teardrop pearl the size of a grape dangled at her forehead. Harris did not need to be told that she was in the presence of one of Ganga Singh's significant female relatives. He smiled broadly and just as he was confronting the challenge of how to address her, he saw her notice his advance. She met him half way.

'I am Sir Ganga Singh's niece,' she announced, speaking a carefree curt tone that was delightfully free of self-importance and simultaneously communicated mild boredom, whether of that fact or the party or life in general, he could not say. She added the hint of a curtsey, 'Princess Padmini.'

Harris offered a polite bob of the head and introduced himself.

Her eyes were large, dark, and rather enticingly emphasised by make-up – and spirited. Yes, they were spirited: Harris noticed her glance with interest over at the headdress of a passing potentate. She missed nothing. Alert and *spirited*. She focused her attention back on him and Harris felt himself wishing to look at her ears, but knew his manners so looked away. For a moment the pain of the tiger toe vanished and even the oppressive heat seemed to lift. He spied a waiter and reached out, retrieving two gins and tonic, one of which he promptly handed to the princess, who took it without hesitation. As the glass bobbed to her full lips, he noticed a tiny diamond nose stud above her left nostril. When in photographs he had previously seen such adornments they had struck him as gaudy emoluments, but in person, the minuscule diamond did nothing more than emphasise the elegant contour of the nostril, and drew attention to the woman's flawless complexion. Great Scott, thought Harris, her skin was as soft as henna-flavoured ice cream.

'Ah,' she announced – evidently placing him. She cast him a mischievous sideways look. 'You are the "famous" British journalist who shot at one of our precious tigers the other day. I hope it brought you pleasure. Between you, my uncle, and the Viceroy, it's a wonder there are any left.' She smiled. 'You're here to interview my uncle, I understand?' These utterances flowed in vowels, consonants and the impeccable falling intonation of any graduate of Cheltenham Ladies' College.

Harris dabbed the sweat that had been coalescing for some minutes on his brow.

'I had the pleasure of meeting his highness this morning –' he noticed the girl looking over his shoulder, rather as if she were looking for someone more interesting to talk to.

She cut in: 'And what about your dashing mountaineer companion? We've been reading about him with interest? Is he here this evening?' She looked about some more.

Harris looked up from her feet, which he was admiring, 'That's a good point – I really don't know where Ernest is.' He frowned out across the room. 'I haven't seen him since the, er, ceremony. Um.' Where was Ernest, as a matter of fact? His mind returned to the task in hand; namely conversing with the beautiful woman directly before him. 'I take it you were at the ceremony –'

'Oh, rather,' she grinned broadly. 'We've not had an assassination attempt here for donkey's years, and all of a sudden, what do you know? Just like a London omnibus, two of them turn up at once. As you can imagine everyone's agog.' Her eyes lit up, then her tone altered and she looked up at him inquisitively: 'But tell me, aren't you astonished at the sheer, blithering incompetence of the man? I mean, he *literally* had the Maharaja and the Viceroy in point blank range and yet he failed. Was a ruddy *imbecile*!'

Her utter contempt was delicious. Harris half snorted his drink, recovering in time to respond: 'That's Marxists for you,' he said, rummaging in his pockets, and producing his cigarette case. 'They're even more hopeless than the other lot. Smoke?' He flicked it open smoothly and she glanced down at the row of beige Turks.

'Are you joking?' she half laughed, her eyebrows arched and looked at him sideways. 'It's bad enough for us to be seen *conversing* with one another – you realise that, don't you? If I took a cigarette from you, they'd assume we were doing much more.'

Harris's throat spasmed – and he coughed hard. She shrank back rather, betraying no sign of compassion, and gazed witheringly at him as he brought his coughing fit under control with a timely application of gin and tonic. She sipped her drink.

Harris's mind was still being flooding with mental imagery, and he emitted a staccato laugh. It was like the best effort of an unlucky jungle parrot on the last day of the mating season. Padmini cocked an eyebrow at him for a moment, and then turned her head away.

He watched her sip her chilled basil and mint tonic and wondered what to say. He took a sip at his own drink, and contemplated the high cheekbones and the cumin-tinged creamy skin. The large eyes were wandering around the room.

116

'I say,' he asked, alighting on a topic. He waited for her attention to restore itself to him. 'Have you read *A Passage to India*?'

The head went back somewhat, causing the headscarf to break on her shoulders and she lowered her drink. 'Are you really interesting in what I think of books, Sir Percival?'

'Call me Harris.'

'Harris,' she nodded. 'If you *are* interested, I feel it's already rather dated. In its depiction of Indians, especially so. If anything they seem more Victorian than contemporary. But of course one doesn't read Forster for reality, does one? One reads him for different truths altogether, and he's good at those.' She sighed. 'As for being an Englishman who puts an Indian at the centre of a book set in India, destined in the main to be read by other Englishmen: he demonstrates rare prescience.'

Harris was still absorbing all of this and nearing the formation of a point that might make him appear erudite and witty, when she added, 'In respect of contemporary fiction, I think the question should be, have you read *Burmese Days*?'

'Orwell?' Harris shuddered. 'God, no. He's not sound at all.'

Princess Padmini lifted her chin, her face registering some surprise. But she said nothing.

'Have you read it?' asked Harris.

'Oh,' she replied breezily. 'Not yet. It's banned here, but I've got a friend bringing me a copy in a few weeks.'

She smiled at him and her eyebrows bobbed invitingly.

'I wonder,' she said, 'if there *is* somewhere around here, after all, that we can go where I can smoke with you –'

Harris chuckled.

'I say,' he said lowering his voice to something approaching an accusation: 'You're not like other Indian women I've met, are you?'

She cocked an eyebrow.

'And just how many Indian woman have you met, Harris?'

He thought for a moment.

'Apart from the woman begging outside of the station?'

117

Padmini replied with the glimmer of a smile.

Harris was suddenly struck by the fear – and it very seldom struck – that he was boring her, so he reached for a banal statement to carry them over until something witty struck: she looked over, her brown eyes caught the light, and he offered: 'Your uncle is undoubtedly a great man and a world figure. As well as being a slayer of tigers second to none.'

'Oh, no doubt,' she replied, flashing him a flawless grin. 'It does beg the question of quite how many tiger skins one man really needs.' She sipped her drink and a thought occurred to her, 'It probably explains why he keeps building new palaces, because he needs more space to carpet.'

Harris laughed.

'Tell me,' she said. 'Did you enjoy killing yours?'

Harris grimaced. 'I don't think *enjoyment* is quite the word.'

'Then why on earth did you do it?'

'I'm not quite sure,' he shrugged. 'Tradition?'

She shook her head, fluttering her elegant eyelashes. 'How patriarchy has survived this long remains a mystery to me.'

Harris gave a double take.

'Are you, um,' he paused, positioning his lips to utter the strange, new word – 'a *feminist*?'

She smiled quizzically at him, rather as if he had said something unworthy of himself, but that was somehow endearing.

'Isn't every women born after 1910 a feminist?'

'Now there's a thought . . .' He glanced down at the toes of his brogues. Golly, his feet *were* hot.

The princess weighed up this comment for a moment, and then laughed. She 'clinked' her glass against Harris's. 'What is it about you English?' she declared.

The congestion of the room and noise began to penetrate his thoughts, as they had before. A grand-looking English couple passed by, pausing to offer the princess a respectful salutation. Next was a small bureaucrat, looking unimpressive in a badly fitting grey flannel suit and spectacles that magnified his eyes so much it was painful to look at them. He floated up toward Padmini but she merely shook her head at him, and he withdrew.

'Who's that?' asked Harris.

'The prime minister,' replied Padmini, sounding utterly bored.

Harris looked back at the man with a little more interest, and pondered making a crack about him being a visionary, but decided that the princess wasn't the sort to enjoy weak wordplay. Then he noticed that his cigarette had amassed an alarming amount of ash. He looked for a receptacle and a uniformed servant stepped forward immediately from the crowd, proffering an ashtray. It might not have seemed like it but they were under close, if hopefully benign, surveillance. If surveillance could ever be benign.

She sighed, and checked her tiny wristwatch – and reached forward and patted his jacket pocket. 'You know, I shall take one of those, as a matter of fact. The whole thing is just so utterly oppressive.'

Harris was just opening his silver cigarette case, when Pagefield intervened, gently grasping the case and taking it from him. He slipped it back into Harris's jacket pocket, and bobbed his head in the direction of Padmini.

'Your highness.' He wasn't here to talk to her, however, and he quickly guided Harris in the direction of the screened window. At that moment a lavishly adorned courtier gently intervened to distract Padmini with a message whispered into her ear.

'On no account,' Pagefield was saying – in that slightly pompous, enervated schoolmaster-ish tone of voice of his – 'are the events of the ceremony to be, er, made public.'

'But it was a public event – about a thousand people witnessed a man attempt to shoot the Viceroy and the Maharaja.'

'That is undeniable, but you were the only *London* correspondent. All the other press are, um, local, and have been hushed up – and that's how we'd like to keep it.'

Harris confronted the massive, impassive face – there were

ever so slightly tragic dried-out trails of sweat running down the sides of it – and mulled the likely impact of non-compliance.

'You might be able to "hush things up" out here,' he said, gritting his teeth. 'But when I'm back in London I can jolly well do what I like. You can't muzzle the free press in the land of liberty!'

Pagefield rolled his eyes and gave a warm chuckle. 'The Viceroy is very good friends with Lord Axminster,' he stated dryly, naming the proprietor of Harris's newspaper. He adjusted his white glove. 'There would be consequences.'

'Consequences!' hissed Harris. He clenched his fist. 'Consequences are so boring.'

Pagefield offered a flat smile, like a mortician delivering a punch-line at an autopsy.

Harris looked glumly out at the sea of faces over Pagefield's shoulder to see if he could see the girl. She was gone – stolen from him in a no-doubt premeditated pincer movement in which Pagefield was complicit. He glared balefully at the British Resident, and snatched a gin and tonic from a passing tray. A search of the crowd confirmed that she had vanished from sight. He drank defiantly.

'Oh –' Pagefield started. He'd thought of something. 'Did you get enough material for your article from your interview with the Maharaja this morning?'

'What?' declared Harris, with a tone of belligerence. 'In all two-minutes of it?'

'I'm sure you've got *heaps*.' Pagefield patted him forcefully on the shoulder. 'You've a seat booked on the morning train for Delhi.'

Delhi? Harris glared at Pagefield. Like hell he was going to Delhi. Not when he had just met the sensational Princess Padmini. We'll see about Delhi!

Pagefield nodded to a passing dignitary.

Harris asked,

'Have you seen Drabble anywhere?'

The British Resident smiled.

'He's on his way to Delhi as we speak.' Pagefield cocked his wrist, taking care not to spill his drink, and checked his watch. 'He took off about half an hour ago.' He offered Harris a broad smile that showed his teeth. 'You see? One down, two to go.'

Pagefield began to edge away.

'B-but why's he flying now? What's happening?'

Pagefield turned back, his frown betraying mild irritation. 'Professor Drabble has been dispatched on His Highness's business,' he reported. 'The Maharaja – and it's up to him – has asked him to follow up on today's unfoldings, shall we say. It's in what one might call a private capacity.'

'Goodness.'

'I know,' sighed Pagefield, rather as if he had just seen an inglorious run-out of his favourite batsman. 'Why they can't just leave it to the professionals beggars belief. But there you go. I'll see you around. Oh,' he added. 'Keep all that under your hat.'

He watched Pagefield saunter off and experienced a peculiar sensation of emotions.

On reflection it was too hot by far to smoke in the durbar hall, plus the conversation with Pagefield had left Harris rather despising everything about the British Raj. It was all very well ruling other people, thought Harris, but being ruled over one-self wasn't on. In fact the direct experience of being deprived of personal liberty left him feeling ghastly. Indeed, it was like a hangover without the pleasure of drinking first. After the conversation with Pagefield a peculiar hollow sickness had afflicted his stomach, reminiscent of the shame he once felt at school for failing to stand up to a particular bully – or indeed, after receiving beatings from masters, which had often happened to him. What had once seemed like an acceptable sanction transmuted itself over the passage of three or so years into a sadistic breach of human dignity. And that was how he felt now, as Pagefield pushed him around. Harris's hand clenched around his icy gin and tonic and stepped out into the closed courtyard.

I wonder if this is what it feels like to be Indian, he wondered. He set his drink down beside the fountain, and quickly lit a cigarette. As he did so a note fluttered from his pocket and floated to the ground . . .

Chapter Twelve

The Maharaja's airfield was a barren, unmarked strip in the desert, remarkable only for the absence of trees and bushes. An air-sock sagged on a flag pole, which cast a long shadow across the shrub in the low evening sunlight. The Rolls-Royce had pulled up by a dusty-looking hangar of Western design, out of which the plane, a de Havilland DH.9, an ex-RAF bomber given to the Maharaja after the war as a token of thanks from the British state, had lately been wheeled.

Drabble was introduced to the pilot, a dirty-looking, stick-thin Welshman named Morgan. He finished his rolled up cigarette and tossed it down before offering his firm hand to Drabble.

'Delhi?' he asked, his eyebrows meeting the fur lining of his aviator's hat. 'Two hundred and forty miles,' he added, more to himself than for anyone else's benefit. 'The DH.9 does 98 knots on the nail, so that's two and a half hours. We should have enough fuel to get there. You flown before?' he asked, as he presented Drabble with a leather flying hat and pair of goggles. He strode towards the waiting aircraft, barking orders to the ground crew as he buckled the chin-strap of his headgear. Drabble followed, climbed into the foremost seat, and his bag was lowered in on top of him.

The propeller was spun, and the engine spluttered into life: a plume of black smoke erupted from the exhausts, then the engine gave a throaty roar. The ground crew hauled away the chocks and the plane skittered out onto the airstrip.

Moments later they were soaring high above Bikaner, the city spreading out below them. From up here it looked remarkable green at the centre with its parks and palatial gardens. The mass of Junagarh Fort dominated the urban outline but there was the other royal palace not far off, set in a broad dark gardens, and various other municipal structures, many completed over the last few years. Beyond the city, the landscape was flat and green – lush, almost, despite the heat. But the full weight summer was still a month or so off. As a young boy, Drabble just about remembered adults complaining of it – or at least, he remembered them talking it about it later. Starting in late April was when the searing sun would start to change this already arid landscape into a dustbowl, until the rains came in July and August, if they came.

Right now the green landscape continued for miles into the distance, growing rapidly grey. Below them were hundreds of farms where families were bringing in the harvest, creating heaps of wheat. From up here Drabble could make out women working in the fields in their bright robes alongside their menfolk – sometimes the evening sun picked out the fuchsias or zinging greens of their headscarves. Over to their right ahead, the silhouette of the plane streaked along the ground, like a flying carpet.

Looking left, towards the horizon in the north, you realised just how contingent on mankind this whole verdant landscape was. For there, the blackish green in the distance met the white beige of the desert, delineating the limits of man's hard-won oasis. After that the productive landscape fell immediately into a sandy, beige void – albeit one dotted with innumerable Khejri desert trees and grasses, which went unchangingly as far as the eye could see. It was said that they could go eight years without rainwater and that their roots went hundreds of yards into the ground.

From up here, there was that striking sense of the scale of India – emphasised by the flat mass of the Thar desert, dotted by trees and occasional villages. Many were no more than small clusters of circular grass-roofed houses with stick fences for livestock.

On and on it went: continuing beyond the horizon. India was more than seven times the size of France and felt like it. In less than the time it took to fly to Delhi from Bikaner, you could travel from London to Paris.

The immense mechanical baritone of the engine just in front of him – on the other side of the instrument panel – was blunted by the earpieces of his thick aviator's hat, which rendered it a repetitive, insistent drone. It closed out all other noise, too, and with the swirling warm wind around his head, and the undulating movement of the plane as it passed through the air – almost like a boat on a big sea – there was something hypnotic about the physical sensation of the flight. Drabble gazed mutely out at the landscape, absorbing its vastness and fell into a mood of melancholy repose.

He had liked the Maharaja: he was a man of undoubted integrity; an individual of passion and drive. Brave, certainly. Not stupid, nor quick to rush to judgement. He could well understand why Harris has travelled a quarter way round the earth to interview him; moreover, he understood why Harris's editor had agreed to it, too – and paid for it. Ganga Singh was a significant figure.

And, if it was your thing, definitely worth killing. As was Mr Gandhi, the undoubted intended co-victim of the bomb plot of Tuesday night. That the same assassin was prepared also to target the Viceroy in what was effectively a suicide mission demonstrated the essential anarchism of his endeavour. It also pointed strongly to the man's associations with Communism, suggested by Goodlad on Monday night. What was highly improbable was that the man was working alone; a fact supported by his knowledge of Gandhi's presence in Bikaner, which had been kept secret, along with the meeting of the Chamber of Princes. There was also the question of how on earth he had gained admittance to the fort, and then slipped away only to reappear for a second bite of the cherry as a photographer.

These facts pointed to collaborators in the household of the Maharaja, a fact that must have occurred to Ganga Singh, and must be a chief point of concern. Secondly – he noticed now that the sun had gone and that the sky before them had taken on an inky blackness – secondly, that collaborator needed by definition to have a corresponding collaborator in Delhi. How, after all, had he managed to escape Goodlad's custody in time to catch the train to Bikaner, presuming that's how he got there? Drabble looked up at the sky above: it was freckled with luminous blotches of blue and dotted with stars.

There was finally the mystery of 'Miss Heinz': her actions proved she had but one intent, to eliminate Drabble in order to prevent him from recognising the would-be assassin on his second attempt and thereby thwarting it. If true, that foreknowledge was proof of the wider conspiracy, but it jarred. How else would she have known where or why to find Harris in the first place? Not only that, but she had performed the pick-up with remarkable aplomb – these people had clearly done their research on Harris. How could all of this have been achieved without some wider organisation at work? The luminous blotches in the heavens above had now vanished, leaving just the stars, brighter and bolder than ever. No. They had, for sure, become involved in a great contrivance, one which Drabble now resolved to untangle.

The answer lay in Delhi, and Drabble had twenty-four hours in hand to find it before the Maharaja himself was due to arrive. For now, the next step was to see Superintendent Goodlad of the Imperial Police. Whether he wanted to or not, he was going to lead Drabble to the answer, one way or the other.

Harris was working his way through another gin and tonic and plotting how to effect another meeting with Princess Padmini. Regardless of the rights or wrongs of it, he was determined.

And he knew few things could counter his determination, once he had set his mind on something.

He looked around for the small bespectacled prime minister – there had been someone calling out for conversation – but could not see him. All he could see was a bobbing landscape of scarlet, sweating English faces – he spotted Pagefield holding court to several Europeans in civilian dress. He saw Colonel Stewart, the head of security and police chief, whose career had presumably hit absolute rock bottom that week. He was conversing with a distinguished looking Indian of about sixty, distinguished not least because of his skull-like head which protruded from a stand-up mandarin collar like a giant lollipop atop a stick-thin body.

Pagefield appeared at Harris's side.

'Who's that?' asked Harris. 'The gaunt fellow chatting with Stewart.'

Pagefield cleared his throat.

'Someone you would enjoy meeting,' he dabbed his cheeks. 'Sir Randolph Sharma-Smith, chairman and managing director of Bombay Cotton Industries . . . one of India's richest men and member of the legislative assembly of the Bombay presidency, no less.'

'What's he doing here?'

'Oh, he's mates with Ganga Singh – who by the way has a beautiful pad on the oceanfront in Bombay – it's one of the places he escapes to in the summer when this place becomes even more inferno-like. I jest not.' Harris noted that his handkerchief was sodden.

'If you think this is hot . . . this is merely the overture.'

'It might be interesting to have an industrialist's take on Ganga Singh's achievements,' suggested Harris, speaking his thoughts out loud. Pagefield was smelling pretty ripe, too. At that moment, an unseen interlocutor addressed the British Resident who turned away, the tan back section of his jacket – which could have been requisitioned from a marquee – was saturated with sweat.

Harris took the opportunity and approached Sir Randolph, who stood alone.

'Sir Randolph,' he beamed, reaching out his hand.

The businessman – shrewd eyes protruding from a skull-like, tobacco-coloured cranium – viewed Harris sceptically, but shook his hand all the same. The grip of his sinewy hand was surprisingly muscular. Harris introduced himself; Sir Randolph's expression betrayed no inkling of interest in his origins or purpose in Bikaner.

'I've been to London,' he sniffed.

'Oh yes,' replied Harris, keenly.

'Never again. Too dark.'

'H'm,' cooed Harris, sympathetically. 'Were you there in the winter?'

'No, it was July.' Sir Randolph pronounced with indignation. 'And the smell . . .' This declaration reached no definite conclusion but he shook his head. 'Now, Oxford on the other hand, Oxford *is* a city.' He smiled, showing his teeth, which were narrow, but in good order for a man of his age.

'You enjoy your work?' barked the tycoon.

'It has its moments,' replied Harris, attempting to inject some jollity into the discourse.

'Really?'

He did not sound like he thought it would.

'Yes, it's the people, mainly.' Something about the immediate circumstances undermined the conviction that Harris would usually bring such a statement – but he pressed on. 'It's a privilege meeting such thoroughly interesting people.'

'I see,' replied Sir Randolph, who was not listening. His large watery eyes were roving around the crowd. As someone who felt himself bored easily, Harris understood the impulse only too well. But he resented it. How dare this fellow give up on him, without even giving him a chance. He saw the tycoon's gaze settle on Pagefield; he faced them but was engrossed in conversing with what looked like a giant pineapple.

'I despise fat people,' Sir Randolph announced, glaring in the direction of the British Resident. 'Fat people have no self-control. I despise people who lack self-control.'

His intense watery eyes met Harris's gaze, 'I know what you mean, Sir Randolph.' He swallowed, 'Cigarette?'

The Indian shook his head.

'I do not smoke,' he stated in his determined staccato English. He gazed severely at Harris. 'I detest smoking. It is an addiction, which by definition requires the cessation of self-control, which I abhor. We are nothing if we abandon our self-control. Even worms have self-control. Surely you are above a worm, sir?'

Harris's eyebrows bobbed involuntarily and he struggled to suppress a grin – not precisely the face of steely self-control, he realised. But this was what happened when he was in the presence of such humourless sincerity. His mind revisited a recent interview with the German ambassador . . .

'Do you not agree?' repeated Sir Randolph.

'Steadfast urbanity is the only solution,' Harris pronounced winningly.

Sharma-Smith inspected him with mild revulsion; his top lip curled, and he pronounced with caution, 'That is a step in the right direction.'

He cleared his throat, a dry rasp, like a lizard coughing in the desert. Evidently unable to spy anyone of interest, the industrialist turned his full attention back to Harris.

'And where is your great friend Professor Drabble, about whom I have heard so much? I am keen to make *his* acquaintance.'

'Oh, you've not heard? The Maharaja's packed him off on a secret mission to Delhi.'

'Delhi –' exclaimed Sharma-Smith, just as Harris was remembering that he wasn't meant to mention any of it. 'What the dickens has he done that for?'

Harris shrugged, and raised his hands, giving him the full Gallic treatment.

'I'm afraid I know nothing more –'

'Don't worry,' continued the industrialist. He sighed. 'I shall raise it with the Maharaja.' His temper was returning. 'Now tell me, Sir Percival; how have you enjoyed your visit to British India and Rajputana so far?'

'In all honesty?' Harris paused. He was seldom entirely honest. 'Apart from the heat, I've loved every minute,' he declared. By heat he wasn't simply referring to the temperature, of course.

As he completed his response he spotted Padmini's profile across the room – above Sir Randolph's shoulder and sandwiched between two conversing heads.

The industrialist nodded.

'India will not be safe until we have stamped out Marxism, Gandhism, and all unspeakable Indian nationalism of any kind,' the tycoon fumed. 'I am as one with Sir Ganga Singh on this: our great country's future lies firmly within the bosom of the British Empire – eventually, one day, we will meet our potential as a self-governing state, for sure, but that too will be within the imperial family.'

Harris was gladdened to hear this from the mouth of such a high-ranking Indian, and said as much. 'Speaking as an Englishman, I struggle to disagree with any of that,' he added cheerily. 'How long do you think it will take for India to gain independence?'

'Independence?' spat Sir Randolph. 'Who said anything about independence? In my view it will be many generations before Indians are ready to take the leap of independence.'

'Oh really? Good, excellent –'

Harris's acquiescence seemed to have an immediately calming effect on the other man's temper. He asked, 'I wonder, Sir Randolph, is the question then, this: when do you think India will attain the same sort of self-rule as enjoyed by say, Canada or New Zealand?'

'Now *that* is an interesting question . . .' Sharma-Smith pinched his lips together thoughtfully so that his mouth resembled that of one of the mummies in Bloomsbury. 'Thirty to forty years, I should think. Any quicker than that would be foolhardy.' He smiled, a flat reptilian affair which offered all the warmth of Leith seafront in November. 'Suffice it to say that it will unlikely occur in *my* lifetime. Which is just how I would like it. Between you and me, Sir Percival, I have no interest in being ruled by Indians –' he shuddered. 'The English are bad enough. People forget, the Mughals were far, far worse. They were greedy, they were indolent. They were parasites. No,' he cleared his throat. 'The prospect of democracy here is frankly terrifying. Indians should be grateful for what we have. Over the last two hundred years, the level of our wealth, education and sheer population have increased immeasurably. Alas, the English have been here so long that people have started to take them for granted. More's the pity.'

Harris listened thoughtfully, half wishing Drabble was present to hear this full-throated support for the Raj. It made some sense: British rule in the subcontinent could not be maintained if everyone was set against them, whatever the perception, certainly prevalent in London, that India had become an ungovernable hotbed of discontent.

'India today,' continued Sharma-Smith, 'is a beautiful rose, one that was transplanted long ago from England and which over the years has evolved into its own perfect hybrid variety. We must preserve that rose at all costs.'

Harris smiled; horticultural metaphors held little interest for him, but he couldn't resist another question:

'Out of interest, Sir Randolph, what's your assessment of the Viceroy's performance?'

Sharma-Smith turned slowly towards him, his expression icy. 'Do not get me started on Lord Linlithgow.' He shook his head. 'If you ask me the rot set in after Curzon. He was the last good one you sent us.'

'And what of Mr Gandhi?'

'Him? Good God,' spat Sharma-Smith. He was speaking loudly now. 'The man's a liability and a fraud. That's the best that can be said of *him*.'

131

Several guests turned to look in their direction. Harris lowered his head self-consciously. He asked,

'Do you think that, um, many Indians agree with you?'

The large round eyes narrowed:

'Agree with me? Sir Percival, do not fib yourself that this is a country where agreement matters. What counts here is *obedience*. The people will obey a strong leader if they are given one.' He took a deep breath and added, almost painfully, 'The problem with recent British rulers is that they have begun to lose faith in their authority. That must be resolved – and resolved quickly if we are to prevent India slipping into the hands of anarchy.'

'I blame the schools,' commented Harris breezily. 'It all started to go downhill when they introduced soccer at Haileybury.'

'Quite,' agreed Sharma-Smith soberly. 'It's just not cricket.'

Harris grinned at that, but stifled it when he realised that the turn of phrase was not a *bon mot* on the tycoon's part.

'Mercifully,' continued Sir Randolph, 'there are pockets beyond British India such as Bikaner which are protected – up to a point, at least – from the insipid influence of British enlightened thinking. Men like Ganga Singh are visionaries and not to be underestimated. They still possess *real* ambition for this country. They may be bulwarks of real India, if all else fails.'

'We can certainly drink to that,' chuckled Harris brightly, raising his glass. He always was more inclined to a happy ending.

Sir Randolph looked down at this drink, his eyelids half-lifted in disapproval.

'I do not drink. I detest . . .'

Chapter Thirteen

Superintendent Goodlad was not at the police station on Chandi Chowk but would likely be found at his club. So said the station sergeant. It was well after 9pm, so Drabble had his bags sent on to his lodgings and paid a call on the policeman as directed. He found Goodlad on the club veranda, seated at in cane chair with a whisky in hand, conversing with another member who resembled the Anglo-Saxon ruling class, right down to the evening dress and the heart attack complexion. On the servant's whisper to his ear, Goodlad's expression darkened – he actually looked almost savage in one fleeting moment – and he saw off his drink at once before getting up. Drabble prepared himself, but as Goodlad approached, Drabble saw his expression soften to something approaching mere detestation.

'Professor,' he stated, not offering his hand and his head bowed forward slightly so that his eyes peered at Drabble from beneath his fair eyebrows.

He waited.

'Do you have a moment to talk?' asked Drabble.

'By all means.' Goodlad gestured towards the lawns which were lost in darkness and stretched out into the night. 'That's probably the safest place to confer around here – there's enough shop talked in this place as it is. Cigarette?'

Drabble declined and Goodlad took out a cigarette case and lit up. They were soon strolling across the gardens, the evening air was hot and far from refreshing. The noise of expatriate conviviality wafted towards them from the veranda, laughter occasionally interrupting the baritone. In the hours since he had left Bikaner, Drabble had had cause to wonder quite how to confront this subject with Goodlad. The man's black leather shoes reflected the lights from club. Drabble noticed the sharp break in the starched creases of his trousers.

'I've heard what happened in Bikaner.' He stopped abruptly and turned towards Drabble. 'You're quite the hero, aren't you? I gather that Lady Linlithgow's been quite shaken up by it all, which is entirely understandable under the circumstances.'

His rage was palpable. 'And then you'll know the identity of putative assassin?'

Goodlad nodded. 'Sohan Choudhury; a committed Marxist and highly effective agitator. He's quite a piece of work. Punjabi,' he added. 'A decided trouble-maker.'

'Well, he won't be troubling anyone now.'

Goodlad nodded, took a deep drag of his cigarette and threw it away. Smoke funnelled from his nostrils, and he added: 'As you can imagine, I've had a little explaining to do – to have had this man in my custody only on Monday evening, and to release him and for him to make, apparently, two separate astonishing attempts, the first that you seemingly thwarted, and then the second one in broad daylight. It's frankly outrageous.' He stopped. 'I mean it. I've been in this godforsaken country for 25 years and I've never heard of anything like it. It's despicable. These people have no idea what we've done for them.'

Drabble remained silent. Their positions were so at variance a discussion of the point would not be of use. He saw the light from the veranda fall across half of Goodlad's face, leaving the rest in shadow. The side he could see conveyed enough betrayal for both. For Goodlad the attack on the person of the Viceroy was a personal attack on him directly – in a way that just did not resonate with Drabble in the least. He realised that Goodlad was waiting for some sort of condemnatory rejoinder from him, which he felt no compulsion to give. The trouble was he saw it from the Indian perspective, too.

Goodlad's rage erupted, and his voice broke.

'My God man, what's wrong with you? Doesn't it make you livid? There were English women and children present, too. It's disgusting.'

Drabble knew that the reply that was true to him was not one that Goodlad could tolerate. 'I condemn all acts of terrorism or acts of brutality,' he replied with studied calm.

Goodlad nodded with understanding, but his eyes glistened with contempt.

'The simple and lamentable fact of the matter is that there was no evidence supposing that this Choudhury fellow was anything other than what we already knew – an active Communist and effective rabble-rouser. But these things are not against the law, so if the Bikaneris let him in, it's their ruddy fault.'

Goodlad lit another cigarette and began to walk.

Drabble asked,

'How do you think he came to learn of Mr Gandhi's visit to Bikaner?'

Goodlad shook his head. 'Who can say?'

'Well the people in Bikaner would have known . . .'

'Right enough – there'll be Communist sympathisers in Bikaner, as anywhere else. What's for certain is that these people don't live in vacuums – they have friends and political associates who hold similarly radical views. Just look at the information that passes around this place,' he added, throwing his head towards the club house. 'People talk.' He took a last drag of the cigarette and threw it down; then he stopped and turned, heading them back towards the light of the veranda. He glanced over.

'Time for a drink, Professor?'

They settled into a pair of cane armchairs in a quiet corner of one of the club rooms, alone but for a quartet of off-duty civil servants in the far corner, playing whist and working their way through a bottle of Scotch.

'The club whisky is perfectly acceptable,' announced Goodlad as the waiter approached.

'That's fine,' replied Drabble.

Goodlad ordered, requiring ice in a separate glass and a jug of water.

He leaned forward and lowered his voice, 'Have you ever heard of an organisation called the Anti-Gandhian League?' He read Drabble's blank expression. '*Good.* I say that because we have striven to nip this vile organisation in the bud – which is how it's stayed. Until now, at any rate.' His voice trailed off as the native waiter returned and set out their drinks.

Once the servant had departed, Goodlad continued: 'The league is an offshoot of the Communist Party of India, itself, as far as we can tell, an obedient offshoot of the Moscow mother ship. Now,' he lowered his voice and dropped an ice cube into his whisky. 'This particular offshoot – as the name implies – is not content with what it regards as the sluggish gradualism of Mr Gandhi's policies towards self-rule and independence. They want it all to happen much *faster*. The league emerged about a decade ago in the Punjab, where they blew up a few letter boxes – nothing too worrying, mercifully. As you would expect, we came down hard on them – gave the ringleaders lengthy sentences and so on – and that was largely that. Cheers,' he broke off from his briefing to raise his glass to Drabble. 'The Communist party endures, of course, but we did not have any grounds before the events of this week in Bikaner to suspect that they were plotting anything more than a new leaflet campaign or causing a few traffic jams with their protests.' He shook his head. 'For what it's worth, the intelligence I've received is that the Russians *are* behind it, stoked up by their doings with the Indian National Congress, no doubt. With Hitler and Musso making lots of noise in Europe, Moscow has wanted to create a distraction for us at least, so they've increased their funding for the party.' Goodlad splashed another ice cube into his whisky. 'Cheers.'

'You can hardly blame the Russians for wanting to spread their creed,' offered Drabble.

'That's an unfortunate fact of life,' agreed Goodlad, his tone rising. He added breezily, 'Unfortunately there seems to be official resistance at the highest level to an outright purge of the Communist party, which in my mind would be the simplest fix.' He sighed, 'We could then simply round up all the individuals concerned and imprison them for the duration.' He gave the resigned look of a priest contemplating an episcopal imposition, 'The supposition is that with the increased funding from Moscow has come the desire for increased activity of the most extreme kind.'

'He who pays the piper . . .'

'Quite.' Goodlad smiled sourly.

This all sounded plausible enough but it didn't necessarily solve the puzzle over Miss Skinner-Chatterjee.

'Does the name Millicent Florence Skinner-Chatterjee mean anything to you?'

Goodlad contemplated this for a moment, squeezed his eyes shut in thought, but finally shook his head.

'She died in Bikaner yesterday – killed in a car accident, a car which she was driving. While trying to run me down in the street, as it happens.'

Goodlad's eyebrows lifted, and he reached for the cigarette box.

'You've had quite a visit, haven't you?'

'I believe she was working with Choudhury. I'm certain she tried to kill me because she knew that I could identify him, and thereby was in a position to thwart his second assassination attempt. I wondered if she might be on any of your lists of Communist sympathisers.'

Goodlad was already reaching in his pocket for a slim notebook. He wrote down the name, with key details.

'I mentioned that she was an Anglo-Indian?'

'A Eurasian?' he frowned, shaking his head. 'They should be on our side,' he said bitterly. 'Communists are like weeds, new ones pop up all the time. Another whisky?'

'Why not.'

Goodlad ordered two more. With his old-fashioned moustache and rather small face, he might easily have been a branch manager of a provincial bank; sitting in a the cane chair, sweating into his dress uniform, he also looked rather small and vulnerable, nothing like the imperious figure that Drabble had seen walk out and confront an entire crowd with little more than sheer arrogance and a swagger stick. There was, however, a powerful brain behind the deep-set eyes. Of that Drabble was sure. And while Goodlad was a committed imperialist, he was also a man of a certain integrity. The question – to which the answer was likely unknowable – was to which cause his integrity applied. Was he, as he appeared, your typical imperialist diehard – the sort who would be wearing down the plyboard in a Tunbridge Wells Conservative club in years to come – or was there more to him? Drabble decided to trust him, or more's the point, at least to *pretend* to. Either way he had to smoke him out.

Drabble looked down thoughtfully at his whisky glass, and levered out another ice cube with the spoon, and dropped it in. He sensed that Goodlad was waiting for him to speak. 'I'm investigating this on behalf of Sir Ganga Singh; if you could find me an address for Skinner-Chatterjee, I'd be obliged.' He explained that she had a Bombay address in her passport, but that she must have been staying in New Delhi, temporarily or otherwise, judging by her luggage. 'It's surely an unusual enough surname. She might have relatives. I've got to try. I'd also like an address for Choudhury or any of his associates in the party.'

Goodlad nodded.

'I'll see what I can do – on condition that you share any information you find with us too. And, Drabble, you mustn't forget whose side you're on.'

He smiled, showing tea-stained, crooked teeth. 'Very well,' he concluded, referring to the clock on the wall. He began to rise from his chair. 'Where are you staying – I'll have anything I have sent over tonight.'

They finished their drinks and got up to go.

Drabble remembered something else he wanted to say.

'Do you know what this is?' he asked, unfolding his hand to show the rose badge that he had found among Skinner-Chatterjee's possessions.

Goodlad frowned down at it irritably – but not before Drabble had glimpsed a decided look of recognition. It was like a shadow passing across his face, gone as quickly as it had arrived. But he knew what it was.

'Is it a brooch?' he asked with interest, taking it up and looking at it under the tasselled light. 'Where did you find it?

He handed it back, but with reluctance, as Drabble explained.

Goodlad showed Drabble to the door, and once again did not offer his hand. He merely nodded his head curtly. 'I'll see if I've got anything on Choudhury and Miss Skinner-Chatterjee. Can't promise, but if I've anything I'll have it sent over to your club tonight. There's a tonga.' He barked an order at the Indian servant at the door, who nimbly dashed off to fetch it. 'Good night.'

The carriage emerged from the inky gloom and Drabble turned back to see Goodlad already heading up the steps and back inside. He saw the creases in the backs of his black dress trousers. It had been an informative meeting. But not, perhaps, without its danger.

Chapter Fourteen

Towards the end of the evening, the crowd thinning somewhat, Harris sidled back over to Pagefield. He was feeling blue. Miss Heinz was dead and, what's more, exposed as a fanatical harpy bent on murder and intrigue. Drabble had gone off to Delhi on an exciting secret mission, leaving him all alone in the middle of nowhere. And the wonderful Princess Padmini had been snatched from his company just when she was getting interesting. Pagefield, looking red, gave him a cheery smile. He had moved on from the heavy-handed admonishment of earlier, eased towards chumminess on a tide of no doubt of gin.

'Princess Padmini –' began Harris.

'Don't even think about it,' cut in Pagefield. He lowered his voice and raised a finger: 'I *mean* it, Harris. If you overstep the mark there'll be nothing I can do to save your skin.' He chuckled, and bumped his shoulder, 'And I don't just mean your *foreskin*!'

Harris scowled; that wasn't funny. A tumult of emotion raged up in him, like a storm wave whipping up over a North Sea breakwater. His hand curled into his fist. He went to protest, when a polite voice cut in:

'Excuse me, Sir Percival sahib –'

Harris turned to see an important-looking Indian of middle years – wearing a moustache and grey-tinted goatee, and filling his elegantly cut suit well.

'My name is Panikkar,' he said solicitously, bowing in acknowledgement to Pagefield. 'I have a request from the Maharaja and only you can assist,' he said smoothly, gently drawing Harris away.

Panikkar led him along a corridor continuing a solicitous dialogue all the while. They turned a corner, shields and memorabilia adorning the walls, and traversed several rooms displaying masses of amour and weaponry, before arriving at a door, which Panikkar opened and led Harris inside. Of all the rooms in the palace, it was the Maharaja's private office – the one in which the two-minute interview of that morning had fleetingly occurred. There was the long green baize-covered desk with the large coloured pencils favoured by Ganga Singh for his note-making, the in-trays and typewriters. At the nearest end of the table stood a silver tray with water jug, ice, and tumblers. But where earlier the room had been filled with light from the courtyard, it was now shuttered and lit by a couple of electric lamps dotted around, giving the large space an intimate warmth despite its size. He noticed several comfortable armchairs about, too, which he has not noticed earlier.

'Please wait here,' said Panikkar, indicating a leather wing-backed chair rather like you might see in the waiting room of a Harley Street practitioner, which Harris promptly filled.

Harris sat down and took out his watch – it was gone nine o' clock – and then ferreted in his pockets for his pipe.

The pipe lit, he got to his feet, feeling boredom coming on, and proceeded to inspect one of the walls. It was coated in photographs which he had earlier not had the freedom to examine. There were photographs of the Maharaja on a howdah atop an elephant processing along the thronging streets of Bikaner – thousands of supporters lining the roadsides. There he was in convoy with the Viceroy – Rolls-Royces instead of elephants this time, more garlands, more camel corps outriders and so on. Here was a photograph taken in the garden of Downing Street with the Imperial War Cabinet, in which a younger-looking Maharaja stood in the middle row in the military uniform of a British army general. That dramatic moustache unmissable.

The door creaked open, he turned; Princess Padmini stood at the threshold, her elegant mouth open fractionally as though she were exhaling, and her large eyes wide – quite as if she was stunned to see him. Plainly she must have arranged this, however. She had changed – switching her elegant fuchsià dress and scarf for a short light tweed jacket and jodhpurs, which stretched over her thighs. Harris felt his lungs fill.

Padmini closed the door behind her and locked it.

Harris grinned at her. Righty-oh.

Without a word, Padmini went over to a low cabinet, from which she nimbly unthreaded a bottle of Glenlivet from a dense thicket of potions. Harris watched her bend down – then averted his eyes: the delicious outline of her jodhpurs left little to his imagination, and made him feel dizzy. She unscrewed the lid as she swayed her hips crossing the room, and was pouring some of Scotland's finest into the two waiting tumblers on the tray before he even had cause to trouble vocal cords:

'You look like you've done this before,' said Harris, swallowing.

She arched an eyebrow and half-smiled.

'I'll let that remark pass,' she pronounced, speaking over the top of tumbling whisky. 'Water?'

'Just a smidge.'

She tilted in just a smidge and handed Harris the heavy glass, taking a swig from her own. Their fingers touched during the exchange – and then met for longer than was strictly necessary. 'Here,' she said, rather after the event.

'Cigarette?' he asked.

'No, thanks,' she said, splashing more water into her drink. 'Perhaps later.' She raised the glass and butted it into his. 'Chocks away! What's in the pipe?'

'Faulkner's Mountaineer,' he said. 'An old favourite. It's rather refreshing.'

She stood close to him, reached forward, and tugged the pipe from his mouth. She put it to her lips, and inhaled slowly – an act which sucked in her cheeks, emphasising her cheekbones and her catlike, almond-shaped eyes. At that moment, her leg pressed against his, and Harris felt the urgent need to take the weight off – but stood his ground. He's met girls like Padmini before, and he knew how not to let it show. He braced himself, watching the smoke billow from the bowl – and fortified himself with a swig of the Glenlivet.

'Like it?'

Her eyes pinched and she coughed hard . . . surrendering the pipe. The coughing fit continued so he poured her a glass of water which he handed to her, rather suavely, he thought. Padmini shook her head at it, and satisfied her throat with the Glenlivet.

Harris resumed his pipe, as she got her voice back. She said, 'I have it on good information that you are leaving Bikaner in the morning.'

'Pagefield has spoken – and apparently there is no recourse to an appeal to any authority higher than the British Resident. Not in Bikaner, anyway.'

'What was your crime?' She settled down onto the chaise longue and unfastened her jacket.

'Fraternising with the natives.' He smiled. 'It's not the done thing.'

She arched an eyebrow at him.

'As far as I can tell, you've not *done* anything yet –'

She slung her jacket to the tiled floor and leaned back, resting her head on her hands so that her white silk blouse betrayed the delicious outline of her pert breasts. She smiled broadly.

'Have you ever made love to an Indian princess before?'

Harris took out his pipe. 'What?'

As the query left his mouth, he registered her statement fully.

'Golly,' he declared, grinning. He looked about for somewhere to put down his pipe, adding, 'I might need to think about that one.' Pipe stowed, he peeled off his coat with all dignity of a man who has spent the last seven hours perspiring into it and reached the end of the chaise longue, where he kneeled, gazing at her beautiful, smiling face. He loosened his tie.

'Don't –' she said, putting her hand out to stop him. 'I never could resist a properly dressed Englishman.'

They lay there, she in his arms, perfectly still. Harris was, rather curiously, not thinking of anything. Not his pipe. Nor his next drink. Not even of his next story. Rather, he lay there, thinking of nothing more than the feeling of her body against his; her smell, and of her soft, rhythmic breathing.

'How soon after conclusion of sexual intercourse do you think it's appropriate to talk about it?' asked Padmini. 'Do you think you can discuss it immediately afterwards?' She moved away from him to get a look at his face.

'It all depends on what you want to say,' Harris averred. 'So long as one is relatively magnanimous. Sex is one of those areas where a little bit of criticism is apt to go a long way.'

'I'll say.' She turned, and pulled her blouse to cover her breasts, which Harris thought was a pity, as they were very nearly the most perfect breasts he had ever had the pleasure of encountering. In fact they were the most magnificent all-rounders; for shape, size and utter poise: they could win gymkhanas, if they had them.

'What are you smiling at,' she asked.

'Oh, nothing,' he said.

She frowned mildly.

'Shall we have one of your cigarettes? Then, perhaps, another drink,' she asked.

Harris did not normally require encouragement in either regards, but he was curious about something else. For the first time for as long as he could remember, he wasn't thirsty – not for a drink, at least. He lit two cigarettes and passed her one, noticing the longcase clock from the corner of his eye.

'Good God,' he declared. 'Did you know that it's two o'clock in the morning?' He began to get up. She seized his hand, and he felt his strength leave him. He fell to his knees on the sofa.

'You can't go yet,' Padmini told him. She smiled. 'We've only just met.'

'You're right,' he said, leaning in and kissing her.

They lay silently, smoking and gazing into the half-light. Harris's mind was at peace but a thought intruded the bliss. He had just had sexual intercourse with an Indian. Surely it went against his notions of racial superiority? He looked over at her. But how on earth could he believe anyone to be superior to this highly intelligent, well-educated, and frankly stunning example of the female species? Good God. He drew on his cigarette, and felt a surge of tension rush through his body. Ernest was *right*. The whole empire business was a whole heap of bunkum – one built upon pillars of bunkum, floating on a vast lake of bunkum-ness. Damn it. Ernest was right. He was always right; damn him.

'What is it, darling?' she asked, before he could speak. She found his face and stroked it. 'You look frustrated.'

'I'm sorry,' he said, with meaning. He turned away, feeling shame and knowing it would be written across it. Padmini reached forward and hooked his chin kindly towards her. She saw the look.

'Oh, that.' She gave a weary laugh. 'Don't worry about *that*. We've always known that you would come to your senses . . . we just didn't know we'd have to fuck you one by one first.'

Chapter Fifteen

Drabble arrived at the Clive Club – which enjoyed reciprocal rights with the Granville in London – and lunged up the marble steps into the unfamiliar lobby. At last he felt he was making progress, and that was reinvigorating his enthusiasm for his task. He turned a corner and stopped dead. Among the assorted caps, hats and umbrella hanging from the hooks along the wall was a burnished, browned pith helmet in the old-fashioned colonial pattern. It was known as a *puggaree* – Stanley had worn one when he went to find Livingstone – and had a pale cloth encircling it. Drabble swallowed. It couldn't be. He approached for confirmation. Surely not. Taking it down, he saw it was from Wrights & Speigels of the Burlington Arcade in London no less. That was a lifetime ago, though; this hat had endured a score and more Indian summers. He peeled back the silk lining and confirmed its owner. Christ alive. This eccentric topee did indeed belong to one very specific servant of the Empire.

He turned to the Indian porter at the counter by the door – and the man caught his expression before he had a moment to speak.

'He's in the bar, Professor.'

'Thank you.'

Without drawing breath, Drabble cleared the mahogany steps, crossed the paved courtyard, and then stood at the threshold of the bar: scanning an array of brown cane chairs and slowly turning fans, and personages dotted about, some lost behind newspapers, some engaged in chatter or games. And he spotted him, sitting there, looking rather pleased with himself. The grey face looked over at him; he was dressed impeccably in a cream linen suit that had seen better days, and his Indian Army tie — broad bands of burgundy and navy intersected by narrow yellow stripes.

'Ernest,' he said, the corners of his mouth curving in pleasure. He got to his feet. 'My boy.'

They shook hands.

'Father,' he gasped. 'How on earth did you find me?'

'Ha!' exclaimed the older man, his eyes twinkling. 'My spies are everywhere!'

Drabble didn't doubt it — after 30 years in the Indian army and then the Government of India, his father knew a great many people. They took each other in for a few moments, and then sat.

In the four years since Drabble junior had last laid eyes on his father, the elder Drabble had aged more than might be expected in the interval. Major Drabble was nearing sixty, and the moustache, once brown, was gun-metal tinged with white. The face that wore it was cracked from years out East, notwithstanding that pith helmet in colonial pattern. There was also something indeterminately smaller or more shrunken about his father — like the chairs at your school when you go back for an old boys' visit. Perhaps years in the persistent heat had sapped him or dried him out.

'A drink?'

Drabble accepted a gin and tonic, which his father ordered. As the waiter retired, Drabble senior looked over sharply.

'You didn't tell us you were coming to India.' The reproach in his tone was unmissable, and justified.

'I didn't want to put you to any trouble.'

'Trouble? Rawalpindi's only five hundred miles, my boy. That's nothing here, you know. I left on Monday. The trains are very good now. The trains *we* have built, I should say, are very good now,' he added. 'Your mother is very upset about it, particularly

147

to have discovered your presence here in the *newspaper* of all places.' He shook his head. 'We didn't think you approved of shooting?' He raised his white eyebrows, mystified, but moved on: 'If she had had time to prepare she would have come, too. As it was she couldn't leave Aziz who is dreadfully ill. I don't expect he'll survive the summer. Did you know that Aziz was unwell?'

Aziz was his father's bearer and had been since he arrived in India in the 1890s.

'I'm sorry to hear that.'

His father nodded dismally, and took up his gin and tonic, which had arrived during this preceding monologue. Drabble watched him savour the mouthful and then reposition the glass with care on the very spot from which he had lifted it. His father's voice altered:

'How do you like India?'

'Very much. Frankly, it fills me with an awesome sense of possibility.'

Major Drabble smiled and there was a youthful glint in his eye. 'Yes,' he said. 'It is an amazing place,' he sighed. He had never quite got over the fact that neither of his sons had followed him in a career out here. 'And I'll tell you this, when we've been given the boot, we'll regret that we didn't try *just* a little harder to hold onto it.'

Drabble arched an eyebrow and lowered his drink: his father had never before conceded even the possibility of the end of British rule. His had always been a Raj upon which the sun would not set. It pleased him, but it was dispiriting to see the fight in his father displaced by bitterness. His father watched him and registered his surprise, but made no comment.

'How long do you think British rule has got left?'

Major Drabble gave a sideways glance. 'Fifteen years, give or take.' He inhaled through his noise and jutted out his chin, pulling the skin of his neck taut. 'We can probably string it out a bit, but it's coming. The India Act more or less makes it explicit. If we wrapped a final handover up with the centenary celebrations of the Raj in 1958, that would be making the best of it. I'll be long gone by then in any case.'

Drabble nodded. His father would be eighty in 1958. So he would either be 'long gone' to that villa his parents had bought for their retirement in Cheltenham or another place altogether.

'When are you planning to retire?'

'Two years. When I'm sixty. That'll be enough.' He repositioned the gin. 'Your mother was desperately sad that you didn't get to see our home, you know. It's gorgeous, particularly the garden. You should see it in the winter.'

Drabble shrugged and offered his father a smile. The major nodded.

'I know,' he said. 'It's time.' He smiled, which caused the corners of his moustache to lift. 'So,' he retrieved his cigarette case from his side pocket. 'What brings you all the way here?'

Drabble set down his glass.

'The official reason is an archive in Bombay that I'm contemplating dipping my nose into – I won't bore you with the detail. But I suppose there are really two reasons: the first you know about; Harris was determined to shoot a tiger –' his father broke into a dry chuckle at the mention of his friend's name – 'and I knew that unless he had someone competent with him, that I was unlikely to see him alive again.'

His father inhaled on his cigarette, and muttered 'true, true'.

'The rest was simply curiosity: the desire, perhaps, to top up my distant childhood memories and see some of this part of the world with adult eyes.' His father watched him closely, but it was impossible to know what he was thinking. It always had been. 'Perhaps I had a desire to come out here again before it's all gone?' Drabble added. 'Then there's the interview Harris has done with the Maharaja of Bikaner – going there seemed rather interesting.'

His father finished listening, and took a drag of his cigarette:

'And are you in any danger of marrying at some point soon? Your mother and I would like some grandchildren to come home to.'

Drabble lifted his eyebrows at that. It would normally take his father several hours to arrive at this point.

The Major stated,

'You aren't getting any younger, I need not remind you. I was – what? – twenty-six when you were born. You're slipping behind the curve, my boy.'

Drabble smiled. 'We'll see.'

Major Drabble nodded.

'Well. I am pleased you've come. India has been my life's work, so it means a great deal to me that you've come out here to see what we've achieved. It's not all bad, son.'

'Few things are,' Drabble fired back, before offering a look of apology. 'Look, you know where I stand. I couldn't change my mind, even if I wanted to.'

His father regarded him coldly. 'I don't doubt it,' he said. He looked away. 'Not that it matters, but India's what put you and your brother through Lancing *and* university. Don't forget it.'

Drabble knew his father would never let him forget it. Smoke filled the void that had seemingly opened up between them.

'What do you know about the Communist Party of India?' he asked.

His father looked up sharply, his eyes appraising him.

'What's your interest?' He broke into a chuckle, 'I assume you don't want to *join*?'

Drabble smiled. That wasn't a bad joke for his father. He would never forget or quite forgive his son's brief flirtation with Communism.

Major Drabble cleared his throat, his features becoming sombre.

'As far as I know, it's a tiny but highly motivated fringe grouping,' he spoke as if reading from a file, 'centred around a handful of highly capable, highly mobile individuals who are not to be underestimated. Most of the important people are under surveillance. Naturally.'

'And what about the Anti-Gandhian League?'

Major Drabble held his son's gaze for a split second and then looked away. 'Never heard of them,' he cracked a smile. 'Now that's a club I *might* want to join.'

'I don't think membership is open to you lot.'

'Us, you mean.'

Drabble shrugged that one off.

'What if I told you that they attempted to assassinate Gandhi on Tuesday night in Bikaner – and then went for Linlithgow yesterday.'

His father stopped midway through stubbing out his cigarette.

'The Viceroy? That's not been circulated.' He drained his glass. 'I've always said that this is what you get if you don't come down hard on people.'

'So you do know them. The League?'

'I might do,' he said, nodding. 'We don't recognise their existence *officially*, but we know about them. They're virtually non-existent there are so few of them, but they're dangerous. Mind you, so is Gandhi.'

'The assassin's name was Sohan Choudhury. He was a Punjabi. Do you know him?'

His father frowned in thought. 'I'd have to check my files – which, alas, are back – did you say Choudhury?' He caught Drabble's nod. 'Christ,' rage entered his voice, and he gritted his stained teeth. 'I hope your use of the past tense implies that he's dead?' He caught Drabble's solemn expression. 'Good.'

Drabble formed his next sentence with care. 'I've been asked to find out more about this Choudhury fellow – what was motivating him, what was behind these attacks in Bikaner.'

'I should think *that* was blindingly obvious,' his father said, with a bleak chuckle. 'By whom?'

'Ganga Singh.'

'Really . . .' his father's chin jerked up irritably, but Drabble could see he was impressed. 'Interesting. Well Ganga Singh is pretty sound.' He cleared his throat. 'In that case, I know just the man you should see. Or at least, I think so. On one condition –'

Drabble nodded, 'Yes?'

'That you share everything you give to Ganga Singh, with us too.'

'Us?'

'Don't start that again. There's an old colleague of mine called Arbuthnot that I know has been in touch with you already. You've still got his details? Keep him informed.' Whatever you might think of the subcontinent, British India was a surprisingly small place.

His father began to write a name and address hurriedly on a piece of paper which he folded tightly and handed to his son. 'See this chap, but tread carefully. He's an out and out Marxist – makes Lenin look like a ruddy monarchist.'

'Right,' the Major grabbed his stick and got up. 'It's late.' Drabble escorted his father to the lobby, where he collected his pith helmet. They promised to see each other again before Drabble left for home, and shook hands.

'Now, my boy,' his father announced. 'A word from the wise. Watch your step while you're out here. Your reputation proceeds you. India is a very conservative place, and people *are* watching –' He smiled cheerfully under his moustache, and they shook hands a second time. Always a sure sign that it would be a long time before they set eyes on each other.

Drabble watched his father head towards the door, and waited till the last of the old imperialist had vanished from sight. He unwrapped the piece of paper that his father had given him and looked down at the name. 'M. N. Roy,' it read, in his father's finely slanted hand. 'The Editor, *Independent India*'. Beneath was an address.

Chapter Sixteen

Harris awoke from an awkward sleep. He discovered that half of his arm was trapped under Padmini's side. That it was a soft, supple, white coffee-cumin infused side made no odds.

He was trapped. He attempted to raise himself up by straining his middle and back, but he only managed an inch or two before plumping him back down. Padmini stirred.

'What time is it?' she moaned, her closed eyes two delectable semi-circles.

Harris strained his neck back to see the clock but the face was not readable from this angle. 'It's getting light,' he managed to add. Her eyes blinked open, and she shot up:

'My uncle –' She rushed over to the clock, and stood blinking at it, her face almost unbelieving. 'It's half past five.' She turned to Harris. 'We've got to move fast. Very fast. If we're found in here we'll have some proper explaining to do – I'm family, I'll be forgiven. But you won't. I dread to think what would happen.'

Harris grinned. 'Not, *"once more into the breach, my friend"*?'

She raised her finger. 'Absolutely *not*.'

They dressed hurriedly, with scarcely a word between them. Then Padmini led Harris through the darkened palace. Despite the early hour there were still a few servants about – those that were shrank from the imperious gaze of Princess Padmini, who Harris felt still looked stunning in last night's jodhpurs. They passed a sunlight dappled courtyard on their right, visible through a carved stone screen, and entered the new section of the palace, where the stone walls smelled as fresh as the carving. Padmini stopped abruptly before the juncture of two corridors. She snapped open a door, glanced inside, and snatched at Harris's lapel. 'Go back to sleep for half an hour on that sofa – then "wake up" and explain that you passed out after getting lost during the party last night. The ballroom is just next door. No one will disbelieve you.'

'And what about you?'

'I'll be fine. I can be back at the Lalgarh Palace within twenty minutes.'

Harris grinned.

'You sound like you've done this before.'

She frowned. 'Never you mind.'

They came together and their mouths sank into each other.

'When will I see you again?' asked Harris. Inwardly he cursed his uncharacteristic eagerness. But he was gripped with fearful sensation. He might never see her again.

'I'll be heading back to Delhi today, and our ship sails from Bombay in a week . . .' his throat cramped. It was panic and a dread realisation struck. This was it. He gazed at her face, looking back at him. It was all at once beautiful, powerful, but also something else. It was everything. She gazed adoringly at him – then she blinked, and he saw her swallow.

'I have to go this instant,' she declared. She leaned forward, and cupping his face with her hands, gave him one last kiss. 'We'll find a way . . .'

Then, as the sensation of her pressure on his lips remained, as her scent hung in the air, Padmini's shape was at the door, and then the door was closed. And suddenly Harris was alone. She was gone.

He felt suddenly inert. A voice in his head told him to run after her; but a countervailing impulse kept him frozen to the spot. He stared gloomily at the closed door. The practicalities of the situation closed in. He was an Englishman living in London; she a minor royal in a minor state in the back of beyond in

154

India. It wasn't ever, *ever* going to be feasible to marry these up, so to speak. Not on the timeline available to him. But they would simply have to find a way. There had to be a way. Yes. He had to see her again.

In that moment his resolve vanished, not all at once, but slowly over a minute or so, his certainty was washed away like the waves overcoming a children's sand castle. There was no way her family would agree. Hells bells. And what about his lot? Uncle Rupert would have plenty to say about it, and he had all the money. This was likely to have been the only bite of this particular cherry that he was ever likely to enjoy, and no amount of wishing would change that. He slumped down into one of the lavish gilded sofas that filled the chamber and buried his head into his hands. He wailed. Acidic, sharp tears pierced their way through his parched tear ducts into his eyes and he sobbed like a caged, injured animal.

He snatched a breath:

'Stop it,' he barked at himself. 'Get a grip.' He stood up, and glared at his miserable-looking reflection captured in a mirror. 'Pull yourself together, Harris!'

He sank down to his haunches, his face in his hands.

'Bahh-hoo-hoo-woo-hoo-wooooo!'

Tears flooded down his cheeks and he dug his fingernails into his smarting face. I have glimpsed happiness, he thought, and she has a name. Padmini! His gaze travelled up to the ceiling – and met the snout of a crocodile, long-since bagged, stuffed and on the wall – a proud part of the Maharaja's game book. Something had happened to his long jaws, which had become shrunken like an over roasted parsnip. It left the poor animal looking faintly pleased with itself.

Harris's flood of tears abated. He stared down at the floor and yawned, droplets of water falling from his face and making tiny splashes on the parquet. He was tired. Very tired. He loosened his tie, slipped off his shoes and lay down.

★

Drabble awoke with a start. There was a noise. He drew back the covers and looked across as he flicked on the electric light, his eyes searching the space of the small club room. Nothing was out of place; the fan turned above his head, distributing a pulse of warm air at even intervals. He drained his glass on the night stand and then filled it again from the water jug, and drained it once more. That felt better. He switched off the light, and lay there in the dark, waiting to see if he heard anything above the whirring of the fan. Eventually he fell asleep – but he dreamt uneasily. The precise contents of the dreams were lost to him, but they left him with an uneasy feeling. And when he stirred again, he discovered that he had only been asleep for a matter of minutes, making the night seemingly endless.

Eventually he awoke for what he decided was to be the last time, with some relief. It was shortly after six and any head start on the sun, would be wise for an Englishman still acclimatising.

He drew the curtains and gazed out up on the dusky court-yard of the Clive Club. Palm trees stood in each corner and a servant was sweeping slowly, and rather ineptly he noted, with a long broom that had barely any bristles. He continued to work. Drabble watched his slow progress, his thoughts returning to the evening just gone. For all his father's visit had been a pleasant surprise, the challenge that he had left him with, had been unsettling. It was never nice to be told to watch your step, even by your father. But that wasn't it. What really irked him was quite what had prompted the old imperialist to say it. Or rather, *who* had prompted it? His father loved him – albeit in his own way – but it was an awful long way to come for an off-chance meeting. That meant either his father was in town anyway, or he had been tipped off or was even dispatched to rein him in. Was that what had happened? The possibility of wider forces at work was faintly unsettling.

The servant began marshalling the derisory pile of debris with slow deliberate strokes. It probably couldn't be regarded as a surprise. Arbuthnot had found them in Delhi, after all, and tried to prevent them from going to Bikaner in the first place. They had been watched. And now, if he hadn't known any better, his own father had come to question him about his investigation, and done a not-so-subtle job at warning him off stirring up any more trouble – unlikely as that would seem. He told himself that it wasn't so, and went to wash and shave. It might not be so. It might be a coincidence. That remained a possibility.

Drabble dressed and breakfasted quickly, collected a letter from the lobby, and then caught a rickshaw from outside the club. It was still early, and there was little traffic about, and the address in the letter was not far away. The journey took them along wide, tree-lined avenues – diplomatic residences and government offices sat back well off the road – and the morning air was cool and fragrant. They soon reached a quarter of narrower streets and blocks, and presently the rickshaw man stopped outside one of these Victorian piles, Montagu Mansions, which in overall design wouldn't have looked out of place in Marylebone. Not for the first time Drabble regretted his decision not to take Skinner-Chatterjee's keys when he'd had the chance. Drabble paid the rickshaw off and rang the doorbell of flat 32. He waited. There was no answer. It was early enough, not yet eight, so he went down the steps and waited in the cool shade: after a few minutes he heard a 'clunk' as the lock within was moved. He darted up the steps, arriving just as the door was swinging open – right into his waiting hand, to hold it politely open for the elderly woman who was exiting with her terrier. Inside, he bounded up the steps . . .

Drabble knocked on the varnished panelled door of flat 32, and then pressed the buzzer, which blared nosily from within. There was no card in the slot and no light coming from the glass panel above the door. He waited. The musty-smelling corridor was gloomy, the half-light interrupted only by the cream, flamed-shaped electric lamps mounted in pairs on the walls every five paces. He pressed the doorbell insistently once more, then waited. Nothing. He glanced one way, then the other – and put his shoulder to the door. Millicent Skinner-Chatterjee's front door yielded easily. Surprisingly easily. He stumbled noisily into the hallway of her flat, and the strike plate of the lock scattered noisily across the parquet flooring. He shut it quickly behind him and put a bolt across. There was little chance that the sound of his intrusion could have gone unmissed, but for now you couldn't tell it was this door that had been forced. A console table in dark wood hugged the wall of the narrow hall, beneath an oval mirror, which reflected a glimmer of light from a glazed door opposite. The parquet then vanished from sight a few yards beyond beneath two closed glazed doors – one going left and one right.

Drabble worked quickly: the door in the hall led to a small kitchen, spotlessly clean and lit by a frosted window, presumably connected to a small courtyard. His gaze settled on four knives clinging to the rack on the wall. From the hall, he went through the door on the right to the bedroom, which was in darkness – the heavy curtains were drawn. He flicked on the lights. This was adjoined by a small blue-tiled bathroom, which like the kitchen drew some light from a small frosted window that looked out onto a service shaft. He contemplated drawing the curtains but hesitated. In the very small likelihood that the flat was being watched, that would be unwise. Then again, were the place being watched, he may well have blown that anyway. He went into the living room – a large space with several assorted wooden sofas and a metal table and chairs at the far end. He drew the curtains, spying a balcony beyond – just enough to get a decent look at the place. He tried the metal door handle: the door out was locked. A dull oil painting of a vase of flowers was hung above the small fireplace, which was clean and looked like it had never been used. Various odds and sods and keepsakes adorned the mantelpiece, along with a wooden clock. Another console table clung to the opposite wall, over which hung an old print in black and white showing a forested coastline with palms and buildings, and a castle – with a deep foreground full of boats under sail. He recognised it to be a drawing of Bombay from the century before.

A low bookcase held several works of literature, with an over-representation of Kipling, which was hardly surprising. There was some Austen, as well as a school bible inscribed with Skinner-Chatterjee's name. Apart from that the room was pretty anonymous – free of personal effects, almost like an unoccupied hotel room just after the maid service. On the wall by the door was a small mounted photograph of Queen Victoria marking her jubilee of 1887; a fan of empire flags framed her and beneath was the legend: 'Queen of an empire on which the sun never sets.' Swathed in muslin and topped with a small decorative crown, the elderly sovereign ostentatiously ignored the lens with considered, miserable severity.

He returned to the bedroom. A pair of ancestors held court in early, lithographic daguerreotype in two separate frames above the small fireplace; on the right was a woman in a voluminous gown and dress of native design with a veil. Her nose and ears were festooned with bejewelled ring-piercings in traditional Rajput style. The image of the man, on the left, showed an Englishman, if ever Drabble saw one. He was balding savagely and dressed in an eighteenth-century-style military uniform – stand-up, braided collar, a string of brass buttons down the front. A sabre perched at his hip; the to-do was finished off with an ornate Masonic apron and jewel suspended from a ribbon about his neck. Drabble looked back at the woman. She was beautiful, and held the gaze of the lens with a knowing intensity. This was undoubtedly quite a match: an adventurer and the daughter of a magnate of sorts. Perhaps this was Skinner *and* Chatterjee?

Several small photographs had been displayed under the glass top of the dressing table: one showed a little girl with dark hair . . . quite possibly Skinner-Chatterjee herself. From her size within the frame and the quantity of hair surrounding her face, it was hard to tell, but the frilly white bonnet and dress placed her squarely in an Edwardian childhood, which fitted. A pairing of two adults, captured in their thirties, was no doubt her parents. From the looks of things, she had inherited her handsome looks from her father, who shared the same high forehead and large, dramatic eyes. They looked respectable enough, he in starched wing collar and she in pearl choker and Edwardian gown. If there were any siblings they did not merit photographic keepsakes. The three drawers of the dressing table contained odds and sods of make-up and various brushes. But nothing else. He looked over at the narrow double bed, and went to the nightstand that stood on the left. Its drawer was empty. Feeling thwarted, Drabble looked about, and headed to the tall chest of drawers, but before he got there he noticed a grilled wooden door indicating a built-in wardrobe, created, it would seem, from a portion of space stolen from the kitchen. A wall of hanging garments confronted him, accompanied by the stale smell of lavender. Below, he saw the floor was taken up with several racks of shoes and a boxed travel typewriter. Behind the shoes, he spotted a cardboard box and dragged it out, finding it full of files and documents.

He skimmed these, seeing correspondence with her bank manager in Bombay; bills for the gas, electricity . . . it was a heap of messy impersonal matters, and he quickly pushed it to one side. Above the hanging rail was a shelf on which hats had been placed: with a scrape of metal he hauled the heavy thicket of dresses, slacks and skirts to one side, and then searched the walls, starting with the back and then checking the sides. High up on the right a small metal door – a safe, with an eye for a key – was fitted into the wall.

So that was that. Anything of interest was likely to be in there, and without a key that was no good to man or beast.

Drabble glanced sourly around the room. There had to be something here. He pushed the cardboard box of household bills back into its original place, and rearranged the hanging garments, before closing the wardrobe. Next he began rifling the drawers of the tall chest starting from the top, finding underwear, nightwear, swimwear, vests . . . He reached the bottom drawer and hauled it free. This was her office. On the left was a stack of blank foolscap paper, envelopes and a book of airmail paper, plus half a dozen spiral-bound notebooks and postcards. In the middle was a pell-mell collection of pencils, pens, ink bottles, and typewriter ribbon. The invaluable tools of a secretary. The rest of the drawer was stuffed with letters, each faithfully kept in bundles secured with rubber-bands – perhaps fifty to sixty in all.

This could be what he was looking for. Drabble tore into the largest one of these. It was a correspondence with an aunt in Lahore. Quickly he established that the topics of conversation were not of use: social life, work – she worked in a typing pool in the government office, it seemed – and her aunt's repeated probing into her love life. On that topic Skinner-Chatterjee was unforthcoming, preferring to dilate upon the joys of the latest gymkhana. Importantly, the letters showed she had been at the Montagu Mansions address for at least three years.

Drabble reached for the next largest bundle.

This turned out to be a saccharine dialogue with a *box-wallah* named Charles Green, from the Army and Navy stores, with whom she was evidently on intimate terms. So the poor aunt had been left in the dark after all. The last latter, from Charles, was dated to December; in it, he expressed his despair at her breaking off of their courtship. Drabble took a piece of paper and noted down his address. Green was in Delhi and might just be useful. He continued to work his way through the bundles but saw nothing of use. There was a friend or two she corresponded with in Bombay; nothing to or from parents, and no sign of siblings. Drabble pushed the drawer shut and felt thoroughly deflated. Where was her address book? She had not had it with her in Bikaner, so it ought to be here. Unless someone had already been in and cleaned the place out first.

He sighed and cast a glance around the room. His gaze settled on the area of the wall behind which the safe resided.

There was still hope. He looked at this watch. It was gone nine, so he had expended over an hour there and gleaned nothing, other than her employment in a typing pool somewhere within the government.

He took another look at the safe. Could it be picked? By him? Unlikely. But by someone who knew about these things? Surely. But where to find such people? Goodlad would know. His father might, too.

He checked the room for any sign of his presence, and returned to the living room. As he did, so a mental picture of Skinner-Chatterjee's set of keys visited him: there was that dull leather key-fob, and then a pair of keys. Neither of them resembled the sort that would fit the hole in the safe door. They were likely, in fact, to be for the building's front door and the door to her flat.

Which made him wonder. Might the safe key be in the flat, somewhere, for safe-keeping, so to speak? It wasn't entirely sensible, but on the whole people were not entirely sensible. He started scanning the sitting room, looking for any pots or boxes that might have been obvious candidates. He checked the small china vase on the mantelpiece and the tortoiseshell cigarette box on the coffee table. Then he went back to the bedroom and revisited the bedside drawers. There were no keys. At the dressing table he tipped out a small ceramic urn filled with coins, paperclips, assorted buttons, hair slides, and so on – but no keys. It was possible that the key was on a necklace or bracelet of course. He couldn't remember now if she'd been wearing one.

The kitchen. He clicked his fingers. The key would be in the kitchen, along with keys to the balcony doors. He knew it. He began in the tea caddy, which contained only tea. Then he searched through the drawers, before moving onto the cupboards. Nothing. No neat row of hooks with a small hoard of keys anywhere.

Drabble looked around. It was time to accept defeat. Time was marching on and he had other things to do. But he didn't like to give in – even if it was inevitable as it seemed it was in this case. He glowered around the sitting room. So near yet so far.

His heart sank and he turned towards the door to leave. Then his eye settled on Queen Victoria and her miserable profile. A thought struck him. He lifted the frame away from the wall . . .

Bingo.

The key slotted perfectly into the lock. Pulling open the safe, Drabble saw a small leather-bound book stuffed with papers. He reached in. Was it a diary or address book . . . a floorboard creaked behind him. Drabble froze – and began to turn. Suddenly he saw a flash of light and everything went black.

Chapter Seventeen

Harris arrived at Bikaner railway station and climbed down from Colonel Pagefield's Crossley, and leaned back in to retrieve his bags. Pagefield did not bother to get out.

'Go on,' he goaded, like a man exhorting his dog to pursue a ferret into its den. 'Don't miss the ruddy train, whatever you do.'

Harris now had his bags out and caught sight of the Maharaja's white-painted train on the platform. Pagefield reached back and slammed the rear passenger door shut. 'Can't say it's been a pleasure having you here, Harris, but it's been an education. Don't come back.'

He tapped the brim of his pith helmet with the pommel of his swagger stick, and muttered to the driver. Harris stood back and the Crossley turned away, leaving him in its cloud of exhaust smoke. Within a few seconds it was just lots of dust, before finally melting into the traffic of camel carts and people.

The station clock stated five minutes after nine, and the heat was already north of a hundred. Harris had been told that it began to shoot up as you reached late March and that was certainly the case. Across the way, a short, pristine red carpet led to the steps of Sir Ganga Singh's carriage – one of four that comprised his royal train. Painted white, twin stripes in the saffron and scarlet of Bikaner ran its entire length just beneath the windows. It wasn't, Harris reasoned, the worst way to be booted out of somewhere – on its ruler's private bloody train. But it was scant compensation for never seeing Padmini again. A white-uniformed

164

servant of middle age with tall and richly embroidered turban approached. He was very tall, even before he added the turban.

'Sir Percival sahib,' he announced, offering a salaam and deep bow. 'His Highness would be most satisfied if you would accept his invitation to travel in his special guests' carriage .' The steward indicated the door adjacent to the one which was fed by the red carpet and flanked by sentries, evidently the Maharaja's private compartment.

He was relieved of his luggage and led up into the train, then handed over to another servant who took his hat and offered him a cup of tea and a copy of the *Rajputana Gazette*. 'Do ensure the milk is severely boiled,' Harris told the servant as he sat in a deep brown leather armchair. He drew a deep breath and gazed out of the window at the station, which was blissfully free of commotion, except for a Rolls-Royce which had just arrived and was being unloaded by more staff. He sighed, and closed his eyes. He was exhausted.

In repose the pounding in the front of his head abated. Then it resumed – as if it resented being forgotten – but at a slightly reduced level of pressure. How much sleep had he had? Three or four hours' at most. And on top of that he had certainly, *definitely*, taken on board more drink than was strictly advisable, especially in this wretched climate. He yawned hard, causing a pain to strike his temples. His eyes opened enough to see the station and another car drawing up. This one had little saffron and scarlet Bikaneri flags on it and he craned his neck to see if Padmini might be aboard. Several men in black morning coats began to alight. He sank back into his chair, despair looming. That was all he needed.

He shut his eyes and attempted to wing his way back to the night that had just been; imagining the feeling of her and the smell of her and the sensation of her against his skin. He opened his eyes, rather as if he was worried that his thoughts were somehow betrayed by his face, and saw the men approach his carriage. As long as it was no one important, it would be tolerable. He could not do important conversation today. He sighed. Given where he was, that was unlikely. His head began to hurt again. Maybe he should just go and hide somewhere, the loo perhaps, where he wouldn't be seen, and where, God forbid, he could be freed of the burdens of human interaction. There was no doubt about it; this heat exacerbated a hangover something rotten. His gullet felt like it had been finely sandpapered, and in his chest was moist with an acidic roasting sensation that got worse when he exhaled. It was all part and parcel of the price one paid for an unquantifiable amount of booze. He yawned, and gripped his chest, which erupted in pain. Christ; he sat bolt upright, clearing his throat hard – too hard, it turned out. The act upset the delicate equilibrium of his innards and an expected discharge spewed up from within, surging up into his mouth. He got his handkerchief to his mouth just in time to catch the fluid which managed to force itself out and, coughing hard, obliged his rebellious body to swallow the balance.

O Lord! His head spun. Would that he could leapfrog the next eleven hours of his life and magic himself into a bath at the Imperial hotel. He heard a noise and looked up – hoping to see the servant arriving with his tea – but instead finding he was being joined in the carriage by Sir Randolph Sharma-Smith, the bigoted fat-hating Bombay industrialist. Joining him was Mr Panikkar, the Bikaneri foreign secretary, whom he had also met at the reception the previous evening – and who'd deposited him in Padmini's care, so he must have put two and two together. Christ alive. Harris heaved himself out of the chair and forced the damp jumble of his handkerchief in to his pocket.

'Sir Percival,' stated Sir Randolph coolly. He regarded Harris severely – doubtless he could smell the sauce on him – and then took up an armchair on the far side of the carriage. Panikkar, waiting his turn, came forward and shook Harris's hand, before taking a seat further along the carriage. Harris settled back into his seat and gazed happily at the chair opposite; in this condition, the very last thing he could to do was to make conversation, and certainly not *polite* conversation, with anyone. He stroked the sweat off his brow with the back of his hand and looked about for the steward. His mouth was frighteningly dry. Where *was* that pot of tea?

He heard the sound of surprised Indian voices – a muffled 'memsahib' said in a pleading tone – and looked up. Princess Padmini, fresh and elegant in a cream linen skirt suit, breezed into the carriage and immediately saw him; her expression remained impassive, but Harris saw a glint in her eye.

'Mr Panikkar,' she exclaimed, coming forward and nodding her head politely – an act met with a deep bow in return. 'Sir Randolph . . . what a pleasure.' They each stood and offered their replies as Harris got to his feet, finding his strength returning. Padmini indicated the seat opposite Harris. He grinned broadly, as she sat down.

The next eleven hours to Delhi were going to fly by.

Drabble's eyes blinked open. He was lying down looking up at the ceiling of Miss Skinner-Chatterjee's bedroom – and he had a sodding great headache. His hand went to the right hand side of the head where the blow had landed and he felt an egg-shaped lump – he checked his hand and saw no blood. His breathing was laboured, he realised, and he felt a trifle rum; queasy if anything. He spread his hands to get up, and suddenly felt a dizzying sensation, rather as if he was looking down from a peak or ridge, and not a matter of inches. He lay back down and checked his watch. It was just after 9am, so he'd only been unconscious for a matter of minutes. This was important, he knew from his climbing experience. It meant that he was probably free from serious injury. He took a deep breath, and tried to raise himself again. This time his arms kept their purchase and the neuralgic gyrations inside his head slowed enough to permit him to raise it and get up onto his elbows, and then to sit up.

Christ alive. He stared down at his feet, getting his breath back. That had taken far too much effort to achieve. He saw the open door of the safe, and remembered. Of course. He exhaled, like a man trying not to be sick. The worst part of it was that whoever just delivered that blow may have quite possibly been lurking in the flat the whole time. Which didn't half give him the creeps. To say the ruddy least.

He half turned and looked over his shoulder. For all he knew the individual might still be here. But he doubted it. Drabble took a deep breath, and got to his feet, steadying himself against the wall. So that was that.

Taking care, Drabble descended the steps outside Montagu Mansions and arrived into the full glare of the morning sunshine. He looked around, probing the landscape for any movement or watcher, and then moved along the pavement, keeping an eye out for taxis. The dizziness had left him, so all that he had to contend with now was an ache in the head and a residuum of nausea. An Indian dressed in a suit and straw hat cycled past, a broad black umbrella held above his head. An Austin Seven came the other way. Up ahead he saw a taxi . . .

It took the best part of an hour to locate the offices of the *Independent India* in the back streets of old Delhi. A white-bearded man with stick-thin legs presiding over the street corner directed him towards a crumbling, unlikely pink haveli off the main drag. After gaining admittance, he found that much of what lay on the inside was dilapidated; the render had fallen from the stone-work and high weeds protruded through the tiles here and there. The *chaprassi* or porter led him through the first courtyard, under the point of a faded Mughal arch, and into the interior, where the sound of desultory typing could be heard. The chatter died as Drabble entered – he saw a large open room dominated by a group of men gathered at a table. Beyond were rows of mainly empty desks, heaped with files and notebooks, wire baskets of copy, and piles of newspapers. And typewriters, of course, one of which was being operated. A fat young man with a narrow moustache and pungent face scowled at him from the table and threw up his chin. He wasn't happy to see a representative of the colonial power in the house. Which was fair enough.

'I'm here to see Mr Roy.'

'Who's asking,' said the fat man. He tossed down his pencil and stood up. Slowly the other four men around the table – old, short, grey, and paunchy – followed suit. They were hardly a menacing prospect but their intent was clear. And Drabble was in no condition for a fight. He squared his shoulders.

'I'm not looking for trouble,' he said. 'I'm only here to ask him for help.'

The men exchanged glances and passed a word or two. The chaprassi looked over at Drabble. The group broke apart.

'All right,' announced the pencil-thrower. He looked over to the chaprassi and jerked his head towards the interior.

The secretary led Drabble through the next Mughal arch, passing a kitchen which smelled strongly of ghee and spice, and out into the sunshine of another weed-infested courtyard. On reaching the next part of the building he pulled back the bead hangings at the doorway, and poked his head inside. There was an exchange and he withdrew, and pulled the beads back for Drabble to enter.

Manabendra Nath Roy sat at a broad desk that like all the others was beset with items and heaps of disordered papers. On the wall behind him were cuttings, a framed front page of the newspaper, and among other artefact, a black and white photograph of himself with Lenin. Roy stood up and stretched his back as Drabble approached. He extended his hand and offered a friendly smile.

'Professor Drabble,' he declared warmly and with rather a lot of teeth.

Roy was tall – six foot at least – and surprisingly handsome, with rectangular, black plastic spectacles that suited him and gave him a technocratic air. His hair was almost black and oiled, and if Drabble didn't know any better, he'd have said he was a politician, not a journalist. He shook his hand.

'Mr Roy.'

Roy indicated a chair for Drabble and called, 'tea' out towards the door. A break of the beaded curtains and bob of the head and the chaprassi was gone on the errand. Roy settled back into his swivel chair and asked, 'How, pray, may I be of assistance?'

Drabble cleared his throat. It had occurred to him, naturally enough, that Roy would not want to cooperate with an agent of the British state. Notwithstanding the fact that he was acting on behalf of Ganga Singh, and not the dreaded GOI, it would doubtless all be regarded as one and the same by someone like Roy. And fair enough, thought Drabble.

'Twice this week I found myself embroiled in incidents involving a young Communist in Bikaner – incidents which would have led to bloodshed and loss of life if he had been successful in his enterprises.'

Roy listened without comment or altering his expression.

'The man was named Sohan Choudhury,' continued Drabble, interested to see if any reaction would register on Roy's expression. 'I don't expect you knew him, but if you did then I am keen to learn as much about him as I can.'

Roy remained utterly impassive. 'Is Mr Choudhury dead?'

Drabble nodded. 'Regrettably so. Shot during an assassination attempt on the Maharaja of Bikaner and the Viceroy.'

Roy frowned. 'When? This week?'

'Yesterday.'

'Yes-yes, the Viceroy was there for the ceremony.' He chuckled to himself, shaking his head, 'How extraordinary. They have done well to keep *that* quiet.'

'Did you know Choudhury?'

Roy shook his head and was about to add to it, when the sound of the beads being parted interrupted him and the assistant arrived with a clinking tray of tea things. This was brought over and tea was decanted with some ceremony. A few minutes later, once the man had gone, Roy added, 'Choudhury is not known to me.

I should add, as a courtesy, Professor, that I would be unlikely to offer you any information if I did know him.'

'What if I told you that he tried to blow up Mr Gandhi on Tuesday night.'

'I would say that I am awfully glad he failed to achieve that objective.'

Drabble added a teaspoon of sugar to his cup of tea and stirred it in. The ache in his head was back. 'I respect your desire neither to help the British establishment in its oppression of India, nor to be seen aiding it in that oppression, but can I take it that you oppose acts of terrorism of this kind? Blowing up Mr Gandhi would not further a peaceful transition to a self-governing India any more than assassinating the Viceroy. On the contrary, both would likely lead to reprisals or a harder line all round. Hardly good for ordinary Indians.'

Roy listened without comment. He filled the pause by turning the tea cup in its saucer.

Drabble added: 'But it occurs to me that this might be just what Moscow wants. They would be happy to stir up trouble here; to hell with the human cost. Stalin doesn't care about human cost – as well you know.' He took a sip of tea and then another and replaced the cup in the saucer. 'You should know that Choudhury was found with Communist party literature on his person. He also had a CPI membership card. If the party is involved, the GOI will find out in due course and there'll be an inquest. You know that.'

'I don't doubt it,' said Roy. He cleared his throat and reached for his pipe. 'Professor, I am no longer a member of the party. Nor do I have truck with Moscow. Not anymore.'

Drabble couldn't resist a glance up at the photograph of Roy with Lenin; the shift of his eyes did not go unnoticed. 'As a result, I have no knowledge of the doings of the CPI or whether one of their number is behind this. I really don't.' He was stuffing the pipe now as he spoke, half addressing Drabble, and half focusing his attention on the task. 'What I feel I *can* say on the

171

matter is that it does not fit with the party that I remember – nor the people that I still know at the top of it. If this Choudhury were a CPI member, then I suspect that it is purely a coincidence. It is, after all, hardly surprising that there are communist sympathisers who are also sufficiently motivated to carry out acts of violence against the Raj and its agents – just as there are many non-communists who are prepared to go to such lengths. It is the nature of oppression. As an historian of the seventeenth century, I would expect you to appreciate that. Indeed, I would argue that it is just good, old-fashioned patriotism. No? As yourself: might not you be one of these men, were the shoe on the other foot? I quite appreciate that the British state would not see it like that.'

'I am not the British state.'

'Yes, yes. I appreciate that you say that, and that you *believe* it, but truly you are, whether you like it or not. And there is no point arguing on the topic.' He waved his hand at Drabble, closing the subject.

'Could Choudhury be a member of the Anti-Gandhian League?'

'I'm not sure that such an organisation exists in a real sense.'

'Not sure, or not prepared to comment within earshot of the British state?'

He smiled, showing his teeth. 'Not sure.'

Drabble drained his cup. Roy – stem of the pipe gripped in his jaws – poured him another.

'What of any other extremist groups?' Drabble asked. 'Are you aware of the existence of any others – individuals who would regard both Gandhi and the Viceroy as their sworn enemies?'

Roy shook his head.

'Do you condemn violence in the name of independence?'

'Absolutely,' asserted Roy. 'But I absolutely also think it will be the only way to make it happen. You British will not leave of your own accord.'

'That sounds like a paradox to me.'

172

'Call it what you wish, Professor. Realpolitik is an ugly word in every respect.'

Roy smiled, and Drabble said, 'It's hardly a convincing renunciation of violence, is it?'

'What do you expect me to say? I reject violence but accept that it's inevitable. I also accept that there will be conditions when it will ultimately be justified. If you're not satisfied, let's call it a qualified renunciation.'

There was nothing to be gained from continuing the conversation. On principle, Roy was not prepared to help. And that was that. But he had helped, up to a point at least. Drabble drained his teacup, set it back down with note of finality to the gesture, and got up to leave.

'Professor,' Roy's tone was now emollient. 'If you would be allow me to offer you a piece of advice . . .'

Drabble halted before the beaded doorway and looked back.

'You are a long way from Cambridge, comrade. Despite appearances, India is not the place for amateur sleuths or nineteenth-century English gentleman adventurers sticking their noses into corners best left unprobed. I would in particular be chary of going around asking questions about the Anti-Gandhian League or the Communist Party for that matter. I say this with no axe to grind, merely to point out that you should be circumspect.'

Drabble stepped into the full glare of the near noon-day sun. He knew he had not got many of the answers he was looking for, but he might have secured one: whatever Roy's protestations, had Choudhury been known to him, he would have conveyed it, either by candidly confirming it or by betraying himself. Drabble took one last look back at the crumbling façade of the offices of the *Independent India*. He reached out and steadied himself against the wall. The searing April sun burned the crown of his head, even through his straw hat. Sweat ran down the sides of his face from his ears and he swore. His head pounded. He should rest and get out of the midday heat. Up ahead a dusty taxi broke through the mass of cycles and carts in the road. He stepped out and flagged it down. He asked to be taken to his club and collapsed into the back seat.

As for Roy's warning? That may well have been sincere inasmuch being what it was presented as, rather than a veiled threat. Drabble decided that it was a courteous warning. Indeed, he suspected that with a little more time, he and Roy might have become friends. But the Raj got in the way of that. As it did with so many things.

Luncheon aboard the Maharaja's express commenced with cocktails at noon sharp in the convivial setting of Sir Ganga Singh's carriage. As well as Harris, there was Sir Randolph Sharma-Smith, Mr Panikkar, the Princess, Singh himself, and his son and heir, the crown prince Sir Sadul Singh, present. Like his father, the crown prince had a fine military bearing, and was a couple of years older than Harris. Probably mid-thirties. The banquet consisted of four courses, all brought out with theatrical flourish by uniformed stewards. The guests talked openly.

Sir Randolph prised a dressed prawn from the embrace of a finely curried egg. He announced, 'The Viceroy is a nincompoop.'

'He's better than the last one,' countered Mr Panikkar, with a dash of resignation.

'That's not hard,' quipped Sir Randolph.

Harris and Padmini's gaze met across the table. She righted a smirk, as the Maharaja cleared his throat in a note of disapproval at the openly disloyal tone of the conversation.

He stated, 'It's abundantly clear that whomsoever has the privilege of being His Majesty's representative in India right now would face disobliging circumstances. Having seen some a dozen Viceroys come and go, I would put Linlithgow in the eightieth percentile. Lord Curzon had most flair. Lord Hardinge was a friend and shrewd, and I am fond of Willingdon. He was a visionary.'

No one disputed the Maharaja's analysis. Harris wasn't sure he had understood it, precisely. The train clattered along; the glassware chimed in time to the bouncing of the bogeys.

Harris said,

'The soup's good.'

There was a general murmuring of approval.

The Maharaja addressed Panikkar, 'Is Gandhi going?'

Harris glanced over with interest: going where? The foreign minister replied that he did not know for certain but did not expand on the where.

'I will cable the Viceroy the moment we arrive to find out,' he said.

'And Nehru?'

'I believe so.'

Sir Ganga Singh nodded, and peered over the Crown Prince, who returned his look with interest.

Sir Randolph shook his head at the steward with the waiting wine bottle. Harris raised his glass eagerly. It wasn't every day that one was served Petrus, after all. And certainly not the 1921. Everyone else took more wine except for the Maharaja.

Sir Randolph said,

'I can't abide Gandhi; the longer he goes on, the more pious he becomes. I fear he's beginning to believe he really is a saint.'

The Maharaja frowned, not unkindly, but everyone knew immediately that he disagreed. The reaction caused Sir Randolph to drop his conceited smile; he ran a finger along the inside of his stand-up collar, and then bobbed at his wine. The stewards were assembled behind each chair and swept away the soup, and replaced it with plates of fragrantly spiced lamb.

'Mr Gandhi is not everyone's cup of tea,' stated the Maharaja as he gathered up his cutlery, 'but he is probably India's best hope of a peaceful transition. We must keep him and his followers in the tent if we are to move towards a new, better future for all India.'

Harris was aware of Panikkar's eyes pinching nervously at the Maharaja and his perhaps unguarded declaration. Harris dabbed the corners of his mouth with his starched napkin and asked, 'And what future do you see for Britain in this future, Your Highness?'

The Maharaja had just taken in a quantity of lamb, so Panikkar pounced. 'I think our position is the one that His Highness has elucidated on many occasions, that the future of India is one of greater autonomy within the British Imperial family.'

Sir Ganga Singh swallowed and cut in, 'And the princes will be a part of that autonomy, all being well. That's how Linlithgow sees it, too. It all hinges on whether we can get the Indian National Congress and the Muslim League to agree.'

'They will never agree,' hissed Sir Randolph. He forked in some lamb and began chewing it spitefully, 'Never in a thousand years.'

The Maharaja's voluminous eyebrows lifted at that, but he said nothing, merely smiling under his moustache. He addressed Padmini:

'And what do think, my dear? You are being uncharacteristically unforthcoming. I trust our Britisher guest isn't making you shy.'

Harris thought he saw the sliver of a smile under the Maharaja's enormous moustache. Did he know? How could he? His gaze stole guiltily to Padmini, who wiped her lips.

'Nonsense, Uncle, but in such august company I hardly think I'm in a position to comment.'

The Maharaja began to chuckle. He enjoyed respectful mockery as much as the next man. 'It's never held you back before,' he quipped. 'Did you have a late night?' He glanced over at the Crown Prince who nodded, smiling as though they were sharing a joke. 'And when precisely did you decide you were going to accompany us to Delhi? What was it you said last week? "Oh, these functions are so tiresome, Uncle".'

The Crown Prince and Panikkar chuckled at that. Padmini reddened, but smiled nonetheless.

'Oh, Uncle,' she cooed, reaching over to pat his hand. 'You know I wouldn't miss the Viceroy's Ball for all the tea in China.' Padmini offered Harris half a smile, and then glanced back at the Maharaja. 'Everyone knows it's the best party in Delhi. And anyone who's anyone will be there. Even the Maharaja of little dusty Bikaner, apparently –'

Silence fell across the table. Harris froze; his eyes swivelled to the Maharaja, and then to Panikkar whose mouth was fixed mid-chew. The Maharaja chuckled, wagging his finger slowly, then the table followed suit. Padmini joined in with a high-pitched tinkling giggle that made Harris laugh . . .

As silence resumed, Harris asked, 'When's the Viceroy's ball?'

'Tomorrow night,' said the Maharaja. 'Don't worry – you are welcome to come as my guest.' He winked at Harris, 'That's if my niece hasn't invited you already, of course.'

Harris's face froze, momentarily, and he forced a smile.

'What's the dress code?'

'Everything you've got,' commented Sir Randolph drily. The Maharaja and Crown Prince exchanged an amused nod. He sighed. 'If only the British put the same amount of effort into oppression as they did into their clothing, the Raj would be secure for another thousand years.'

Chapter Eighteen

Drabble alighted from the taxi and was wearily climbing the steps of the Clive when a voice assailed him:

'Professor Drabble!'

He turned to see an Indian rush towards him from the shaded portion of the pavement, a broad smile across his face. He swept off his cloth cap. 'Oh I am glad to see you, Professor sahib,' he declared with a lilting Indian accent. 'Let me introduce myself: I am Dr Jignesh Gupta, of Benares University. I have something very particular to discuss with you. You will not be disappointed, I think.'

The man's face was agreeable; a semi-circular smile crammed with teeth was at home in a lantern jaw; small, academic eyes glinted behind metal-rimmed spectacles which sat on a straight nose that had a small swelling at the bridge. He wore a dark brown suit that was a touch heavy for the season and his face was streaked with sweat. He looked like he could do with a drink.

Drabble frowned. 'How did you find me?'

'Ah,' Dr Gupta grinned. 'I had foreseen this, and understand your suspicion,' he titled his head solicitously. 'I read about you in a thrilling report of the shooting of the man-eating tiger with your companion, and then recognising your name from my area work, resolved to meet you and ask you about this matter which is, coincidentally, rather pressing.'

'But how did you come to find me here?'

'Forgive me – I looked you up in *Who's Who*, and they list your club as the Granville.' He grinned. 'Everybody knows that the Clive enjoys reciprocal rights with the Granville, so I guessed, and then I was able to ascertain through a cousin of mine that you have in fact been in residence here.' He smiled broadly. 'You can imagine my satisfaction at discovering this fact.'

That was all plausible enough, but, of course, wasn't *entirely* satisfactory: but then, things in life seldom were. Drabble said wearily,

'Did you say Dr J Gupta?'

'Yes, Professor sahib, Jignesh,' he smiled.

'As in "The authentication of treaty of the East India Company of 1658"?'

The man beamed, his teeth shone with pride.

Drabble shook his hand. 'Shall we pop inside? I could do with a cup of tea.'

Dr Gupta's suddenly expression changed, and glanced nervously towards the club entrance as if temporarily glued to the spot. Drabble's gaze travelled up the steps of the club and back to Gupta.

The penny dropped, and Drabble shook his head.

'You're joking?'

'I'm sorry, sir, but they would not welcome me. Indians are not permitted . . .'

'It's me who should apologise.' Drabble swore under his breath. 'Is there somewhere –' He broke off, his fist clenched. 'Sod it, Gupta. Come on, let's see if we can't cause a small revolution.'

Drabble led him up the stone steps. At the entrance he paused at the porter's doorway and asked for the book, signing Dr Gupta in. He turned it back, and the Indian porter saw Gupta. His eyes widened.

'Sahib, it is not permitted –'

'Come on, Doctor,' instructed Drabble and he walked on.

★

Moments later, Drabble and Gupta arrived in his room. He plucked a bottle of water from the icebox and poured two glasses, which they both drained.

'Thank you, Professor,' declared Gupta with relief when he placed the glass down. 'I must say it is a privilege to meet you. I am a decided fan of yours, if you don't mind my saying, especially your recent monograph on Cromwell. Most enlightening.'

Drabble thanked him and replenished the tumblers.

'Likewise, your work on the East India Company is very interesting – I had little idea, for instance, of Cromwell's interest in it.'

Gupta beamed.

Drabble handed him his refilled glass: 'You'd better get to the point before the porter gets someone else involved. Mind you, I am happy to take the consequences for my actions.'

Gupta took a cardboard cylinder from his bag; it was perhaps some ten inches long, and he placed it on the bed carefully. With a serious glance back over at Drabble, he peeled away the rubber stopper at one end and upended it, inserting his bony fingers to draw out its contents.

A burgundy cloth roll emerged, which Gupta delicately laid down on the bed and proceeded to unroll. Drabble watched his draw the layers back. It was a large photograph of what appeared to be a document . . .

He stepped forward. 'Good God – is that what I think it is?'

Gupta moved aside to allow him to examine it closer. His eyes ran across the pinched Latin writing, long since faded, the words *Carolus Secundus* – Latin for Charles the second – leapt out. Drabble read the inscription quickly . . .

'It appears to be a codicil to the marriage treaty of Charles and Catherine of Braganza . . .' his voice rose with excitement, 'relating to the seven islands of Bombay.' He looked over at Gupta. 'Doctor, what is this?'

'I believe it is precisely what you just said, Professor: a supplementary agreement to the treaty of 1661 between the kingdoms of England and Portugal, relating specifically to the terms of the grant of Bombay to the British crown as part of the dowry.'

Drabble was already aware of the terms of the famous dowry, which included the handover to Britain of various Portuguese possessions, in return for Charles taking Catherine's hand in marriage – and agreeing to an alliance with Lisbon. The grant of the seven islands of Bombay had eventually led to Britain gaining control of the entire city and province which formed the basis of the Bombay Presidency and thus one of the corner stones of what was to become the British Raj.

'Hang on . . .' Drabble read quickly. 'It seems to be laying down conditions for the grant of Bombay's even islands to the British crown.' He paused as he translated the Latin text. He pulled out a notebook and began copying down the inscription.

'It says,' his tone rising in disbelief, 'that "neither the Britannic Majesty nor his successors may grant ownership of the seven islands of Bombaim to any other potentate, other than the King of Portugal or his heirs and successors". Goodness. How intriguing.'

'Isn't it just,' agreed Gupta, his eyes glistening. 'My question, Professor, is do you think this is an authentic document?'

Drabble gave a staccato laugh and stopped writing his notes. 'I see – well now . . . from the photograph at least, the vellum looks as it should; Charles the Second's seal is correct, and the Latin is certainly bad enough to be of 1660s vintage. But it's possible it could be a forgery. I'd have to see it to offer a final judgement. I would love to see it. Do you have it?'

'The original is in the hands of a collector who asked me to verify it – though I have seen it and believe it to be legitimate. He told me only that it had been unearthed recently among a cache of papers relating to the construction of Bombay castle. For reasons of privacy the collector has asked that I do not divulge his identity.'

Drabble did not usually regard secrecy in such matters as a positive sign, and said as much. Gupta shrugged – seemingly keen not to appear to be unkind or judgemental, perhaps – and said, 'But I am nonetheless pleased to have seen such a document.'

That was undeniable. Drabble said, 'The only way to attest to its authenticity is to have it looked at by specific experts – and I would anticipate they're most likely to be found in England or Portugal, which could present some practical challenges. I can think of one philologist I know at Cambridge already; he'd give his eye teeth to get his hands on this.'

If it was real it was certainly a 'discovery'. 'On the basis of essential appearances, and probable age, it certainly *looks* legitimate. But to be perfectly frank, this isn't exactly my field.'

'That's what I said,' Gupta grinned and shook his head. 'Historians are so predictable.'

Drabble took a few more quick notes and then began to fold the burgundy fabric over it.

'Do you think, if it's genuine, that it would carry legal force, hypothetically?'

His words hung in the air for a moment, before Drabble had time to marshal his response. 'That's a very good question, Doctor – but it's *definitely* not my field.'

Gupta gave a noncommittal shrug, and finished putting the photograph away. His reaction made Drabble wonder if that was the question he was really looking for the answer to all along. If it were, then what Gupta, or rather the document's owner, needed was a constitutionalist. Drabble could recommend one or two for that. 'Now,' he said. 'Dr Gupta, I think we should both vacate the club premises before we are asked. And I don't know about you, but I could also do with some lunch.'

They drew barely a comment from the porter at the door. He instead produced a letter for Drabble. It was not, as he first thought, an expulsion notice for flouting the club's racist bylaws. Not that he would have minded. Rather it was from Goodlad and contained an address for Sohan Choudhury. He had proved as good as his word.

'Lunch is my treat, Doctor,' said Drabble as they exited the club, 'and then I have a favour to ask of you.'

Drabble and Gupta sat at a wooden table in the midst of a sea of such tables under a broad iron ribbed roof. Native waiters passed to and fro holding trays of food and cups of tea aloft. Drabble was the only European he could see, which was refreshing after the last fortnight. Several metal bowls and platters containing several vegetarian dishes lay between them, along with a pile of chapatis. The conversation flowed easily.

There was no way that Gupta's appearance at the club could have been coincidence or the result of his detective work and luck: it had to be connected to whoever gave Drabble the bump on the head that morning. The question was, how? And, quite naturally, Drabble was convinced that Dr Gupta was an unwitting part of whatever conspiracy it was.

Drabble ladled more of the bitter-tasting dahl onto his plate and proceed to gather it up with the strip of chapati. 'Notwithstanding the need to protect the wishes of your, um, the owner,' – he avoided the use of the word 'patron' but he guessed that was a more accurate description of the relationship – 'but it may help me attest the document's provenance if I were able to meet them to see it and discuss it further. I am due to remain in India for another week or so, if that would be of use.'

Harris was gazing from the window being rocked gently by the train, and feeling pretty postprandial about the world, when she appeared next to him. It was warm, very warm in the cabin.

Padmini leaned in.

'Do you want to come to the terrace?'

'The terrace,' asked Harris, with a bob of his eyebrows.

'I'll show you.'

Harris stirred himself from the armchair and they made their way through the next carriage, passing along a corridor in the Maharaja's private quarters, and arriving at a door at the rear end of the train. Padmini opened the door, and air buffeted into the vestibule, then they stepped out onto a covered balcony, where the airflow settled.

Alone, Harris took her hand and pulled her close to him. She kissed him, and pressed herself against him, then broke away.

'God, you're a good kisser,' she declared.

They closed up again. Harris felt her hand going for his waistband.

'Steady on,' he clucked, snatching a glance towards the door.

'Everyone's sleeping,' she hissed, stepping in closer. He looked over at the door, seeing if there was a way to lock it from the outside.

'No one can see us,' she declared, half shouting, and taking his hands in hers. Harris decided to give in. It was an easy decision. Of course. She was beautiful, insistent, and this might be their last chance of anything quite so intimate. Silently, she pressed her hand to his chest and guided him around so that his back was to the door; her hands went to his flies and she dropped to her knees.

'Steady on,' gulped Harris again, moving to raise her.

But Padmini resisted and moved quickly.

'Good God,' he uttered, with a tremor. He gasped and looked up at the wooden-panelled ceiling of the open terrace, and then breathing, took in the vista.

The railway tracks led away, winding all the way to the distant horizon like a vast long tail from the rear of the train. The tracks bisected a vast landscape of brown desert, spartanly dotted with trees and occasional dunes rising up like hills A family of camels charged across the tracks just behind the train and then fell quickly into the distance, the sandy trail visible behind them. Harris steadied himself against the ridges of the doorframe, and glanced down at Padmini. He inhaled sharply. In the distance the railway tracks suddenly veered up from the dusty soil, and curved into the sky in a corkscrew, followed by the trees, sandy landscape, camels, and all . . .

★

A painted Ganesh in bright fuchsia, green, and gold was affixed to the lintel above the front door of the house that according to Goodlad, Sohan Choudhury had called home. Drabble checked his wristwatch. It was approaching 4pm. The house was narrow and consisted of two storeys, marked out by two shuttered windows, one above the other, looking out onto on a quiet dusty side road. A bull nibbled at weeds protruding from the ground several doors down. Most of the brown paint had peeled from the front door, leaving the bare wood on show.

Drabble had not revealed to Gupta the actual purpose of the visit, rather had enlisted his help in finding Choudhury's home without exploring reasons, but on the basis that he knew he might well struggle to find it alone and time was short. This proved a worthy concern: Choudhury's dwelling was located in a district little frequented by Europeans, where what little signage there was incomprehensible to Drabble. He had some Hindi words from his upbringing on the cantonment but that was it.

He knocked and waited. Nothing. He confirmed that they were unobserved, and put his shoulder firmly to the door. The dry, elderly doorframe gave in easily and he stepped inside – barely giving Gupta a moment to protest, which he did.

'Professor!' he stammered, but hurried in after him, bewildered.

Drabble stepped into a darkened room, lit only by the searing shaft of light from the door which showed him his angular silhouette across the floor: a small teak table and chairs occupied the space before the shuttered window to the right. On the wall two carvings of Hindu deities looked down – Drabble spotted the four-armed god Vishnu, with his discus and mace, and then Saraswati, the god of learning, among other things. He fitted the bill for a schoolmaster, Choudhury's given occupation.

Drabble took out a box of matches and lit a candle on the table, and then pushed the front door closed, and jammed a chair against it to prevent anyone following them in. He would not be making that mistake again.

'*Professor!*' whispered Gupta. 'I insist you tell me what is going on.'

'We'll just be a minute, Doctor . . .' Drabble proceeded into the interior of the property. 'Follow me.'

They entered the next room; a bedroom – a low bed crouched along the far wall beneath a small framed photograph of Stalin. There was a wardrobe, a desk, upon which stood various books. Topmost was an battered copy of *Das Kapital*, marked as the property of a library somewhere in Delhi, by a label pasted into the inside cover. There was also a pile of Communist Party of India leaflets, the sort that were being handed out at the demonstration Drabble witnessed on Monday night.

The next door opened to a box-room, in which there was a bed but little else, and then they were in the kitchen. Flies buzzed noisily around the open fireplace and an array of various aged pans and urns stood dotted about the floor or on shelves or low tables. There was a strong smell of spices and curry – but also something acrid. Drabble unfastened the window and threw open the shutters, sending the flies into a frenzy and letting sunlight surge into the cool room. Grasses sprouted through the mud and piles of litter strewn across the earthen back yard, where freshly laundered cloths hung from a line. There was a dark dress and light man's shirt.

'Professor –'

Gupta's tone was urgent, and Drabble saw immediately what it was.

An elderly woman lay motionless on a bench by the far wall, almost as if she were sleeping. Her eyes were open in alarm.

'She looks as if she were frightened to death,' stated Gupta.

The woman looked about sixty; Drabble noticed that her jaw was gritted as he took up her wrist and felt for a pulse. He laid her arm back down. There was no apparent stiffening of the joints, which told you something, too.

At first glance there was no signs or marks of injury, then he felt a large egg-shaped bump on her head, just beneath the start of the hairline, in the gap of grey before the her headscarf. The injury was consistent with being struck by a right-handed person who was somewhat taller than her – she had seen whoever it was, too, and the horror on her face registered the imminence of the strike. On this basis it was perfectly possible that whoever dealt this blow might be the person who dealt one to him earlier. Mind you, saying that they were looking for a right-handed person of perhaps a little over six feet in height hardly narrowed things down very much.

He bent down to the fire; the embers were still warm. Whatever had been in the pot above it was now reduced to a blackened mass, but the thick pot had the echo of the heat left in it.

'What a mess,' said Drabble, in conclusion. It was possible that the blow had not been intended to kill the woman, of course. Just as the blow directed at his own head had presumably been intended to stun. Or perhaps not. He took the candle and returned to what was presumably Choudhury's bedroom. Light filtered in from the kitchen, showing details denied by the candlelight: the bare rendered walls, the brightly coloured rug, a wooden carved icon of Ganesh similar in style to the ones in the front room, propped up on the desk.

'We shall have to notify the authorities,' he heard Dr Gupta say from the kitchen. 'This poor, poor woman. She reminds me of my mother,' he added sombrely. 'She has a kind face, does she not?'

'She certainly did,' replied Drabble, a touch coldly, he realised. He was inspecting the other items on Choudhury's desk. A fabric-bound hardback copy of Lenin's *What Is To Be Done?* in English translation. There was also a copy of *Oliver Twist*, inscribed with Choudhury's signature, in the short pile, along with copies of *Paradise Lost* and the *Canterbury Tales*. These were consistent with his occupation as an English teacher and likewise inscribed with his name. He checked the Marx and the Lenin and noted that Choudhury had inscribed neither, which might mean they were borrowed, or that he did not want to betray his ownership of them by writing his name in them. That was a possibility. After all, Communist Party membership was banned, and for all Drabble knew, the books might be, too.

On a short shelf was a copy of *Kim*, by Kipling, and several books in Hindi script that Drabble did not understand – and a copy of Forster's *A Passage to India*, which Drabble had read not long ago and enjoyed. He held the candle close to the picture of Stalin and called out: 'Can you give me a hand with something, Doctor?"

Gupta came and Drabble handed him the candle; he lifted Stalin from the wall to examine the fixing and its reverse. There was nothing to see. He asked about the books.

'Hindu religious texts,' declared Gupta. '*The Bhagavad Gita*, and that is . . .'

So Choudhury was far from being a hardened atheist, although it was perfectly feasible for him to be a committed Marxist and maintain some religious faith. He motioned to Gupta and started to head out. Drabble felt suddenly exhausted. The visit had been a disappointment. He felt he knew no more about Choudhury than had had before they arrived. All it had done was to add to the misery of the mystery – another death, quite possibly that of Choudhury's mother. 'Come on, Choudhury,' he said. He scowled around the front room one last time, hoping to see something that would transform this state of affairs. But the place was void of useful detail and what detail there was could hardly be trusted. The place had been sanitised, a process which presumably took in eliminating the elderly woman. If that was true, it painted a bleak picture of the people they were dealing with.

Drabble arrived at the front door, and waited for Gupta to join him.

'Come on,' he repeated, addressing the interior. The doctor arrived; Drabble could see he was not happy to leave the old woman there, but Drabble did not have time to get involved. He checked his wristwatch. It was nearly five. He was due to report to Bikaner House at seven. Whatever the niceties of it, they simply did not have time to get involved with the police in this issue. In fact, with the little he had discovered of the authorities, the police might be the last people he should get involved.

Drabble opened the front door, letting in the glare, the heat and the cacophony from the street and stepped into light – but immediately halted.

Six native policemen, their putties lined up perfectly, stood to attention under a European officer, probably no more than twenty-five.

'Professor Drabble,' the lieutenant declared, squaring his shoulders at him. He touched the peak of his service hat with his cane. 'Lieutenant Nettleton, sir –' He offered a nod towards Gupta. 'Doctor. I'd be obliged if you would come with us.' Nettleton motioned towards a car and military lorry. 'Transport standing by. I think we'll leave this lot to the police, don't you?'

Crammed into the back seat of an unmarked white Morris Oxford – with a native police constable for company – Drabble and Gupta were driven slowly through the early evening Delhi traffic. The heat in the car intensified as it inched its way through the bazaars and thoroughfares of the old part of the city. There where glimpses of the Red Fort between the pedestrians, hawkers and rickshaw drivers. Then they made their way into the new city, where the roads were wider, traffic more spartan, and skies that much bigger. Nettleton did not volunteer their destination, and it seemed somehow beside the point to ask. Drabble could sense that Gupta was afraid. The interior of the Morris was hot – just as it was outside of the car but even so he sweated prodigiously, and stared blankly ahead, clutching his leather case on his lap, blinking occasionally.

Drabble shot him a tight smile. It was going to be all right, he declared.

At least, he sincerely hoped they would be.

The Morris circled a roundabout and then proceeded at 30 miles per hour along a broad tree-lined boulevard; at the end of the road Drabble saw parks and fountains and well-dressed Europeans perambulating under umbrellas as if it were a Forster novel.

They cut betwixt two parks and then turned right, passing under the shadow of the imposing Lutyens arch commemorating Indian's Great War dead. The Morris headed up Kingsway, a stately thoroughfare that would not have looked misplaced in one of Albert Speer's fantasies. It was a drive that he had covered part of during his Monday evening outing, and it had lost none of its impact. In the distance was the dome of the Viceroy's palace – silhouetted by the evening sun that swept a gold blanket across the heavens.

The Morris, escorted by the canvas-covered Bedford truck, continued in stately convoy along Kingsway, turning neither left nor right, and all the while the great round-topped dome of Viceroy's House grew in size and sheer architectural magnificence. They passed neat parks with immaculate lawns, leisured pedestrians, official cars and checkpoints manned by soldiers; Drabble saw large ministry buildings in stone like ducal seats set back from the road.

They halted at the high wrought iron gates of Viceroy's House. Nettleton wound down the window and exchanged a few words with the Indian sergeant at the sentry post. The gates went up, and they resumed; now reaching some ten miles per hour. Gupta swallowed.

The car stopped at the foot of a deep, wide set of stone steps. Nettleton and the driver got out smartly and opened the doors for Drabble and Gupta, who alighted. Drabble looked up at the broad columns, rows of shuttered windows and arches. It was a vast deliberation in rusty sandstone; a gargantuan riot of neoclassicism, of Mughal and Hindu architectural flourishes all bundled up in one immense imperial fantasia. Whatever you thought of the Raj, this was an astonishing testament to a fusion of peoples over time. Drabble suppressed some conflicted pride.

Nettleton led them up the deep flight of stairs into the colonnaded entrance of red-orange sandstone palace. Beyond the columns was a broad opening with double doors, and a desk, where a uniformed commissionaire sat, attended by various native staff – runners, telephone operators, and so on.

Nettleton announced them, and received a officious nod.

'Go through, sir,' said the commissionaire.

Nettleton led them across a broad marble hall similar in dimensions to Trafalgar Square. The interior space was circled with attendants in tailcoats and guards in tall bright turbans and ornate uniforms. Flagpoles sprung out from the cornicing encircling the chamber in a crown of Union flags. Drabble tore his eyes away. It was sickening. He focused on the dark sweat-patch on Nettleton's spine and followed him to a staircase and up to the first storey, which like everything else in this structure, was three or four times the size it needed to be.

They walked along a black-freckled white marble corridor, tall doors leading off in both directions. Drabble sensed this was the administrative zone of the palace, its functional heart. Nettleton stopped, ordered them to wait and disappeared inside one of these unmarked doors. A reedy gramophone rendition – William Walton's *Crown Imperial* if he wasn't mistaken – spilled into the corridor, along with sunlight before silence and the gloom was restored.

Drabble and Gupta shared a glance. The doctor grinned nervously.

The tall door swept back, causing them both to squint. As the blanching faded, a small man looked up from his wide desk, situated in the middle of an office larger than a squash court and flooded with light. It was Arbuthnot.

'Professor Drabble,' he declared cordially. 'Doctor Gupta . . . come in.'

They sat down in the comfortable club chairs pulled up in

front of his broad desk, and Nettleton was dismissed. As an impeccably liveried steward served tea, Drabble noticed a Mughal era portrait of Tipu Sultan, the so-called Tiger of Mysore who had posed the last real obstacle to the East India Company in the 1790s. There was also a copy of Thomas Jones Barker's *The Relief of Lucknow.*

'They help me to keep a sense of perspective,' announced Arbuthnot, with a smile. He offered the sugar to Gupta. 'I have a fondness for Tipu Sultan,' he continued absently. 'He was a brilliant man, and very nearly didn't lose. I mean to say, he wouldn't have lost if he hadn't been in an unwinnable situation.' The full grey moustache dipped.

'A little like we are now, you mean?' stated Drabble. Arbuthnot did not miss the coldness of his tone and his forehead ruffled accordingly, but whether he was communicating disbelief or opposition Drabble could not be discern.

'How so?' he replied.

'The Raj can't go on,' Drabble asserted. 'The superstructure is jolly impressive – the frills, the tassels the lances, *this place –*' his eyes circled about the room, 'but the foundations are withering. And you know it, probably better than most.'

Arbuthnot eyed Drabble and sipped his tea. He glanced over at Gupta, then addressed Drabble.

'Do you know whose the office is through that door?'

Drabble's eye followed his to the tall dark door under carved Grecian scrolling and lion and unicorn in relief.

'The Viceroy,' stated Arbuthnot. 'And do you know who's in there?' He turned to the door on the opposite side of the room. 'The Commander-in-Chief of the India, Sir Robert Cassells.'

'So that's what they did with him,' sniffed Drabble. Cassells had been a prominent general during the Great War.

Arbuthnot drained his teacup, and moved around the front of his desk, where four pipes of differing styles were arranged on stands. He perched at the corner of his desk, took up one of these, and lit up. Smoke clouded from his mouth and nostrils.

'I think, Professor, it would do you no ill to have a greater appreciation of the context under which we operate.' He looked over at Gupta, and smiled. 'Needless to say, what I am about to impart is highly confidential and were either of you to repeat any of it, I would be bound to deny it, and throw every effort of the GOI at rubbishing your public standing at the risk that others might.'

'I have your meaning perfectly,' said Gupta.

'Good,' Arbuthnot inspected the bowl of his pipe, presenting a clear view of the curl of silvery grey hair crowning his head, then drew on it. He went over to a vast map of the subcontinent that hung from the wall, crowding the corner, and mused upon it.

'The official policy of the government of British India is simply this: to extricate the United Kingdom of Great Britain and Northern Ireland from the Indian subcontinent with all practicable haste. That this has to be achieved without loss of face, or loss of life, or without ceding control of the subcontinent to a third power, goes without saying. But, to be crystal clear, if we could effect the change with those stipulations, then I assure that this would happen tomorrow. Today, if possible.'

He turned to face them. Drabble shook his head.

'I don't believe you.'

'It is true.' Arbuthnot was in earnest. 'Hard as it might be to believe – Dr Gupta, I sympathise – but this has in fact been the position of the government since before Lord Curzon was here. First we had the Morley Minto reforms of 1909, extending the parliamentary franchise to Indians, then the Montford reforms of 1919 went somewhat still further, and finally – notwithstanding the efforts of Mr Gandhi and the Congress party – we were finally able to introduce the 1935 Government of India Act, which is an altogether new territory. The governance of India is a journey, one that will hopefully see us departing in,' his lips formed an 'oh' and his eyes swivels towards the ceiling, 'in about

1950, following the next big Act, which I anticipate in about 1947 or so.'

He sighed, and gazed over at the Tiger of Mysore. 'It will depend on a few diehards in the House of Lords, and perhaps just a little on whatever Comrade Stalin decides to get up to next, but if both are quiescent – then who knows?' He shrugged cheerfully and inspected his audience.

'It won't be easy,' he continued. 'It's probably the biggest foreign policy challenge that the British Empire has had to deal with since 1776. But at least we have a plan this time. A plan, I might add, that puts us on the right side of history.' He smiled.

Arbuthnot reviewed his onlookers, his pipe stem braced between his teeth.

'Now, I fully appreciate that the appearance of GOI policy is one that we might characterise as status quo prolongation,' he turned to Drabble. 'But that is assuredly *not* the case.' He nodded meaningfully at Gupta. 'The reason I'm sharing this with you is not so that you can go forth and undermine a highly confidential purpose of British policy, but because I need to acquire your trust, and experience has taught me that offering an important confidence is often the most efficacious means of achieving such a state – especially when the confidences accord with the wishes of the listeners. More tea?'

Harris filled one of the leather armchairs in the saloon cabin of the Maharaja's train like hippopotamus recovering from the mating season. He was still processing the thoughts and sensations of the last twenty-four hours, not least the very last hour or so, on the viewing platform at the rear of the train with Princess Padmini. She had retired – his trail of thoughts paused, he gazed out of the window at the trees in the dusk – following the climax of those proceedings. Good God. He closed his eyes and relived the moments at the rear of the train. Was this normal? Was this the way people made love out East? They had the *Kama*

Sutra, of course, a document so inflammably erotic that it was banned. This explained the appeal of colonial service.

From the window, dark silhouettes of the huts and trees passed by in a blur. He would have to get up at some stage. He looked down at the whisky in the cut glass tumbler on the table before him. He didn't even have the energy to pick that up. His arms lay heavily on the chair; perhaps this is what paralysis feels like, he wondered. The glass of whisky was simply too far away. Far too far. He yawned; this time his eyes began to water and the entire back of his mouth began to tear itself apart. God it was hot. That was part of the trouble. This whole bloody country was so hot. It was maddening. No wonder people just got gobbled up by it. It was either that or they perspired away – disintegrated like some victim of a chemically astute killer who rinses his victim away diluted by acid down a plug hole. Except in the Tropics it was the heat: once one's body was so utterly voided of all moisture, there was nothing left in it to bind the flesh together. It was like returning to dust without observing the usual traditions of death and cremation first.

He decided to smoke. His left arm felt like it was being pressed down by the weight of several pigmies. With enormous effort he managed to lift it and slide his hand down to his coat hip pocket, where it located the pipe. He managed to get this out, stifling another yawn, through gritted teeth. Next he had to find the tobacco and matches. The even more dormant right arm refused to budge. Harris groaned and got it going by shifting his shoulders. Eventually he filled his pipe and lit it.

Christ alive. The only thing to combat heat like this was *more* heat. If his skin had sweated out everything possible, let's see if he could squeeze any moisture out of his lungs. He drew the hot spiced smoke into his mouth and inhaled . . . ah, rejoice! He closed his eyes and leaned his head back, feeling the oppressive exterior heat abate against the equalising force of the tobacco. The train was passing a shanty town of tarpaulins and tents that stretched far towards he horizon, where the green hills rose up dark in the dusky light. From the window he could see flames flickering between the crouching figures attending the smoking fires, and he could catch a whiff of wood-smoke and something else – ordure – through the open window. A small boy, probably no more than four or five, ran along the side of the encampment waving a stick being pursued by a small, hairy dog.

This scene of abject poverty distracted him but briefly. He drew again on the pipe, closing his eyes and in that moment glimpsed Padmini's face, soft and olive-hued in candlelight. Her chin reared up, and then her throat, and sternum and her surprisingly pronounced breasts – soft, pert and voluminous . . .

Harris cleared his throat and opened his eyes, adjusting himself in the seat. Out of the window the encampment had gone, replaced by the order of a whitewashed town – neat roofs of houses and civic structures encircled domes and minarets that showed it to be a mainly Muslim settlement.

He braced his eyelids open, against the drowsiness of the atmosphere, and took another draw on the pipe. The alarming fact was that Padmini was not a mere plaything, not some toy for the playing of life's greatest game. Though, he knew, she would be a first-class example of such if she were. No. Princess Padmini meant much more to him that that. He felt it in his bones – and in the pit of his stomach – that that was so. He swallowed and caught his throat, a spark of panic suddenly erupted within him. But how could it be? How could he be – he paused, fearful of his own thoughts and feeling his throat tighten – in *love*? And not just that, but in *love* with an *Indian* woman?

It went against everything he had been taught since he was a boy. The white races were superior, they said, and for evidence look no further than the fact that the white nations controlled everything and had all the stuff. The wily Japanese put a bit of a spoke in the works – true, but then, frankly, they had defeated the Russian navy in 1905 using ships we'd sold them. And they, anyway, were yellow, which was only *off-white* when you thought about it, so they were very nearly part of the white brigade.

That was the orthodoxy, anyhow. Whites were top of the pile and the darker you got, the further down the food chain you were.

The train clattered across an iron suspension bridge spanning a deep gorge. Trees of such great size and leaf loomed out from the gloom, and Harris imagined the great tumbling waters below. Nothing could be heard over the dirge of the steam engine, which he now glimpsed up ahead as the tracks curved around a great hillside.

Plainly, the orthodoxy was tosh. Complete and utter codswallop. Were the Romans in any way superior to the Ancient Britons or Gauls, or had an accident of history merely offered them certain advantages that gave them a head start? Were the Greeks superior to the Romans? Probably. They certainly wrote better plays and produced better philosophers. But not, ultimately, intrinsically.

So were white Europeans in any way superior to Indians? No. He shook his head, as if the physical gesture would aid mental assimilation. It meant that the whole argument of white racial supremacy *was* bogus. Utterly. It was a cloak of unbounded absurdity that was intended to disguise an uncomfortable truth that there was no moral justification whatsoever for our rule in India – or anywhere else for that matter. We ruled India because our guns were bigger and fired faster than theirs.

And as a result, *we were in the wrong*. Harris pulled his pipe from his mouth, his lips parted in mild horror. We. Were. Wrong. Meaning that nauseating little fakir Mr Gandhi was right. Christ alive. Harris braced his shaking hand and drew manfully on the pipe. He wasn't a nauseating little fakir after all. The man was a bally hero.

And whatever we said to justify it? Oh, the railways; oh, the hospitals; oh, the schools, oh, the primitive structures of representative democracy . . . Look at all the amazing things we have done for these people! It didn't matter a fig. The French, doubtless, would have done an efficient job at administering Britain had they won the Napoleonic wars. They might even have done something about the food.

Harris suddenly felt rather sick. Everything he held to be true was wrong. And if he hadn't known it before, he did now. His feelings for Princess Padmini proved it. One plus one equals two. Ruddy hell. The sooner we got out of this mess the better. Christ alive. What a mess. But the bigger question for him was, how on earth could he and Padmini be together? Her family would never permit her to marry him. Almost certainly never, anyway. His family wouldn't like it either, but they would jolly well have to lump it; and if Harris never had to see Lord Uncle Moneybags again, he could live with that, too. If that was the price for having Padmini. But would she marry him?

Harris caught his reflection in the window: he had gone quite white.

Arbuthnot remained silent as he poured a fresh cup of tea for Dr Gupta. The china spout was narrow so the fluid was dispensed only slowly, and he was using this delay as a means to build up to something. That was Drabble's read. He watched Arbuthnot conclude the ceremony and take up his seat.

'I have spent 42 of my 63 years in India,' he declared importantly. 'I was born in 1874 to parents themselves born in the early years of the reign of Queen Victoria, meaning they were the recipients of Georgian values. Britain didn't become Victorian, I would say, until after the repeal of the Corn Laws, and then only slowly so. Until 1870, if not later, England was a land of boot-scrapes and country parishes where the parson and the squire rode to hounds. I believe that this has had a bearing on my life.' He paused for effect. 'My father's father, General Sir Augustus Arbuthnot, was born in 1801 and came to India for the heyday of the East India Company, eventually retiring to Shropshire in 1834, on an estate the size of a small princely state, currently enjoyed by my older brother, the third baronet. India, gentlemen, has been in my family for more than three generations.

And we have done well out of India and India, I believe, has done well out of us. I love India, and have made my life here. But, gentlemen, the world is now different, and we *are* going to change with it before it's too late.'

Arbuthnot paused, and appeared to be looking at the portrait of George VI that hung in the dark-wooden recess. Drabble asked,

'What has all this got to do with us?'

Arbuthnot's silver eyebrows lifted and he rotated his chair to face Drabble.

'You have in your possession a small artefact,' he said, reaching his open hand forward. 'A brooch or badge, of a rose, I believe. May I see it?'

Drabble hesitated before setting down the teacup and saucer. The item was his only proof of something that he suspected was afoot – evidence perhaps of a conspiracy that united Miss Skinner-Chatterjee and Choudhury in a common purpose and which doubtlessly included the very people who had knocked him unconscious that morning, and made short work of poor Choudhury's mother.

'Please show it to me,' said Arbuthnot. Drabble reached into his inside jacket breast pocket and from the buttoned section within, took out the brooch. It was perhaps a little over half an inch long, finely carved and a dark shade of vermillion. Arbuthnot took it gratefully, and pulled on a pair of heavy reading glasses.

'An English rose entwined with Indian shrubs,' he declared. 'How fitting.' He swept off his glasses, and emitted a long sigh. 'We have heard rumours of a so-called Rose Conspiracy for some time now,' he offered a flat smile beneath the solid grey moustache. 'But I have never – nor has anyone to my knowledge – actually seen this totem of their existence.' He swallowed.

'I have a bump on the side of my head that also proves their existence,' said Drabble. 'And I've seen two of their assassins at work. They're real enough.'

Arbuthnot nodded and replaced his turtle-shell spectacles to examine the brooch again. He turned it in his fingers, rather like an archaeologist examining a vital fragment of portent. His breathing changed, and he laid it down. 'These people must be stopped.' He set down the glasses and squared his shoulders at Drabble. 'I'll speak candidly. We know nothing about this organisation, let alone its precise intentions. We do not know, for instance, if it is in the pay of a foreign power – be it the Soviet Union, Imperial Japan, or perhaps Hitler's Germany. They all look,' he glanced over at Gupta, 'over at the British Raj with jealous envy. And regardless of what they may promise, liberty for Indians is not on their agenda.' He shook his head. 'The best clue we have, as you know, is that they may have Soviet connections, because of the Communist sympathies of Choudhury, but, to be honest, that might be a red herring.'

Drabble wasn't convinced either.

'Choudhury's collection of Hindu texts and various religious decorations did not accord with the hard-line, diehard atheism one comes to expect with a stringent Marxist position. Nor do I believe he was known to M. N. Roy. The other question mark over it being a Soviet show was the absence of any corroborating evidence among Skinner-Chatterjee's possessions. All I found there was a patriotic portrait of Queen Victoria.' Again, hardly conclusive. The book in the safe would have confirmed it, of course. 'I don't suppose you know anything of Miss Skinner-Chatterjee's life that might be useful? I got the distinct impression that her flat had been swept – perhaps by your investigators?'

Arbuthnot shook his head.

Drabble didn't know whether or not to believe him. For the first time it dawned on him that the events of the day proved one point beyond doubt: the conspiracy, whatever else, was still very much active. He said:

'I am due to report to the Maharaja of Bikaner on what I have discovered thus far this evening . . .' he referred to his wrist-watch; he would need to head straight to Bikaner House from here in all likelihood. 'As you are doubtlessly aware, alarmed by the two incidents in Bikaner, he asked me to investigate the matter further for him here.' Arbuthnot's eyebrows lowered, and Drabble finished there. He did not understand what that portended but guessed it was disapproval.

'What do you make of the Maharaja?' asked Arbuthnot.

'He seems to be highly enlightened, and frankly surprisingly pro-British, but then, I daresay the superstructure of the Raj preserves his enhanced position, so you're in it together.'

Arbuthnot half smiled.

'Ganga Singh is a good man,' he pronounced. 'He *is* pro-British, but not to a fault. And to speak freely, I am fairly certain that he is *not* involved in any of this. He may well – after all – have been killed or injured by the grenade that Choudhury was going to throw during the meeting of the princes with Mr Gandhi on Tuesday night. To contemplate that being a feint is I feel beyond absurdity.

'There must, however, be a connection with Bikaner, because whoever Choudhury and Miss Skinner-Chatterjee were working with knew that the princes would be there, and that Mr Gandhi would be there, too. The co-conspirator must have given him access to the royal premises, too. And then there's the question of the attempt on the Viceroy's life; that *must* be subordinate operationally,' he declared. 'Because Linlithgow's visit would never have occurred had the first attack been successfully concluded.'

'It's a bit of a tangle,' continued Arbuthnot moodily. He sighed. 'Would either of you gentlemen care for a cigarette? They're rather good.' He flicked open the lid of an ornate silver cigarette box. Gupta accepted, Drabble did not. Smoking and high altitudes did not mix. A billowing cloud of purple-grey smoke wafted towards Drabble, as Arbuthnot continued his thought. 'On the basis that neither Choudhury nor the Skinner-Chatterjee woman have any pre-existing connexions with Bikaner, then I think we can for certain say that there *must* have been someone in Ganga

Singh's court or the British Residency who knew what was happening and tipped them off. That is certain. And likely as not that is the reason that Ganga Singh has asked you – and not one of his own – to investigate.'

That made sense.

'Have you got much to tell him?'

'Nothing, really,' confessed Drabble. 'Nothing more than you know. Perhaps that's not surprising. I'm not a detective. I'm a historian.'

Arbuthnot nodded.

'I know what you are, Professor.' He smiled at Gupta, then addressed Drabble, 'Do this for me. Go to Ganga Singh as you have agreed, please, and tell him everything that you have told me or that we have together discussed. Do that. But while you are there, be alive to the fact that there is someone quite close to him who is surely the Bikaneri connection. That someone brought Choudhury and Skinner-Chatterjee in – and got Choudhury inside the palace grounds. And that somebody may well be critical to locating the individual operating somewhere here within these very walls – or near to them – who is also part of this conspiracy. *That* is the person we all need to stop – and fast.'

He cleared his throat.

'Bikaner may yet lead to Delhi. I therefore urge you to help us find the heart of this conspiracy, before it is too late. There is also something else that you should know: tomorrow evening, the Viceroy is hosting his annual ball. A thousand of the most important dignitaries, military and civil officers, politicians, religious leaders and business magnates will be there. It is a would-be terrorist's fantasy.' Arbuthnot pressed his hand to the neatly arranged hair crowning his head. 'They were unlucky in Bikaner. They might not be unlucky again.'

The Maharaja's train arrived at New Delhi station stopping on a platform already dressed with a red carpet, and a fleet of waiting cars. The party was driven along broad thoroughfares of the imperial capital, and arrived not long after at Bikaner House, Singh's New Delhi powerbase. Princess Padmini made the journey in a limousine reserved for the women of the household. Harris had joined Colonel Stewart – who had been marooned in a different carriage for the journey – and Mr Panikkar in the third limousine, behind the Maharaja and Crown Prince, and the womenfolk. The servants followed on behind. No one spoke in the car as they proceeded along the highways of the imperial capital. Harris gazed from the window of the Rolls-Royce with wonder at what he saw. The vastness of it all exceeded his expectations . . .

They circled the corner of grassed park, turned again and were suddenly sweeping in between a pair of his sandstone gateposts. Bikaner House, the Maharaja's recently built New Delhi palace, presented a single façade, which wrapped around them, creating a geometric forecourt, one fringed with palms and lush foliage. About forty members of the household staff, dressed in white jackets and narrow trousers with red and saffron silk turbans stood in a line, waiting to greet them with libations and deep bows.

It took about ten minutes to get inside. Once ensconced they were shown to their rooms; Harris's was large enough for a set of tennis and had three tall windows overlooking the park with a clear view of the India Gate. Elsewhere he could see the ornate crenulations and exotic roofed towers of various official buildings over the treetops. It was impressive. Aside from the politics, we had done a bloody good job here. He sighed. It would be hard to walk away from it.

Harris threw himself down into a armchair beneath the nearest electric fan and got out his pipe. It was seven o'clock. Dinner was at eight. He had nothing to do till then but dream of Padmini.

A small black bird, with rather a refined head shape and sleek beak, landed on the windowsill and bleated a few times in Harris's direction. It puffed up its wings, as if to spring into the room, and Harris grouchily launched himself from the chair:

'Shoo!' he cried, his arms akimbo.

The bird flittered away and Harris found himself at the window, scowling for the contemptuous avian. Feeling somewhat better about the world – he had conquered one potential hazard – he glanced down and spotted Captain Dundonald far along the gravel pathway below in conversation with another man, one dressed in the tan uniform that was the essential colour scheme of British rule in India. His face was lost to the shade of his pith helmet, but Harris could make out the shoulder strap of his leather Sam Browne, and from the physical proportions Harris guessed it might be Colonel Stewart. The pair stood close together. Dundonald's hands were positioned on his hips, foreshortened below his shoulders, his head turning alertly from side to side. They were in close conference.

His interest was piqued. His eye caught movement and the small black bird flew back towards his window – straight at him. He cursed and flung his hand out towards it, causing it to veer off. Below the heads bobbed upwards and the men hurried off.

Harris peered back down just in time to catch them clearing the corner. He pondered it, then the scene distracted his thoughts: beyond the grounds and tress, the sounds of the metropolis were insistent. Growling traffic, droning, the laboured cries of beasts of burden, the call of hawkers, whistles and more. Somewhere on the floor above, amid all the cacophony, would be Princess Padmini. His heart swelled at the thought of her. What was she doing? He sighed and drew on his piping, strolling back towards the vast double bed. He propped the pipe on the night stand, exhaled plumes of greyish blue smoke and plumped down on the soft cotton sheets. Was she, at this very moment, lowering her perfect cinnamon hued body into a vast copper bath, coated in rose petals? He sighed and imagined the cleft of her bottom sinking beneath the surface of the water, swallowing her up, covering her stomach and inching over her perfect breasts, touching, moistening her nipples, and then running like an incoming tide all the way to her throat . . .

This was not helping. Also he had to change for dinner. And he could probably benefit from a bath. There was no avoiding it. His heart sank and he lay back down. Harris liked the Maharaja enough, but the whole court business was getting him down. The foreign secretary – Panikkar – was a joyless cove and a half. Then there was the Crown Prince, who seemed nice enough but was rather standoffish and only talked about shooting and not much else. There was only so far you could go on the strength of killing things. Then there was the frankly vile Bombay businessman Sharma-Smith, who was quite literally about the most hateful specimen of manhood you were ever likely to come across. And the there was Captain Dundonald. Harris shook his head. He didn't like him either. He wasn't about to forget his unseemly carry on with Miss Heinz, or whatever her real name was. The sly cove.

Harris sighed. The others were decent enough. Especially the old Maharaja. Yes, Ganga Singh was all right, but he was apt to make one feel rather inadequate. He'd shot three tigers in five minutes, after all – among about two hundred in all. Harris had needed Drabble's help to shoot his. Harris sighed again, this time rather self-pityingly. It was all too shaming. Still he had landed one good shot. That was something. It was all flooding through his mind at a rate of knots . . .

Oh well, he thought. Thank goodness Delhi was a damned sight cooler than Bikaner. That was something. Also the continuous presence of camels was beginning to get him down. And sand, too. Harris began running a bath . . .

'Now, Dr Gupta,' declared Arbuthnot, taking up the ornately carved meerschaum pipe that was one of the collection that stood along the front of his wide dark polished desk. 'Would you do me the kindness of explaining your presence in the company of Professor Drabble, here? Are you also an historian by day, and an amateur sleuth by night?'

The question seemed to wrong-foot Gupta. He shot a look at Drabble.

'Go on, Gupta. Show him the codicil.'

Gupta turned to Arbuthnot.

Whatever the possible connection and risks, Drabble had decided matters had gone too far *not* to trust Arbuthnot. Well, up to a point, at least. It was one of the mottos of his late climbing companion Hubertus. He said people were like ropes. You had to be very sure of them before you trusted them with anything, let alone your life – but then you had to watch them carefully. Drabble wasn't sure about Arbuthnot, but he knew well enough that he was dangling by something now, and it would better hold or else.

Gupta reached for his bag and took out the cardboard scroll case. Grasping it like a cleric approaching an altar with a relic, he approached Arbuthnot's desk, a rather obsequious smile written across his face. The bureaucrat cleared a space on the broad desk, moving files to one side, as Gupta unbuckled the case and slipped out the sheet and unrolled it. Arbuthnot snatched up a broad magnifying glass and scanned it keenly and he gasped with pleasure.

'Incredible,' he declared. He chuckled, his voice rising with incredulity, '"neither the Britannic Majesty nor his successors may grant ownership of the seven islands of Bombaim to any other potentate, other than the King of Portugal." Well that's a turn-up.' He laid down the magnifying glass and took out up his pipe. 'Professor, what do you make of it?'

Drabble hesitated. He shared a glance with Gupta.

'On the strength of what we can see in the photograph, there's no reason to suppose that it's not the genuine article.'

Arbuthnot regarded him coldly and cleared this throat.

'Do you concur, Doctor?'

Gupta, who still stood next to him, nodded. 'Yes Sir,' he said.

'I am grateful for Professor Drabble's analysis. He has great experience in this field.'

'I can claim no senior expertise in palaeography, but I have seen my fair share of documents of this era.' Drabble turned back to Arbuthnot. 'Do you think it carries any legal force?'

The Portuguese were still owners of three colonies on the west coast of India, of which the largest chunk was Goa. King or no king, they would certainly be interested by the document if and when British rule in India changed. While hardly current, this 276-year-old legal amendment to the marriage treaty of Charles II and Catherine of Braganza was potentially incendiary.

Arbuthnot sucked thoughtfully on his meerschaum.

'Absolutely not.' He swallowed, an act which caused the lined skin at his Adam's apple to contract like an exhaling octopus. 'Anything of this kind has been superseded by the 1858 Government of India Act.' He frowned in thought, as if weighing this up, and then gestured irritably towards the vacant chair with the stem of his pipe. 'Do sit down, Gupta. Now, tell me, where on earth was this unearthed?'

Gupta paused before he spoke.

'All I know is that which I have been told. That it was recently unearthed by a collector in Bombay. More than that I do not know. I have seen the original and it looks genuine to me. Plainly no one has seen this for a hundred years or more – perhaps longer . . .'

'And who is this collector?'

Gupta hesitated and looked over at Drabble. He frowned. Plainly whoever this person was they did not want him revealing their identity.

Arbuthnot repeated the question, this time more forcefully.

'Come, come, Doctor,' he added. 'Time is precious.'

Gupta looked down at the marble floor; his narrow shoulders drooped.

'I have been bound to confidence, sir,' he swallowed fearfully and lifted his eyes to meet the ferocious stare of Arbuthnot. Gupta sighed miserably:

'It is Sir Randolph Sharma-Smith, Sir. The industrialist. I dare say you are —'

Arbuthnot snatched up the large black Bakelite phone on the desk. 'Send Nettleton in, please. And fetch me the Chief Justice . . .' There was a pause as whoever was on the other end of the line replied. Arbuthnot's face coloured and his voice rose with incredulity. 'I don't care who he's having cocktails with. Tell Sir Maurice that it's urgent.' The receiver landed heavily on the cradle. 'Lord strike me down,' he hissed. 'Who the hell do judges think they are?'

Arbuthnot looked over at Drabble and Gupta and, with his neutral expression restored, stood up. 'Thank you for your time, gentlemen.' Behind them they heard the door open, and Arbuthnot smiled and looked over their shoulders. 'Lieutenant Nettleton. Please convey Professor Drabble and Doctor Gupta to their next appointment, which,' he referred to the clock on the wall, 'I expect will be at Bikaner House.'

Gupta got to his feet and started for the desk, leather scroll case in hand.

'Thank you, Doctor,' stated Arbuthnot. 'I'll keep this for now.' Drabble saw horror inform Gupta's features; his eyes widened, and he swallowed, as if he were about to be sick. His mouth opened to speak but no words emerged.

Arbuthnot nodded.

'Don't worry, Doctor. It will be perfectly safe here,' he said. 'You can return in the morning to collect it. And if *Mr* Sharma-Smith wants his photocopy in the meanwhile, he knows where to get it. Do feel free to tell him when you see his this evening.'

They began to move towards the door; Drabble turned back:

'Who is this man, Sharma-Smith?'

He caught Gupta looking over, and registered a fearful expression on his face.

Arbuthnot said, 'He is the owner of the Bombay Cotton

Company – and a close friend of Sir Ganga Singh's, hence his presence at Bikaner House. He's on first-name terms with the Viceroy, too, and I shouldn't wonder Sir Maurice Gwyer, our dear Chief Justice. Suffice it to say, *Mr* Sharma-Smith is a man with many interests . . .'

Gupta added meekly, 'And not a man to be trifled with.'

Arbuthnot looked over sharply, his eyebrows lowered.

'Indeed, Doctor. Rather more pertinently, in respect of the codicil anyway, he is also of Portuguese descent, which is rather coincidental, is it not? Don't let the "Smith" deceive you. The man's about as British as the Kaiser.'

Chapter Nineteen

Flaming beacons – yellow tongues licking the sky hither and thither – lined the driveway to Bikaner House, sending flickering light over the fronds of tall palms and other exotic, architectural foliage that sprang up from either side of the drive. The Morris crunched over maroon gravel turned black by the pitch dark sky and drew up at the main steps, where a uniformed attendant – wearing a broad sash in the saffron and red of Bikaner – swooped open the door.

It was shortly after seven. Drabble and Gupta, both in black tie, were led through a marble lobby large enough to have parked four of the Maharaja's Rolls-Royces side by side, and straight into an adjoining room where drinks were taking place. The noise hit them first: it was a wall of low murmuring voices. Then he saw it: a shimmering chandelier, crafted from a strange stone or shell, sprinkled a pale golden light across a carpet of conversing heads beneath. Some of these heads twinkled with their finery – bejewelled turbans, or robes embroidered with gold or silver – or they glistened from wax or sweat. Which made sense. The salon was a sauna and Drabble fingered the collar of his shirt, releasing his neck from its close embrace. He scanned the room: among the native finery were English officials in scarlet or navy – glittering in golden and orders depending on whether they were army or diplomatic – and the occasional dinner jacket of a box-wallah. Finally, there was an occasional tiara atop the head of a European guest that caught the light.

Drabble felt a tap at his shoulder. It was Ganga Singh.

'Maharaja,' he offered a bow.

Ganga Singh replied with a kindly dip of his heavy eyelids – as if to say, 'too much' – and nodded towards the exit. They followed and followed him out to a dark terrace, where the breeze reduced the temperature to something altogether more manageable.

The Maharaja offered them the choice of a selection of cigarettes plus cigars of various sizes and took out one of the largest for himself. Gupta overcame his nervousness to take one. The Maharaja glanced over at the cane chairs. 'I prefer to stand, if you don't mind,' he said, before introducing himself to Gupta.

'I am chancellor of Benares University,' said Singh.

'I know, sir,' said Gupta, grinning from ear to ear. 'You are very highly regarded in the institution.'

Singh swiftly turned to the matter in hand.

'What have you got for me, Professor? I have had security doubled as a precaution. You should know that I have a telephone call scheduled with the Viceroy later so your intelligence will be transmitted to the highest levels.'

Drabble began by summarising the events of the past evening and day. 'The evidence for a conspiracy linking Miss Skinner-Chatterjee and Choudhury is greater than ever – but what the impetus for the conspiracy is, and what its precise ambitions are, are still unknown.' He explained the bump on his head received at Skinner-Chatterjee's flat, and the apparent murder of Choudhury's mother. Next he produced the badge. 'Arbuthnot in the Viceroy's office confirmed the existence of what he called the Rose Conspiracy,' Drabble added. 'They are not afraid to hurt people to get their way. What their ambitions are, I cannot say – whether it is the prolong the lifespan of the Raj, as Miss Skinner-Chatterjee suggested, or to hasten its demise, more consistent one might think with a Swaraj campaigner like Choudhury, remains a matter for conjecture. All we know for certain is that their victims to date include both Indians and Europeans and they are not afraid to resort to violent means.'

The tip of the Maharaja's cigar glowed. He exhaled, then took the badge and inspected it under the light. He nodded thoughtfully and then returned it.

'And how have you managed to become embroiled in this matter?' he asked Gupta.

Gupta bowed, before he spoke.

'I sought Professor Drabble's expertise with a certain historic document,' he started. 'And, um, rather unfortunately I have ended up with rather more than I bargained for.'

Ganga Singh clapped him on the shoulder.

'In for a penny, in for a pound.'

Gupta smiled weakly. 'I should like to speak discretely to one of your guests, if I may,' said Drabble. 'Sir Randolph Sharma-Smith,' he continued. 'Is he here tonight?'

Ganga Singh's heavy eyebrows lowered and he looked to both Drabble and Gupta.

'Sir Randolph? By all means, he is one of my guests of honour – but you can't possibly suspect him of involvement?'

'It is a separate matter, sir, but it would be premature to go into further detail. I give you my assurance that no slight would be caused. Will you effect an introduction?'

The Maharaja regarded Drabble sceptically, and drew on his cigar.

'Very well,' he said. 'Wait here.'

Harris had bathed and then changed into his best double-breasted dinner suit and highly starched boiled shirt, with patent leather shoes. From his neck hung his K, which added a severe amount of gravitas to any sartorial effort, and in his left-hand hip pocket was his best cigarette case, fully loaded with twenty unfiltered Jasper & Justinian fine blend hundreds. All in all he was feeling rather dapper.

He spotted the vile Sharma-Smith hurrying from the room

in the wake of a flunky – excellent, that was one tremendous bore removed – and relieved a garlanded waiter of a glass from his silver salver. He took the top off the chilled gin and tonic and merged into the mass of chattering guests, his gaze gently roving the crowd for Princess Padmini.

Looking through the mass of faces and tiaras and turbans, the first person he recognised was Dundonald, now changed. Harris scowled. The bounder. Still, the man had a healthy sweat on, which made Harris smirk and reflect that no amount of acclimatisation could help you in certain situations. He was looking pretty animated – no doubt he was boasting about his heroics yesterday morning at the unveiling ceremony. Yes, he was the sort of cove who would show-off about that sort of thing. Very undignified. Harris advanced into the crowd and peered around a head to see who he was speaking to . . .

'Sir Percival,' boomed a voice. The noise collided with his eardrums just as he spotted Princess Padmini – composed and utterly beautiful - in enthralled silence staring right into the cove Dundonald's moist, pink face. She looked like she was hanging on his every word.

'Sir Percival,' tried the voice again, obliging Harris to turn. Before him stood a sinewy red-faced man of about fifty-five. Dense gun-metal hair, reminiscent of a wiry terrier, was parted and cut short to his head, but this and his face were positively drenched in sweat already, however, so one had only to worry about his heart, and he smoked a foul-smelling cheroot in a cigarette holder. He wore a navy velvet smoking jacket with frogging and the busy, inquisitive expression of a man who is looking for his keys. 'I hear you nearly got eaten by a tiger, what?' He nudged Harris's elbow painfully. 'Easily done old man. No shame in it. I've nearly been gobbled by one of those ruddy beasts myself once or twice. It happens.' He coughed. 'It wouldn't be fun if it didn't, would it?'

Harris raised his eyebrows and his interlocutor realised his small omission.

'Sir Richard Powell,' he said proudly, as if that should mean something to Harris. It didn't, but Harris knew well enough not to show his ignorance by admitting it. Instead he adopted impressed expression and shook the firm hand that was offered.

'Delighted to meet you,' declared Harris winningly. He looked over at Padmini who still appeared to be captivated by Dundonald and found something to say: 'I never knew you were friends with the Maharaja —'.

'Oh, Ganga Singh and I go back a long way,' grinned Powell, showing some fine, even teeth. 'You have to be friends with everyone to get on India, don't you know?'

'I dare say you're right,' replied Harris, losing sight of Padmini.

'So how is my old friend Lord Trychester?'

Christ alone knows, thought Harris; the proprietor of his newspaper certainly did not deign to talk to his staff of reptiles, as he regarded them.

'In rude health,' he proclaimed buoyantly.

'And the *Evening Express*?'

'Never better,' grinned Harris.

'Not gone wobbly on India?'

'Absolutely not,' quipped Harris. 'Stiffer than ever!'

'Good,' bellowed Powell. 'Can't abide people going soft on India.' He shook his head. 'Everywhere you sodding well go in the old country, people are going soft. It's like a disease of some sort.' He took a good go on his stout cigarette holder. 'I mean to say, they've literally no idea —'

Harris looked over for Padmini, thinking of the good he could do her; instead he saw Dundonald, now listening, his caddish eyes glistening. Harris cursed.

Powell droned on: 'I mean, they haven't got a clue what absolute savages these wogs are, particularly when left to their own devices.'

'Absolutely,' agreed Harris, feeling increasingly like he was having an out of body experience. 'Have you been to Bikaner?'

he asked. 'They've got schools, hospitals, electric lighting in the streets – and I think they even built their own railway.'

Powell's head retracted and frowned at Harris . . . his mouth then broke into a broad smile. 'Ah, well, Rajputana is *different*. They've been civilised there for a long time, and they've learnt quickly, too, don't forget.' He patted Harris's upper arm somewhat abruptly. 'But trust me. You don't know India like I do. For the most part, if we weren't here these chaps would still be living in mud huts and subsisting on *chhana masala* – if they were lucky.'

'I've had some rather good chhana masala,' stated Harris, his eyes observing a confused, puce frown unfold on the face before him. Harris grinned, and Powell chuckled hard, his eyes lighting up:

'Very funny,' he proclaimed. 'Now . . .'

Out on the terrace, Sir Ganga Singh excused himself and made for the door. 'I shall return to the party, but I very much wanted you two to meet.'

Sir Randolph Sharma-Smith nodded in acknowledgement of the Maharaja and then regarded Drabble gravely. His prominent eyes flicked severely to Gupta, and then back to Drabble.

'I've heard rather a lot about you from one place or another, Professor Drabble.' He clicked his fingers at the turbaned servant who waited at the door. The man swooped over and Sharma-Smith ordered a drink. He left them alone on the terrace.

'You have reviewed the codicil?'

'The photograph of it.'

'Your assessment?'

'First, tell me. What's your interest?'

'My interest, Professor? I'm sure Gupta explained? I'm a collector.'

'Ah,' replied Drabble, his tone indicating that he understood this to be explanation adequate enough. 'I wondered if you thought it might be an insurance policy?'

Sharma-Smith's eyelids closed to slits and he emitted a staccato laugh, like a dog's bark before it was sick.

'Most amusing,' he declared. He took delivery of a martini glass from the waiter. 'Alas,' he proclaimed, 'you see before you a keeper of Britannia's flame, Professor, a believer that she shall continue to rule the waves – even if various portions of its own political elite appear to be losing their backbone on the issue. Gupta –' he glanced over at the doctor, who lowered his gaze.

'I see,' said Drabble. 'I take it you don't believe in Indian independence?'

'Of course I believe in Indian independence, just as a child believes in the tooth fairy, or in Father Christmas.' He smiled, showing narrow teeth that were pointed. 'It'll never happen. I certainly have no intention of being here to see it,' he added. 'And if you knew India as I do, you would have no hesitation in agreeing with me.'

Drabble noticed Gupta take a long drag of his cigarette.

'Surely, it's inevitable?'

Sharma-Smith shook his head.

'This is precisely what I believe is wrong about the younger generation of Englishmen. You have lost your stomach. You are just so defeatist.'

'I call it being rational.'

Sharma-Smith reviewed Drabble over the top of this glass. He said:

'I believe that we can easily maintain or *finesse* the status quo for decades yet to come.' He cleared his throat. 'At least 1984 is my guess. Perhaps we can forestall it to the end of the century.'

That made Drabble's eyebrows rise. It was the very date that Miss Heinz had specified during their discussion on the train to Bikaner.

'You find that surprising, Professor?' chuckled Sharma-Smith.

'I do,' replied Drabble. 'But not for the reason you suppose.'

216

The magnate's eyes glistened.

'And what of Indian self-government?'

'Oh, that –' Sharma-Smith brushed it off. 'It is the same difference as independence.'

Drabble cocked an eyebrow at him. 'A rose by any other name?'

For a moment, Sir Randolph paused, his gaze pinched curiously at Drabble. Then he nodded. A peculiar, almost lascivious smile came to his lips. 'I couldn't have put it any better myself,' he said curtly. He turned on his heel and walked from the terrace.

'Don't forget to pass my regards to your proprietor,' repeated Powell as he broke away from Harris and moved off. 'Sir Randolph,' he boomed on seeing the other arrive in the salon.

Harris watched him stride off in the direction of the bigoted, boggle-eyed box-wallah, and resumed his search for Princess Padmini. He scanned the room without success. Either she was lost behind the sea of heads or . . . or worse, Dundonald has managed to lead her away somewhere. Harris clenched his fist. The man was a rascal – a repeat offender. Harris began to edge through the crowd towards their last position, sliding inelegantly through guests, muttering 'sorry' and 'pardon me' as he did so. He wasn't to be defeated.

It was all too hot for this sort of thing. His button caught on the gauze sash of a lame-gowned Englishwoman, which he realised only after have caught her wrist and sent her drink flying. He apologised again, and then looked around for Padmini: there was still no sign of her. Dundonald was nowhere to be seen either. The cad. Harris felt his temper rising. He took out his cigarette case and lit up a Jasper & Justinian.

A flushed European woman in a long sequinned dress with what appeared to be a bird of paradise emerging from her silver turban burst into raucous laughter. Several heads looked over. Harris could not see anyone he recognised. Then he spotted the Crown Prince, Sir Sadul. He was being talked at by a pair of self-important looking Britishers – GOI by the looks of their stiff winged collars and superior expressions. Harris shook his head. Back home these people – invariably the product of middling sorts of public schools – would be grovelling their way through professions in the provinces. Out here they were lords.

He sighed. Perhaps that's what the Empire was really for? Off-shoring all the arrogant, sharp-elbowed bounders who were likely to vex one? If that was the plan it wasn't working; there were still plenty left at home.

'Harris,' said a familiar voice, and a friendly hand clapped on his shoulder. He turned:

'Drabble!' He felt himself gladden – like an Ulsterman arriving at the Pearly Gates and discovering St Peter dressed from head to toe in orange. 'By Gad, it's fantastic to see you – and who's this friendly-looking fellow?' He extended his hand to Gupta.

Gupta introduced himself.

'Ah, another historian? Just what we need,' grinned Harris, showing all his teeth. 'Right, there's someone I simply must introduce you to.' He scanned the room, looking for Padmini, but again he couldn't see her. Nor could he see Dundonald. A shadow passed across his world, like a sinister foreign body eclipsing the earth in an HG Wells story.

Drabble read his friend's mood, and Harris noted his concern –

'Not to worry,' he declared, batting on. 'Later – now, we need more drinks. Come Gupta.' He clapped his hands together and dragged them towards a turbaned waiter with a tray of drinks wider than a squash court. 'What's your poison?'

The Maharaja's feast was a ball. But in terms of promoting their investigation it was a drag. Drabble and Gupta sat together at one end of a very long table, which seated about a hundred guests on either side. The Maharaja was at the centre, flanked by Sir Sadul and a senior British diplomat, judging by the extreme frogging in gold, then the two self-important officials Harris had clocked, and then they fanned out into several other representatives of Indian princely houses, then the more eminent of the box-wallahs. Chief among these were Sharma–Smith, who sat several seats down from the Maharaja – indicating to Drabble both his enormous wealth and favour among Ganga Singh, but also in wider elite circles. The Maharaja's table setting in Delhi would certainly not ignore those niceties. Dotted among these were men were womenfolk – European wives in the main. But among their number was a handsome young Indian woman who wore a trouser suit that wouldn't have looked out of place in a Max Ernst painting or strolling along Berlin's Tiergarten. Her hair was cut to a bob, and – goodness – now you mentioned it, she was really very attractive. There was a petulant cast to her expression, too. He looked over at Harris. He was gazing at the girl – soppy eyed with a face that evinced decided adoration.

Indeed, Harris spent most of the dinner gazing like a doting canine in the girl's direction. Drabble shook his head more than once – either in despair or in the hope of discreetly drawing his attention. But it was not good. Seated next to the woman was Dundonald, he whose timely shooting had saved lives – and rather prestigious lives at that – at the unveiling. Unfortunately, though he was a good shot, he was a bad sport. No, no. Drabble did not like the cut of Dundonald's jib. Not for one second.

All the while, when not conversing with Gupta, Drabble endured torturous conversations of such stilted formality one might think one was in London. It would all be over soon.

Meanwhile he pondered Sir Randolph, whose profile he could observe six or seven chairs along. Drabble had also remembered something very important. Among the papers he had found in the cardboard box of bills and official correspondence in the back of Skinner-Chatterjee's wardrobe were payslips from the Bombay Cotton Company.

Was it seriously credible that he was materially involved in the conspiracy? He had no evidence for the fact – apart from the man's peculiar interest in the Portuguese past of Bombay and his discovery of the divorce codicil. But he had also been in Bikaner, of course, and was a confidante of the Maharaja's – which would give him privileged access to information relevant to the conspiracy. Given his name, if not his appearance, he was Anglo-Indian, which gave him something else in common with Skinner-Chatterjee.

And then there was the 1984 prediction.

And he had baulked at the 'rose' comment . . .

Oh yes, he had. In that moment, like a dog at Crufts refusing a hurdle, the man had baulked. And that signified something. And that something could surely only be the word-association itself. But it was not proof. It was little more than guesswork.

Drabble looked along the wall of overfed, over-privileged and over-bejewelled diners before him and shook his head. In truth there were many people in this room who had a stake in preserving the status quo. It was New Delhi, for God's sake. Everywhere you looked there was an imperialist or a collaborator. He glanced down the way towards Sir Randolph, seeing his angular nose, his mouth opening as a bony finger raised before it. He was definitely involved. He also had a motive that possibly explained the otherwise conflicted nature of the two attacks so far: if you want to preserve the Raj, which he most definitely did, then both Gandhi and the Viceroy – who after all is attempting to enact the British strategy of gradual withdrawal – were your foes. And why would he want to preserve the Raj? First, because he was an Anglo-Indian, his precarious status relied on the racist hierarchy of British rule without which he would be rendered neither one of us, nor one of them.

Second, it was possible that he would face economic ruin if the bonds of Britain and India were unravelled.

But this was all fine supposition. Now Drabble had to find the evidence.

'Are you looking forward to the ball?' asked the women

opposite. Her head was topped with a tall tiara that looked as if it was wearing her, rather than the other way around.

'The ball?' asked Drabble, before remembering.

The tiara rolled its eyes, and the face gave up on him for his ignorance.

'The *Viceroy's* ball,' she said, twinkling as she bobbed her head forward importantly. '*Tomorrow* night.'

After the ladies left the table, the depleted ranks of male diners reached for cigars and a broader conversational canvas, and leaned back in their seats with brandy. The Maharaja, at the centre, was surrounded by a core group of admirers, courtiers, and allies about a dozen deep. Drabble was sitting just beyond this ring of loyalty.

Harris, still seated on the far side of the Maharaja's party, looked gloomily at the empty seat beyond, occupied until recently by the young woman. Or he seemed to be daydreaming when not occasionally glowering over at Dundonald. Yes, indeed. Drabble knew it. He was mooning over the girl. Doubtless there was a story to tell, and Drabble would hear it. More than once.

Gupta stifled a yawn and was about to ask him a question, when the vacant chair to his left was withdrawn and an Indian of about 50 sat in it. He brought the chair forwards and deftly nudged his large round plastic spectacles further up his strong nose.

'I'm Panikkar,' he announced. 'I believe you were coming to visit me on Tuesday evening.'

He smiled and offered his hand. Drabble shook it and introduced Gupta.

Panikkar said, 'I've been eager to meet the man who successfully breached the palace security arrangements and then managed to escape our prison block – quite the double, even for a sahib,' he smiled and drew on a cigar the size of a carrot.

Drabble offered him a courteous bow. 'The pleasure was all mine.'

Panikkar's expression changed. 'More importantly I wanted to acknowledge your intervention at the unveiling. Perish the thought of what might have been had you not been there.'

'Or Dundonald, had he not shot the assailant.'

The older man nodded and his large eyes blinked slowly – an action magnified by the powerful lenses of his spectacles. It made them resemble specimens under the gaze of a microscope.

'I gather you saw Arbuthnot today . . .'

Drabble didn't dispute it, and waited for him to continue.

'An intriguing man, in many respects?' Drabble confirmed this with a nod; Panikkar tapped the end of his cigar on an ash-tray proffered on a silver tray borne by a waiter.

Drabble said,

'He told me that Delhi is of the opinion that there is a member of the conspiracy in Bikaner. Likely as not in the Maharaja's own circle.'

They both glanced over. Panikkar said from the corner of his mouth,

'Take your pick.'

The foreign secretary turned back to Drabble and smiled, showing his teeth. He looked over at Gupta, and acknowledged him for the second time in the exchange.

'I take it, Professor, you will be travelling back to England via Bombay?' he suggested. 'Did you know that the Maharaja has a rather superb mansion on the beach there? It's where he escapes the summer heat of Bikaner. Can't say I blame him.' Panikkar drew on the cigar and surveyed the ceiling, his pressed his fore-head thoughtfully, and then his solid fingers pressed the top of his head through his thinning hair.

He sighed:

'Reminds me – have you been introduced to Sir Randolph Sharma-Smith?' He glanced over conspiratorially. 'Fellow just speaking now. Intriguing gentleman. Rather an *explosive* tem-perament, if you get my drift? Big in Bombay, too. Big everywhere.' He pushed his spectacles up his nose. 'His family have been doing the laundry since the Mughals were in charge.' He offered a flat smile to Drabble, and began to rise from the table. 'I think I'm right in saying that his firm – the Bombay Cotton Company – is even doing the laundry for the ball tomorrow night.' He shook Drabble and Gupta's hands, and said under his voice, 'You might care to bear that in mind . . .'

He had gone before Drabble could reply. Drabble turned to Gupta and then back at Panikkar, watching him stroll down towards the other end of the table. On his way, he clapped one of the fellow diners on the shoulder and then fell into conversation briefly with Ganga Singh.

Drabble turned to Gupta. 'Did you catch that?'

A broad U-shaped smile broke out across Gupta's face.

Chapter Twenty

Drabble and Gupta alighted from the tonga and gazed up at the Indo-Gothic façade of the Bombay Cotton Company's building in old Delhi, which stood overlooking the river. It was a mansion-like structure and resembled Harrods, with ornate brickwork, columns, and domes. Yellow electric light shone in the tall windows: it was clearly a place of frenetic activity. From within came the sound of engines and machinery: smoke and steam emerged from vents, pipes and open windows. This was an operation on an industrial scale.

'I expect they work through the night,' remarked Drabble, remembering his visits to Derbyshire to see his mother's family's mill.

'Sir Randolph is famous across all India,' announced Gupta.

They passed along the front of the building, which was in darkness: the entrance to the offices was closed. Reaching the corner of the building they found a side street – unpaved and smelling strongly of excreta – but lights shone out from the interior, from tall doorways. They heard the sound of an approaching vehicle and stepped back. A van purred around the corner, and then turned cautiously into one of these entrances. Drabble and Gupta hugged the wall and proceeded.

Peering into the open doorway, Drabble saw a large hangar-like space, filled with about a dozen lemon-coloured vans: their rear doors were open awaiting cargo, and sweating Indian workers – many dressed in barely more than rags – hurried back and forth loading cases of laundry into them. The cases were the size of tea-chests and it was heavy work, especially in north of a hundred degrees Fahrenheit.

Suddenly Drabble registered the presence of a tan-uniformed overseer strolling among the workers. He was a Sikh, tall and broad-shouldered, and his height was emphasised by a high turban. A coiled whip rather incongruously hung from his belt. The arrogant expression on his bearded face said it all. Drabble muttered under his breath.

'Let me see,' declared Gupta, peering around his shoulder.

Drabble withdrew, his mind swimming with thoughts. The growl of an engine awoke him, and he yanked Gupta back – just as a van surged out and shot past them up the lane, spreading the yellow headlights over the far wall. They clung to the shadows.

Drabble ventured back to the corner and looked in again. The vans were queuing up in four bays, and being loaded with wooden chests bearing the company's logo. The porters brought the crates from doors leading off inside, and as each van was filled by five or six of these crates, its doors were slammed shut and the vehicle growled from the bay . . .

In the furthest bay, he saw, instead of a yellow van, a high-sided canvas covered military lorry had been reversed in. Here a pair of porters was lifting down a company tea-crate from its rear and doing so with great care. Drabble watched them carrying it slowly towards one of the yellow vans. They looked to be struggling under its weight – even though there were two of them on the task and they were carrying it with the sort of judicious care that one would reserve for Grandmother's finest porcelain, not tablecloths. Reaching the rear end of the small van parked next to the lorry, they set it with due effort and precision into its rear compartment, and then slid it inside. A second pair of porters then arrived with another crate from the lorry, and loaded it into the same van. One of the men then climbed in and began bracing the boxes' straps before re-emerging a minute or two later. The doors were shut, and the overseer bellowed at its driver. The van's engine started, its lights firing up, and out it went.

Drabble stepped back into the shadows as the van swept past. In the moment it was gone, he returned to the corner. The two porters were now over at the lorry again, lifting down another crate like the one before. They began to carry it over to another of the vans. Whatever was inside those boxes, was a damned sight heavier than napkins . . . or table linen for that matter. The tall Sikh went over to the lorry and did an audit of its contents, referring to his clipboard. He called over to a pair of porters and summoned them. There had to be a way in.

Drabble glanced over at Gupta. 'Can you climb a tree?'

'What?' Gupta grasped Drabble's meaning and frowned up at the side of the building. 'Is that really, absolutely necessary?'

What had he done to upset her? It must be something– otherwise there was no explanation for it. Harris checked his pocket-watch. It was a little past eleven. Everyone had turned in, more or less. Harris had, by his own admission, become somewhat lachrymose during the course of the evening and had hung about, just in case she might put in another appearance. But no. He sighed and decided to take himself off to bed.

It *was* silly, of course. Probably nothing more than a lovers' quarrel, if indeed it was that. Yet the simple fact was that he had heard nothing from Padmini since the 'end of the train' moment, and despite the joyful outcome of *that* encounter, the whole thing had played on his mind. Why had she avoided him? Had she had a change of heart? It had quite vexed him, he realised, as he looked down at his empty cigarette case. He had quite exhausted his supply of Jasper and Justinians.

But then he had returned to his room and discovered the note from her lodgèd under this door. Ah the joy. Ah the heart-lifting elation. He scanned the short letter and then pressed the letter to his mouth, closing his eyes and inhaling the rose-scented paper. Goodness. O Padmini, you do love me after all!

He re-read the note under the light one more to time, to relish the words and her unusual angular hand. 'I miss you, my love,' she gushed, making his heart surge. 'I cannot wait for us to be together again —' Nor can I, he thought, NOR CAN I! 'Meet me at midnight in the library — and we can start a new chapter, all over again!' Harris chuckled with excitement. He checked his watch: just time for a quick ciggie. He took one from the cigarette box and went to the window: O, what a world it was. O, what a life! O, what a life it was . . . his heart swelled as he contemplated Padmini. Her beauty, her intelligence, her grace, her slim legs . . .

He gathered up his stick and trod carefully along the corridor, making great pains not to disrupt the silence of the night. The marble floors were solid — there were no unfortunate floorboards — oft the bane of a young bachelor's in England — but there was the distance and relative gloom to contend with. Following the mighty baroque balustrade, he reached the top of the stairs and the banister— which he cradled as he descended in near darkness. After some forty or so stairs, he hand arrived at the mighty newel post, a vast alabaster pepper grinder.

There were some lights on downstairs, presumably for staff who would still be tidying up. He moved quickly, pleased not to have been detected and reaching the door of what he hoped was the library, was pleased to confirm it as such and get the door opened and closed behind him with minimal auditory alarm. A low lamp had been left on in the room, presumably for the benefit of any guests who found themselves unable to sleep, and his eye fell upon one or two of the broad sofas that might do nicely for the assignation that was to follow. He rubbed his hands together in anticipation and looked about for a drinks trolley.

Then he noticed a narrow doorway between the bookshelves: lined with books it led into a recessed library space that was in darkness and was easy to miss. It gave him an idea. He slid into the small alcove and waited.

Just then, the door of the library opened – the latch scraped the lock as though whomever had opened it had pushed the door fractionally too soon. He held his breath. He would let Padmini come into the room, and settle, just as he did, before surprising her. The question was, how *precisely* would he surprise her? Should he leap out? H'm. That might cause her to scream, which would not be optimal. Mind you, she did not strike him as a screamer. Not like that, anyway. Perhaps he should cough, or make a low animal sound, something that might alarm her gently. That was it, he would make a low growl like small dog – a Pekingese, for instance. Yes, something yappy. Getting into character, he raised up his hands like paws and prepared to unleash his best canine impersonation . . .

'Is everything in readiness?' asked a voice. It was male, Indian-accented, and certainly did not belong to Padmini. Harris dropped his paws and cut short his breath.

'Very nearly,' replied another voice, this time English. And Harris recognised immediately. It was Dundonald. Blast it. He knew the cove was up to something. He always had. Harris clenched his fist and resolved to act. 'Amrit has confirmed that the vans have been loaded and are being conveyed to the Viceroy's House as we speak.'

'Excellent,' replied the first voice, with repellent, villainous gloating that made Harris's lips squish together like he was at panto – and for air to rush through his teeth –

'What was that?'

It was Dundonald – a torch light shot through the gap in the doorway. Harris looked back but all he could see was darkness. He looked back at the light, which was growing in intensity, and – panic rising – hurried into the pitch black passage, his hands out before him.

'HARRIS,' hissed Dundonald, as the light swept over him and projected his shadow along the floor beyond. 'Stop right there –' Harris heard the metallic sound of a revolver being cocked behind him. He started to turn.

Just then there were new footsteps: and the electric lights were switched on. Harris knew this was Padmini.

'Sir Randolph,' he heard her declare. There was surprise in her voice, and disquiet. 'What's going on here?'

Before he could shout a warning, he heard a thud – the dull impact of a dense object striking something solid, like a bag of sugar hitting concrete from a first floor window. It was followed by the deeper sound of Padmini's body landing on the floor.

Harris clenched his fist and glared at Dundonald.

'You'll regret that, you cur,' he hissed.

'Not before you do.' Dundonald holstered his Webley revolver and pulled out a stout wooden truncheon, and without hesitating struck Harris across the forehead. As the pain registered in his frontal lobes. Harris's knees failed him – and everything immediately went black.

Drabble looked up. The moon was large and milky in the inky black sky. He had got his hands up to the stone ledge and left behind the security of the cast-iron drain pipe, his left foot finding solace on a gargoyle's horned head. There was a great deal to be said for neo-Gothic architecture, and when you threw in pipes and other industrial protrusions, it became even more accommodating.

Drabble reached the second floor of the Bombay Cotton Company's palace, where a window was cracked open enough for him to slip in his arm and haul himself over the ledge. He climbed inside, and then looked down and saw Gupta about half way between his position and the ground. The historian had made good progress to the first floor window, where a wide ledge offered sanctuary, but had been unable to clear the rather challenging overhang leading to the second. That was fair enough. Drabble had conquered harder overhangs thousands of feet higher, but that didn't make it any easier for the newbie.

'Use the gargoyles,' he cried in hoarse whisper. 'I'll be right –'

Drabble noticed the tall overseer stride out into the lane, the light from the delivery area casting a mighty shadow of him on the wall of the adjacent building. He looked around suspiciously, perhaps he had heard something – Drabble froze – and then stalked back inside.

Drabble lowered himself into the darkened room – a vast office, from what he could tell, with rows and rows and carols, on which were set tall typewriters. It was a typing pool – perhaps the very one that Skinner-Chatterjee had worked in. His eyes adjusted to the low light and he skirted the edge of a row and followed the middle aisle all the way to the end. Here, in increasing darkness, he eased open the door leading to a corridor within. It was all in complete darkness. He would have to do his best. Taking long, light steps he hugged the wall, and hoped he would find what he was looking for – a way down. He counted his steps and proceeded with care. He reached a corner some twelve paces further along, and then moved in a ninety degree angle in a perpendicular direction from the one he begun on. The darkness began to lessen – it might have been his imagination – and then he saw the light. It radiated from a staircase leading down to the next storey. Bingo.

He was at the top of the flight of stairs. He stopped and listened. There was nothing. Nothing, apart from the distant sound of heavy machinery that he had heard from outside. That must presumably have been part of the boiling or washing mechanism of this vast factory laundry. His heart was pounding as he descended slowly, carefully taking each dark step at a time. The noise of machinery intensified and he saw down over the floor to which below. It was a clerical area, like the upper storey, but the middle was an open gallery which looked down upon the brightly lit distribution area. From up here he could see over the top of a high internal wall, beyond which were industrial washing facilities, with the four production lines of vats, boilers, and dryers, constantly lost and then reappearing amid clouds of steam.

The air thickened with the smell of detergent and soap, rinsing his nostrils. Drabble remembered Gupta, almost certainly still trapped on the first floor . . .

He saw the overseer stride across the loading area; now he carried a black metal box, rather like a travel typewriter case. He slotted this into the back of one of the last remaining yellow vans, next to a tea crate and then closed up its doors. He slammed on its roof and shouted over to the cab of the military lorry, as he paced around and got into the van's passenger side. The lorry's diesel engine fired into life and growled, spewing out a choking black exhaust. It surged from the building into the dark lane. The overseer's van, purring into life, followed it out.

They were too late. Drabble hurried back and found Gupta: he had reached the window on the second floor. Drabble heaved him inside.

'I thought you'd forgotten me,' he protested, recovering his breath. 'I saw the lorry go – have we missed the boat, Professor?'

'I fear we ma –' Drabble led them from the office and out to the gallery. He saw immediately that all was not lost. Looking down, the loading area was bright and now largely deserted. One last van stood waiting for a delivery, its doors open.

'Come on, then,' grinned Drabble. He motioned to the van and took down one of the yellow company caps that the drivers wore. 'There's only one way to find out what's in those boxes . . .'

The yellow Bombay Cotton Company van spat into the dirty lane, its dim headlamps transforming it into a narrow tunnel of light. They skidded into the main road at full tilt. Drabble was at the wheel. Gupta wore a company cap and was threading his arms into the sleeves of a Bombay Cotton Company shop-coat. The van bounced along the unmade road, and veered. Drabble jerked the steering wheel.

'These potholes are rather serious,' he exclaimed.

'Yes,' whimpered Gupta as his head collided with the roof of the cabin. 'I blame the authorities.'

The headlamps captured the tasselled flanks of a camel surging

231

into the middle of the road; several others cantered beyond. 'Hell's teeth,' Drabble swore as he stabbed the brakes and swerved to miss. 'Camels.'

'Dromedaries, as a matter of fact,' interjected Gupta, bracing himself against the dashboard. 'Camels have two humps.'

They bounded over the ridge of a pothole at speed – both of them got air in their seats. The van landed hard.

Drabble jammed his foot to the floor, and they overtook several tongas, and carts, and then a rickshaw on the corner. He snatched the wheel, as a police car came screaming towards them the other way. Their wing mirrors clipped.

Drabble shouted to be heard over the straining engine:

'If my guess is right. Those vans were heading straight for the Viceroy's House.'

'How can you be so sure?'

Drabble looked over.

'That's what we're going to have to find out.'

He was satisfied there was enough evidence to support the move. Between Arbuthnot's reaction to Sharma-Smith, and then the man's own behaviour on the terrace, not to mention Panikkar's unsolicited intervention after dinner which had led them here – this was a worthy avenue of investigation. Obviously they would have some explaining to do if they were caught. But then that was a small price to pay.

Drabble flicked the wheel and overtook a slow-moving pair of rickshaws. Coming the other way was a open bus; he swerved the van back into their lane, coming in close to the rickshaw-wallahs who shouted at him in protest.

They hit the ridge of another pothole and the van jarred violently.

Drabble swore.

'If you don't mind my commenting,' remarked Gupta, 'I think you might want to conserve our tyres, even at the expense of arriving a few minutes later. After all the ball isn't till tomorrow night.'

Drabble eased his foot back off the accelerator.

Then he shook his head and stabbed his foot back to the floor.

'What is it?' cried Gupta. He was wide-eyed, and the van jolted violently on another bump. Drabble gripped the wheel, his knuckles whitened.

'If you were planting a bomb,' he thundered, 'might you be tempted to detonate it sooner rather than later, in order to reduce detection time?'

Slowly Gupta looked over, as though he hadn't quite heard: 'Who on earth said anything about a bomb?'

Chapter Twenty-one

Drabble and Gupta shot along the Kingsway and passed under the India Gate. Glowing lamp-posts lit the route of the highway at the far end of which – roughly two miles away – stood the Viceroy's House, the symbol of British dominion in India.

If there were an explosive device in the building, and if it were detonated tonight, then the Viceroy and the Vicereine were both in considerable danger – quite apart from their domestic and household staff, the senior equerries and ladies-in-waiting and so on. Drabble felt his mouth going dry. Depending on the size of the charge, an explosion could kill the best part of a thousand people, some of them the most pivotal individuals responsible for the administration of the Raj.

And that was just the start. Imagine what would happen if such an atrocity were achieved. Uprisings might be expected elsewhere, copycat bombings might be inspired, and there would be reprisals by the authorities – quite possibly from outraged hardliners. Think back to Amritsar in 1919 and multiply it. Bumping off a constable in some remote hill station was one thing, but blowing up the King-Emperor's representative in India along with his wife while they were abed was quite another. As Harris would doubtless remark, it's just not cricket.

He glanced over at Gupta; the poor fellow's face was full of dread. As well it might be. The doctor caught Drabble's look, and said: 'These are dangerous men, are they not? What can a couple of seventeenth-century historians hope to achieve in the face of such desperados?'

Drabble changed gear at the roundabout and the van's engine revved powerfully. They followed the broad road around the left side of the palace complex, hoping it would lead them to a service entrance. Much of the looming structure was now in darkness, save for the occasional light from a burning beacon, lamp-post or window. Drabble took a deep breath. He was exhausted but the imminence of their arrival gave him the jolt of adrenaline. Somewhat after the event, he found himself registering Gupta's pessimistic declaration. 'Don't worry doctor,' he replied. 'We have the element of surprise – and *that* is everything.'

Gupta frowned gloomily. 'It didn't help Tipu Sultan.'

Up on the right he saw a break in the high railings and a lay-by with two striped sentry boxes. Drabble pulled over, stuck his head out of the window, and barked,

'Delivery.'

The young British army soldier had already clocked the van, and took one look at Drabble before stepping back and waving them on. The barrier went up, Drabble lifted the clutch, and they slipped along the driveway between rows of palm trees, tyres crunching over gravel, towards the dark outline of the palace.

The road snaked through the trees, skirting several low buildings, most in darkness. Suddenly the vista opened up, the fronds of the palms parted, and they were at the rear entrance of the palace: four or five doors were opened, with bright light shining out from within. Native porters rushed back and forth with deliveries from vans and lorries. A European commissionaire, clipboard in arm, stepped out from the melee and held his hand up – commanding them to halt. Drabble stopped and his face leaned in to the window – the generous white moustaches of a man in his late fifties. He was a Londoner.

'Did you get lost?' he cried, clocking Drabble. 'Right, round to the side with you – no need to traipse this lot through the kitchens. There's an entrance to the ballroom on the north-west corner. Go on. We've two 'undred tables to set before morning.'

They left the din of the kitchen bay, and drove in darkness now along the palmed lane that evidently led to the far side. Gupta broke the silence:

'What are we going to do when we get there?'

Drabble glanced over. 'Have a look around – see what's what.' He fired the doctor a reassuring smile. 'Did you notice if there was anything in the back?'

A pair of bright headlights shone directly at them, forcing Drabble to shield his eyes and pull over. A yellow Bombay Cotton Company van swept past, followed by another – and then another passed. Its driver waved and Drabble nodded in return.

They took the next right turn and arrived at a small paved parking area. A single wall-mounted light showed a two of sets of double doors that were set low in the red brickwork. Drabble and Gupta took an armful of table linen each – enough to plausibly argue one's presence – and headed straight for the doors, which were three steps below ground level.

Drabble cracked the door open and looked inside: the service space was lit with wall lights, spaced at regular intervals travelling off left and right along a broad corridor. Another corridor went directly ahead under the heart of the building. Pipes and cabling crowded the walls and interrupted the line of the ceiling. From here, what might resemble neo-classical take on Indian architecture on the outside, more closely resembled the service decks on a ship. And there was something else – besides the smell of disinfectant and the ubiquity of grey paint – there was a hum, a low drone of machinery, a note that might go almost unnoticed until you noticed it. Then you would struggle to get it from your ears.

If you were going to hide a bomb, where would you put it, if you wanted maximum bang for your buck? In a building such as this – one quite so large – you would reasonably need to place it relatively close to the intended targets of your attack. To ensure success, that is. That much was obvious.

Drabble glanced at Gupta and motioned towards the passage-way heading into the midst of the building.

He wasn't sure there was any point in carrying the linen any more, but neither of them was yet ready to relinquish the best first line of defence from enquiry.

Anonymous doorways led off in either direction, none appearing particularly meritorious of investigation. Drabble hurried. Gupta panted beneath the weight of table linen.

'Where do we even start, Drabble?'

Just as the question weighed in the air – and Drabble wondered quite how he would answer it – a staircase hoved into view. The steps were covered in green linoleum and led up to a mezzanine level above – where they could see a pair of double doors.

Drabble went up, and listened at them carefully, then – hearing nothing – eased one open. He was at the far end of a vast ballroom; twelve magnificent chandeliers hung from an ornate mosaiced ceiling, emphasising the sheer scale of the room. Beneath their glare servants were spreading tablecloths and laying scores of tables – they glittered with glassware and golden plates and dishes. Here and there stood vases sprouting great exotic flowers in bright tropical colours. This, clearly, was to be an immense gathering of truly imperial proportions.

Gupta arrived at Drabble's side, and gasped at the sight. The nearest table had been laid: a golden figurine of a Greek god or similar was the centrepiece, with fourteen gilded seats around it. Drabble took in the room: there must be fifty to sixty tables – including a long top table at the far end. All told that room would seat more than eight hundred. Maybe a thousand. He plucked up the menu standing on the table nearest: it showed the date, and introduced the jamboree: The H.E. Viceroy's Imperial Gymkhana Ball.

He inspected the menu – noticed that the third course as a cheese soufflé – and set it down. A sense of foreboding was over-hauling him. His eyes travelled from the cream card, along the maroon table cloth, and descended to the polished floorboards: somewhere – presumably down there in the bowels of this building where they had come from – was the means to blow this entire shooting match into the stratosphere. Just imagine. Accomplish that and you would be eradicating, at a stroke the elite strata of the government of India. Say what you like about the Raj, say what you like about the injustice of it, but that was a ticket for anarchy and prolonged bloodshed. Christ alive.

Suddenly there was a shout: 'Oi! You!'

Drabble looked up: a red-faced Englishman of medium height, arms lifted in uproar, marched towards him.

In a moment, Drabble realised that he, as an European, quite possibly had no business being dressed in the uniform of an employee of the Bombay Cotton Company – and certainly not doing anything quite so menial as carrying around table linen. Furthermore, he knew that no amount of explanation would resolve the logical inconsistency of his position. He looked over at Gupta and hissed: 'Run – *now!*'

Drabble hurled the bundle of linen in his arms at the soldier – glimpsed the dense pile collide with him – and leapt for the double doors. He galloped down the stairs, three steps at a time, half dragging the Indian academic with him.

'Come on, Gupta,' he cried, veering right along the corridor. 'We don't have time for officialdom.'

As he spoke he heard a loud blast on a policeman's whistle. Just what they needed.

Drabble raced ahead, pipes and wiring flying by in a blur. They needed an escape route from the corridor – somewhere to hide or better still to lead them to wherever the bomb might have been placed. Gupta panted behind him, catching his breath. There had to be somewhere to run to . . . They passed a stair-case, which would have led back up to the ballroom.

'OI, YOU!' cried the apoplectic voice. 'Stop where you ARE!'

Drabble didn't look back: the end of the corridor approached. Here there was another choice: left – he presumed towards the exterior of the structure – or right, towards the middle of the building. He ducked right, swinging his arms as he opened up into a full sprint. Seconds later his eyes zeroed in a manhole that lay dead ahead. He broke step, decelerating rapidly; Gupta almost tumbled over him. They had perhaps five seconds.

Drabble levered open the cast iron cover: metal steps led into darkness.

Gupta slipped into the hole. Drabble followed and dropped the cover, leaving them in darkness. He hurried down the rungs after Gupta, and found the ground some eight or nine steps down. Gupta was there, breathing heavily.

Footsteps clanged over the cover above them.

'Keep moving,' said Drabble. 'I don't suppose you've got any matches?'

Above them, they heard a metallic scrape, and light flooded in – they stepped back into the shadows.

'I know where you vermin are,' shouted the guard with a tentative ecstasy. 'And you ain't going nowhere,' he crowed. 'Not now anyway.' He slammed the cover down, plunging them in darkness. Drabble cleared his throat. He could hear Gupta breathing heavily.

Above they heard the sound of scraping, and then Drabble figured it out; it was the sound of a heavy object being dragged across the manhole cover.

'That's just what we needed,' announced Drabble. 'A jobs-worth. Gupta, tell me you've got a pack of matches on you . . .'

To Drabble's relief, Gupta did have matches, and they were not in a sewer. There was not even a whiff of excreta, which given where they were was pretty surprising. It did beg the question of quite what the purpose of this underground service tunnel *was*. Looking at the dark brickwork, illuminated from a flaming Bombay Cotton Company cap, the space certainly could have been a sewer.

'We should look on the bright side,' said Drabble under his breath.

'And what bright side is that exactly?' asked Gupta.

'We could be knee-high in shit – or being marched off to a prison cell.'

Gupta sighed. 'There's still plenty of time for either eventuality.'

Drabble chuckled. 'I'm beginning to like you, Gupta: you have a fine streak of optimism.'

'There is a third eventuality of course,' added Gupta. 'The bomb has already been set up, and will be set off before we can actually find it. Then we will either be killed outright in the blast or buried in masonry.'

Drabble stripped off his yellow coat and handed it to Gupta.

'Be a good fellow and tear the arm off that, will you?'

They advanced in silence, they were approaching another cast iron cover overhead.

'What are you looking for?' asked Gupta. Drabble heard the sound of tearing fabric.

'I'm exactly not sure,' he said, arriving at a door. 'But I'm sure we'll know it when we see it.'

He reached down to the steel door handle and turned it . . .

Chapter Twenty-two

Harris became aware of himself. It wasn't a nice feeling. To begin with he wasn't quite sure that he liked what he found. In fact, he was certain he didn't. First, he felt sick, a little at least. And then he recalled that he was stirring from a forced slumber. His jaw ached for some reason, and, yes, his head – he stopped moving his jaw because it pulled at the tender skin on his scalp – hurt. A lot. He had also been drooling, which was never a good sign.

Harris's eyes started to find their feet: he was in a large concrete-floored room, a storeroom if he didn't know better. The ceiling was low, and there were electric lights along the bare brick walls. The place seemed to be filled with various boxes. He sighed. What had he got himself into?

He looked down and saw that he was seated in a wooden chair. He couldn't see his arms, he realised, then noted that they were tied together behind him. Another bad sign. He leant forward and made visual confirmation of the fact that his feet were lashed to the front legs of the chair at his ankles. That was all distinctly suboptimal. If he had to be a prisoner, it would at least be civilised to be able to smoke.

And once again Drabble was nowhere to be seen. As usual. His mind returned to the incidents of the December before, when Drabble had managed to be absent while Harris was on the receiving end of a run of disobliging treatments. Typical Ernest, he concluded. Always ruddy well turning up late to take the glory . . .

In that moment, the events immediately preceding this involuntary loss of consciousness flooded back. That's right. Dundonald, the cove, came at him with a wooden truncheon of all things. What a ruddy thug.

And the cheek of it. It's one thing to have a disagreement with a fellow and to resort to fisticuffs. But it's quite another to raise a bloody bludgeon against him – as though he were some common footpad or other. That was too much.

A sudden realisation interrupted this bitter assessment. What about Padmini? He had heard her voice just before that cove had smote his own head and knocked him out. Whatever had happened to her? He cast around quickly for her . . . but instead of the beautiful princess his gaze settled on the half a dozen or so tea crates arranged at the centre of the room. They had been levered open and various red and black wires protruded from them. His gaze followed the jumbles of wires along the floor and over to a trestle table on top of which sat an unusual-looking metal box.

His eyes darted back to the tea crate closest to him – at the pair of red and black cables that spiralled from its top, and then travelled along the floor. He looked over. Cables led from a metal box on the table back down onto the floor to a squat rectangular battery, the sort of thing one might find in a tractor requiring a particularly exorbitant level of electric charge. Additional cables led from other tea cases. In all there were six. What on earth could all this lot be . . . for? And what part did the battery play? His eye went back to the metal box on the table – he spotted a lever on it, that stirred a worrying thought. He looked over at the tea crates. He'd wager they didn't contain Darjeeling, Orange Pekoe, or Assam. No indeed. He now noticed they were branded with the words, 'Bombay Cotton Company'. They didn't look like they contained bed linen either.

The name was familiar to him, for some reason. And then it came to him: Sir Randolph bloody Sharma-Smith.

The bastards. He looked back at the crates, the cabling, the lever and the battery. He was no expert but . . . *this looked very bad indeed*.

That was it. Harris looked up at the heavens – or rather, the low ceiling. Sir Randolph was going to blow up all the fat people . . . No, no, that's not it. Surely not. He looked over at the wires, the battery – that lever. No, that *was* it. Oh, Lord. It had to be stopped . . .

'PADMINI!' he cried, the word aggressing from him, like a dog having a stick yanked from its jaws.

Behind him he heard a muffled voice: Padmini?

She sounded sleepy, drowsy perhaps. He pressed his feet to the ground and pushed up in a bid to pitch the chair around. He was partly successful, then tried again. Pivoting around he saw her, bound like him to a chair, and sporting a bright, peacock-hued black eye. His fists clenched and he hollered, 'Dundonald, you bastard! Where are you? DUNDONALD?'

Harris's head fell; crushed with pain and a sudden thumping headache. He swore under his breath. And then he struggled to lift his head to Padmini. He saw her; she looked pitiful, but curiously defiant – uncowed by the ungentlemanly attack on her. Hear, hear, thought Harris as he noticed that her mouth was filled with a handkerchief – one of his own, to make matters worse – which rendered her attempts to speak dull muffles.

He clenched his fists. By Christ, Dundonald was going to pay for this outrage on Padmini's honour. Look at her; his poor, dear, darling Padmini, reduced to this! Harris suddenly remembered his walking stick – one of the finest he could buy, and with his foot injury essential. Ah, his hand metaphorically went to his chest, he saw it propped by the wall. Thank goodness. He couldn't go anywhere without *that*.

'So you are awakened, Sir Percival,' declared a dry, Indian-accented voice. Harris recognised it at once to belonging to Sharma-Smith. Rage erupted from him:

'Now listen here, you dratted cur, you despicable, scrawny wretch –'

243

Sir Randolph stepped nonchalantly into view, just as Harris's voice reached exit velocity. 'You abominable turncoat!' he bellowed. 'You jumped up, power-crazed, fat-loathing box-wallah. I don't care what you do to me – I am I dare say deserving of whatever fate you enact - but Princess Padmini is innocent; furthermore she is of noble, royal Rajput stock and I demand she be released this instant. *This instant*. DO YOU HEAR ME?'

Sharma-Smith rolled his eyes. He wore a beige suit with a stand-up collar, and a slightly long tunic in the Indian style. It almost had a military bearing, such was its Spartan beigeness. He raised his hand to command Harris's silence.

But the journalist kept going. He saw Sharma-Smith's hand fall, like that of a starting official at a race deprived of his pistol, and felt a sudden jolt to the back of his head . . .

The door was locked and Drabble did not think it worth forcing. 'We can always come back,' he said to Gupta. 'Come on.'

They moved along and before long reached another door. Drabble tried this one. It was also locked.

'Pretty soon that British soldier will arrive, having followed us,' panted Gupta. 'I fear Professor, that we have been misled. Regardless of the unusually heavy and I confess suspicious-looking boxes we observed, there may be no plot. Panikkar might have it wrong.'

Drabble took half a step back, and kicked the door before him as hard as he could. It flew open – its lock shooting from the door, and scattering across the floor inside. Drabble stepped forwards after it, holding aloft the burning torch. Nothing. Just an empty storeroom. 'Christ,' he swore.

He hurried on. He had taken perhaps a hundred steps since first entering the tunnel network. They had passed two large storerooms, which must have been situated beneath the grand ballroom, but they must soon – if not already – be passing the end of the room. If the bomber was planning to take out the ballroom tomorrow night, then this was the sweet spot. If he was going to explode his bombs sooner, then closer to the centre of the structure would be preferable.

But Gupta *was* right. The guards would soon be upon them, too. They could not go back now, for fear of running right into them. The only route for them, probably, was to take the next available set of steps and return to the floor above and hope to evade whoever was there. They might then double back and make it to the van and escape. That was one possible plan.

The corridor now bent back the other way – meaning this was the end of the line. Then Drabble saw it: a door that had a light shining from under it. He stopped. It was definitely a light – a low yellow glow that could not be denied. He doused the torch:

'Gupta!'

The doctor fell in beside in.

Drabble gripped the door handle and sprang into the room. He saw Dundonald stepping back from Harris, who was out cold, his head hanging limply forward. Next he spotted the diminutive frame of Sharma-Smith and saw him turn towards them – the outline of his bony head emphasised by the clean lines of his dark brown, minimalist suit.

'Professor Drabble,' he called, exultant. Drabble saw he had a silver pistol in his hand, trained on them. 'Come in.' He motioned with the gun. 'Doctor, shut the door please. Did you grow up in a barn?'

Sharma-Smith approached Drabble.

'Don't think I won't shoot because of the guards. I will,' declared Sharma-Smith. 'I can shoot you dead *and* set the fuses on these explosives in five minutes flat – and be gone before anybody is any the wiser.'

His eyes glinted voraciously, like a starving man glimpsing a banquet table. 'I know,' he said, 'quite impressive for a Eurasian box-wallah of indeterminate Portuguese, British, and Indian ancestry.'

Well, Arbuthnot had said the man was of Portuguese descent – notwithstanding the Smith, which was doubtless garnered in the two and a half centuries since the Brits had displaced the Portuguese, Drabble thought.

Sharma-Smith gestured with his gun towards a pair of chairs by the wall. 'Dundonald,' he said. 'Restrain Drabble and Gupta. If they begin to make any noise knock them out. Don't hold back.'

Dundonald forced Drabble into a seat and quickly began to bind his wrists. Sharma-Smith offered a satisfied smirk: 'The time of fat white sahibs is fast coming to an end in India – one way or another. Your culture has glutted itself and become obese. Let the purge begin.'

Dundonald yanked the rope at Drabble's wrists with excessive force, tying them to the legs of the chair. They were locked. He moved on to Gupta, as Sharma-Smith announced:

'We have enough TNT here to blow Lutyens' dome not just to smithereens but to Darjeeling. And as the dust settles the English will either come to their senses and remember themselves – inflamed by indignation and rage – and avenge themselves upon the Marxists and nationalists who they believe perpetrated this abhorrent act of naked aggression on the capital of this empire – or they will fail. My hope is that the English will be saved from themselves. Perhaps the sound of the explosion will be loud enough to wake your leaders in London and restore them to their senses.'

'And what if it doesn't. What if the fat white sahibs just decide to call it a day? What then? The likes of you – the slighted and overlooked not-quite-Indians – will be in the worst position. Neither them nor us, your communities will suffer most, no? The British won't have you. The Indians don't want you.'

'Don't worry, Drabble,' Dundonald cut in, 'we're not going anywhere. If London does throw in the towel, there's enough of us left to make a damned good fist of it. And we'll jolly well go down fighting if we have to.'

'You mean like poor Miss Skinner-Chatterjee has already?'

Dundonald's face flashed with anger. Sharma-Smith cleared his throat and eyed him. 'If all else fails, Drabble, as you yourself said, we have an insurance policy. The Portuguese have always been trustworthy – and we can always do with stout souls like Captain Dundonald here.'

Dundonald finished securing ties around Gupta's wrists and went to the fuse box, where he began checking the cabling. Drabble knew they didn't have long.

He cried,

'Your insurance policy isn't worth the paper it's written on, Randolph. It's a fake – and even if it weren't, it still wouldn't carry any weight. If you think the Portuguese are going to attempt to assert their rights, you've got another thing coming.'

Sharma-Smith glanced at his wristwatch.

'I wouldn't be so sure about that, Drabble,' he declared. 'You may discover that five million Portuguese have got more gumption than forty million Britishers put together.'

'Be that as it may, Randolph – you and your followers will be dead long before Lisbon can come to your rescue. Enough of the right people suspect what you're up to . . . Panikkar, Arbuthnot . . .'

Sharma-Smith's nostrils flared. 'Enough,' he snapped. 'By the time they've finished picking up the pieces of the Raj's exploded ruling class, the next phase of my plan will be in force. Dundonald?' he declared, checking his wristwatch again. Dundonald looked up from the fuse box and nodded. He was making final adjustments.

'What about Choudhury?' barked Drabble, eyeing Harris. He still wasn't moving.

Sharma-Smith looked back.

'What do you think? The Left can be bought like everyone

else.' He chuckled contemptuously. 'As it happens, they're a good deal cheaper.'

'So he *was* part of your conspiracy?'

'No. He was simply a useful idiot, like so many on the Left. Dundonald?'

'One second, sir —'

Sharma-Smith sighed, 'You see, Professor, it is amazing what you can get for 50,000 rupees, especially from a committed Marxist. It's just a disappointment to me that poor Comrade Choudhury was seemingly incapable of achieving his mission, even with the help of the late Miss Skinner-Chatterjee.' He shook his head. 'If he had, we should not have had to go to all of this trouble, and we'd already be free of Mr Gandhi.'

'Who else is involved? Colonel Stewart, Pagefield . . . Arbuthnot?'

Sharma-Smith simply shook his head, rather as if the question were beneath him, and looked to Dundonald, who was awaiting his command.

'Do it now,' said Sharma-Smith, checking his watch again.

'Yes, sir.'

Dundonald pushed the lever over; there was the whisper of a metallic rasp, and the timer started ticking.

The two men headed towards the door, which scraped opened. The tall Sikh overseer from the factory entered, bowing his head to pass under the doorway. Satisfaction arrived on Sharma-Smith's face.

'Amrit,' he declared warmly, before breaking into Hindi. He spoke fast – Drabble caught a word or two, half-remembered from childhood – it was clear that the man was receiving a set of instructions. At length he gave a deep bow, and Sharma-Smith and Dundonald left. Amrit bolted the door after them and then stood in front of it, his arms folded. A sentinel of doom.

★

Drabble stared over at the purring timer – the small hand progressed very slowly anticlockwise towards twelve o'clock. He called over to Gupta.

'Does this man really intend to die here with us?'

Gupta looked at Amrit and suddenly broke into Hindi.

Amrit stood motionless, like a soldier standing to attention outside Buckingham Palace. Gupta shook his head.

Drabble cursed. He didn't need a translation. 'I'm sorry, Doctor. This is all my fault.'

'You can't take the credit for everything,' grinned Gupta. 'Do you know how long we have left?'

Drabble strained his head around to get a better angle on the timer.

'I can't see it.'

'About five and a half minutes,' declared Padmini, as she finishing spitting out Harris's handkerchief. 'Dundonald set it to six minutes –'

Gupta burst into Hindi again – now shouting, pleading with Amrit. But again the man didn't even acknowledge the appeal. He stood unmoved, unflinching, his arms folded and his face fixed with stoic finality.

Christ alive. Drabble felt beads of cold sweat trickle down from his armpit, down his side. He pulled at his wrists straining until the muscles in his arms burned, but Dundonald's ropework locked them fast. He glanced around the room once more: Harris out cold; the woman battered and tied; Gupta as much use as himself. What were they going to do? How the dickens were they going to get out of this? Rather more importantly to the world at large, how were they going to prevent the two thousand occupants of this building getting wiped out by this bomb?

'TEETH!' He lurched forward. 'Come on, Gupta!' He sprang forward again, using his toes and throwing his head and chest forward, pecking forward and gaining inches with the chair each time. 'We can use our teeth. Come on!' he yelled, gaining another couple of inches towards the fuse box.

Gupta followed suit, bucking forward in his chair and roaring in determination.

'I'm coming!'

Padmini saw what they were doing and started towards the fuse box . . .

Amrit broke into laughter and shook his head at them. But as they made progress, he stepped forward: he grabbed Drabble just as he closed on the table and flung him backwards, somer-saulting. Drabble landed hard on the chair and cried as the wooden frame splintered under his weight.

Amrit turned and kicked out – stabbing his foot into Gupta's chest. The doctor flew backwards like he was on rails and then went over.

Padmini got her mouth to a red cable and began to yank at it from the battery –

Amrit seized her shoulder and span her round, and silenced her with a ferocious slap.

Drabble was on his back, his chest heaving. The chair was shattered beneath him with his legs still attached to its legs. Inside him something was crying in pain – it was not just the chair that had broken in the fall. He heard Gupta groan and saw him lying on his side, blood streaked across his face. Padmini was silent – Amrit began dragging her and her chair away from the fuses. Her body looked limp. The Sikh was methodical, you had to say that for him. Harris was still out cold, his face cast in faintly infantile expression that made Drabble wonder if he'd taken a severe hit to the head.

Drabble wrestled his hands free from the broken chair-legs, wrenching the rope bindings with him, – and sprang from the floor, dragging pieces of the chair with him. He leaped up onto Amrit's back, throwing his hands around the man's neck. Amrit roared: he gripped Drabble by the wrists, suddenly making him the prisoner again, and charged backwards, slamming Drabble against the wall. Once, then twice – then a third time. Drabble cried out in pain and collapsed to the floor gasping for air.

Amrit chuckled and rubbed his hands together. This was all too easy for him. He strode back over to the table and stood guard in front of the fuse box.

'I say,' announced Harris, looking about him and clocking Amrit. 'This isn't the Granville. I could have sworn I was in the long bar . . .'

Amrit watched Drabble get to his feet. Drabble knew he was watching him still as he ferreted out a decent wedge of timber from the shattered remnants of the chair and weighed it in his hands. It was better than nothing. He looked up – the Sikh grinned and beckoned Drabble forward with a twitch of the fingers.

'Four minutes left,' cried Padmini. Amrit glanced over . . .

Drabble lunged with the chair leg, striking the big man. It almost bounced off him. Drabble scuttled backwards. Amrit surged forwards, overstepping Drabble and snatching hold of the end of the leg, which he threw off into the air.

'My stick,' bleated Harris, coming to his senses. 'My walking stick!'

Drabble dived for Harris's stick, rolling out of Amrit's grasp. Despite his size he moved quickly. Scampering from his reach, Drabble weighed the stick in its hand. In itself it was useless, but . . .

Amrit charged.

Drabble dragged the pommel free from the stick, drawing out a two-feet long blade, which flashed in the light just in time to pierce Amrit's sternum. The point broke Amrit's charge; he halted and seized Drabble by the throat. His hands clamped around Drabble's neck and squeezed. He began to smile.

'Three minutes,' cried Padmini with effort. From the corner of his eye Drabble caught movement. Gupta was crawling towards the battery. But he was never going to get there in time.

Unable to draw breath, Drabble felt his strength draining away. He roared but it came out as a whimper – and rammed the blade home with all his might. Amrit grimaced – showing a fine

251

set of cream-coloured teeth – and his eyes narrowed as if he'd just eaten a particularly tart lemon. But his grip did not flinch.

Drabble was fading fast. He gave up on the sword and began pulling desperately at Amrit's powerful wrists. They were like cricket bats. It was no good. Drabble felt himself weakening. Amrit's smile widened, showing yet more creamy white teeth. Then his face started to fade . . .

'The pommel,' panted Harris. 'Drabble,' he shouted, 'THE POMMEL!'

'Two and a half minutes,' cried Padmini.

Drabble's eyes blinked open and looked down at the pommel of the sword stick, spying a notch in the brass design. It was a lid. He summoned his last strength, flipped it back, and then walloped the whole caboodle upwards, towards Amrit's face. A brown cloud of snuff filled the air between them and Amrit threw his head back in agony, staggering. Drabble's nose erupted in a spasm of spiced tobacco but he knew it was coming. He filled his lungs and then lunged towards Amrit, seizing the swordstick.

'AHHHttchew!' Amrit sneezed powerfully – in a different context it would have whipped up petticoats – and his head snapped forward . . . onto the point of Drabble's sword. It struck him dead centre of the forehead. His eyes blinked, and then flickered shut. The giant collapsed to the floor.

'Two minutes!' Drabble, gasping for air, sneezed. He staggered to the fuse box table – whipped the lever across – and then started tearing at the red and black wires, snatching them from terminals on the top of the battery. His eyes followed the rest of the nest of wires that led from the fuse box. Without a power source, they were harmless – he knew this – but he tore them from just in case.

Just then the ticking of the timer stopped . . .

He leaned forward onto the table, his chest was pounding. His throat was on fire. He was panting like he'd just done the hundred yard dash. He looked over at Harris and grinned.

'Ruddy hell,' declared Harris. 'You snuffed him out!'

252

Gupta was getting to his feet and looked down at Amrit, the blade protruding from his forehead:

'Good grief,' he said, shaking his head. He clutched his side painfully.

'Right,' announced Drabble, going over to Padmini. 'We need to raise the alarm – and get this battery as far away from this lot as possible . . .'

Epilogue

The Viceroy wore the uniform of the diplomatic service – all navy blue and gold frogging down the front, topped off with a slim black bicorn hat armed with enough goose feathers to give flight to a family of birds. Where there wasn't frogging there was a blue sash and glittering jewels of four or five orders. The Vice-reine wore white and a heavy tiara and silk gloves. In the front row was the Maharaja of Bikaner, Sir Ganga Singh, encrusted with jewels and accompanied among others, including Panikkar.

The Viceroy completed his oration and invited Sir Percival Harris, already dressed in a blue satin cloak with gold collar, to present himself at the podium. Harris obliged, walking a little heavily on his stick – overdoing it a mite, thought Drabble. He knelt before the podium on the purple velvet cushion, then stood, with his head bowed at the neck. The Viceroy solemnly invested him with the star and insignia of a Knight Grand Cross of the most exalted Order of the Star of India, the Raj's greatest honour. Harris stood, with difficulty, and then stepped back before bowing from the neck and walking away. Gupta went up next, and was invested as a Companion of the Order.

The ceremony complete, the Viceroy invited the solemnity of the occasion to be lifted somewhat by a round of applause for the new members of the order – but also for Drabble. The mention of his name caused him to shudder, as did the applause, but he nodded awkwardly at the gazes which unavoidably caught his. The applause faded away and people began to disperse.

Arbuthnot sauntered over and stood by him, watching the gathering in his half-amused manner. 'The Viceroy was rather put out at your refusal of a decoration,' he volunteered. 'So we've arranged a gift for you.'

Drabble, who had been watching Harris shaking hands with the Maharaja at the front, and was half wondering what was being said between them, now turned to Arbuthnot, who added, 'It's a Rolls-Royce Silver Ghost . . .' He smiled. 'We didn't think you'd object. I've ordered you several years' worth of tyres, too – they can be cripplingly expensive. I mean it, you should see what we spend on them.'

Drabble was lost for words.

'Thank you,' he managed at last.

'Don't thank me,' responded Arbuthnot. 'Thank the Viceroy.'

He offered a benign smile.

'May I ask if we know what Sharma-Smith's grand plan was?'

'What, after they'd blown everyone of any significance in India to kingdom come? I'm not sure. I don't think their plan amounted to much more than seeing what would happen.' He sighed. 'Far be it for me to speculate but I expect that given the right circumstances, various reactionary forces may well have presented themselves. Fortunately it never happened.'

Drabble nodded. He understood. The radical right, just like the left, was never too far away.

'Among the younger generation – men like Dundonald – I think there's a minority who are determined to hold on to India, whatever the costs,' Arbuthnot continued. He shook his head. Plainly, he did not have a plan for what to do with them.

'What's to become of Sharma-Smith and Dundonald?'

'We've thrown away the key,' pronounced Arbuthnot. 'The hunt continues for co-conspirators. Despite your concerns, Colonel Pagefield was *not* involved. Oblivious, I think it's fair to say.'

'Better to be safe than sorry.'

'And incidentally, Superintendent Goodlad is clean, despite circumstantial evidence.'

'Despite it all,' said Drabble, but he was pleased. He had some hope for Goodlad: you might not agree with him, in fact, you probably oughtn't, but he was straight, and that was something.

Drabble and Arbuthnot exchanged another glance and then the older man, and slipped away into the crowd. Drabble was left with the cloying feeling that something important had been neglected.

He did not have long to dwell on this omission before Harris came bounding over. They shook hands and Drabble congratulated him heartily. 'So we shall have to call you Sir Sir Harris, from now on? Or knight, knight, perhaps?'

'Double tosh,' sniped Harris, who extended his hand warmly to Doctor Gupta. 'Congratulations, Gupta,' he bellowed. 'Well deserved!'

The doctor's arrival reminded him of what he forgot to ask Arbuthnot.

'Gupta, did you ever hear about what happened to the codicil?'

His expression confirmed Drabble's suspicion.

'Lost for good, this time, I expect, Doctor.'

Drabble looked over at Harris and saw a bleakness on his face – written in the sombre creases around his eyes. His friend was anxious – and his eyes flitted over their shoulders as they talked. He was looking for Padmini. Drabble recognised it immediately. It was as if he had ceased to be happy unless he was in her company. Her apparent absence from the ceremony had, Dabble feared, robbed it of any pleasure for his friend.

'Everything all right?' he asked when Gupta was drawn away by well-wisher.

'The phantom toe's playing up, that's all,' he sniffed. 'They said it would.'

For a newly minted grand knight he looked pretty miserable, thought Drabble. Which was pretty rich. He was about to comment when his friend's features brightened. The lights switched on – and he almost burst past Drabble.

'Padmini,' he erupted, reaching out to take her hand. She curtsied and Harris responded with a bow. They came together again after this, but she was conscious of the company and – Drabble realised – Harris's lack of tact. His eyes were gazed upon her – nothing else visual was working its way to his brain. 'Padmini,' he repeated. 'What's wrong?'

'Darling . . . I wanted to congratulate you,' she turned her head away, but not before Drabble saw a tear loosed from her eye. It shot down her cheek and lodged in the gauze of her veil. He inhaled: she was an exquisite-looking woman. Her skin was like silk stretched over velvet. He had no idea how Harris did it, but he did.

But Drabble could see that this was not to be Harris's day, Knight Grand Cross of the most exalted Order of the Star of India or not. They stepped away from the crowd surrounding them, but Harris's voice carried. It always had since the first day they had met in the dormitory at Lancing all those years before. For all Drabble knew it had carried – probably in the womb.

'Padmini, I have a ticket for you,' he pleaded. 'Come to England with me. We will be married there, properly,' he added tactlessly. She turned her face away again, and gripped his hand. A handkerchief appeared from nowhere, and she dabbed her face.

'Darling,' she declared. 'You know I can't come with you. There is far too much to be done here. India is where I belong.' She indicated the Maharaja and Viceroy, in close conference. 'My uncle cannot reign for ever. Nor will the Viceroys. This is my world, and I need to stay in it, to do what I can to shape its future.'

Harris stood there, his mouth open, tears streaming down his face.

'But . . . but . . . but –'

She collected his hands in hers and pressed them to her breast.

257

'Go back home – back to *your* world,' she said. 'You will always be in my heart, Harris. You will always be my Star of –'

Padmini's voice failed her, and she turned, striding away.

Harris watched her – in her haste she collided with a man looking the other way, but even that she did with grace. A second later she was through the door, and then even her shadow had vanished. Harris's knees felt weak; he inhaled, remembering to breathe . . .

Drabble put his arm around his friend's shoulder. Harris looked over at him, his streaming eyes red from tears, and Drabble's heart filled with love for his friend. Oh, goodness, he thought. Harris had it bad, and this was just the beginning.

THE END

Author's Note

Enemy of the Raj began forming in my mind more than a decade ago when I visited an exhibition. Among the paintings, bejewelled swords, and shining silver Rolls-Royces, was a glass display cabinet containing an astonishingly alive-looking tiger. That's not surprising, since it was a real tiger – albeit one that had been dead for a century or more.

It was there that I learned for the first time about a man called Sir Ganga Singh, the Maharaja of Bikaner (reigned 1887-1943) and a man who plays an important role in this book. I discovered that one of his claims to fame was that he had shot three tigers in five minutes: not an easy task (nor one likely to be repeated) and this led me on a journey. First I bought a 1927 manual on how to shoot tigers and other feline game (panthers are tricky), written by Colonel A. E. Stewart of the 3/10th Baluch Regiment. *Tiger and Other Game: The practical experiences of a soldier shikari in India* is an amazing book; quite awful of course, but in tone of voice and authority, it is offers a peerless masterclass in attitudes of the time towards 'natives' and animals. With Stewart, I learned how to shoot tigers – and panthers and other game too – but also how to think my way into the minds of the ruling class of British India. (On the subject of tiger hunts, there's a minor debt also to Saki, and his short story 'Mrs Packletide's Tiger'.)

In preparation for this story I also read the 1937 biography (more of a hagiography, really) of Sir Ganga Singh by his then foreign secretary, K. N. Panikkar. The Oxford-educated

Panikkar, who also appears in the book, later became prime minister of Bikaner and subsequently, following the independence of India in 1947, represented the country at the UN. Then, after the formation of the Indian Republic in 1950, he served as ambassador to China until 1952, and later still to France. Panikkar's *His Highness The Maharaja Of Bikaner: A Biography*, cemented my interest in Ganga Singh and all that is written about his achievements in *Enemy of the Raj* is derived from this and other historical documentation and my research trip. He was a pioneer in terms of civil engineering but also in terms of civic institutions. He was also a patriot, albeit in the unusual context of British rule in India, and he was a thoroughly good man, even if today we find his ardent sportsmanship distasteful. (He shot something like two hundred tigers in his sporting life.) As described in this story, he went off to fight for the Empire in the Great War, and he was at the peace talks in 1919 and signed the Treaty of Versailles. He really was a statesman on the world stage and counted Lloyd George and Clemenceau among his friends. And as I discovered in a visit to Bikaner while researching this book, he is still rightly an esteemed figure there and its university was recently renamed in his honour.

The Maharaja also saw that things were changing, and was a man with a plan – as alluded to in the story. Of course, the Second World War happened, taking possibly doomed plans for Indian federation with it. It was more devastating and life-changing than anyone could have imagined, and finally tipped the scales on Britain's grip on power in India but also underscored the moral undeniability of national self-determination. Other real life figures brought to life include, liminally, Lord Linlithgow (Viceroy 1936-1943) who did indeed unveil an equestrian statue of the Maharaja to mark his golden jubilee in 1937. The speech he gives in Chapter Ten is based on the report of the event given in Panikkar's biography. One other real individual portrayed in the book is– M. N. Roy, the editor of the weekly, *Independent India*. He is worth a book of his own – having been a committed Marxist and gone to Russia to meet Lenin (he founded the Communist Party of Mexico and of India) he eventually turned his back on Communism and became a radical humanist.

The reading list for *Enemy of the Raj* also included E M Forster's *A Passage to India* (1924), which, of course, is quite, quite brilliant; and *Burmese Days* (1934), by George Orwell. Both expose the hypocrisy of colonialism from a valuable contemporary point of view. Another important source was *Plain Tales from the Raj* (1975), by Charles Allen, based on the first-hand memories of Britons in India. The behaviour of Superintendent Goodlad during the protest on Chandi Chowk in Chapter Two, for instance, was based on a recollection in those pages. Devotees of Kipling might notice faint similarities in the childhood story of Drabble getting lost in the jungles with aspects of the story of *Wee Willie Winkie* (first published 1888). The shooting of the snake in his bedroom as a boy also comes from a story repeated in *Plain Tales from the Raj*.

There is a great deal of nostalgic feeling about Britain's legacy in the Indian subcontinent, and to my mind, not quite enough contrition. That the worst of it was done in the days before we ourselves were as civilised as we are today is relevant. It is also worth remembering that it isn't so very helpful to judge the past by the standards of the present. Nonetheless, even within the light-hearted setting of a piece of entertainment such as a Drabble and Harris novel, I wanted to address the darker side of British rule in India, and in a broader sense, colonialism, and to do something to address the slew of nostalgic versions we are assailed with. It's also worth seeking to understand how it came about and was administered, often by good people just like you and me. In a transparent sense that is the task of Superintendent Goodlad in this story: he is a good man doing bad things. And there would have been many like him. In the 1930s there were in the region of a hundred thousand Britons in India, ruling a landmass populated by well over three hundred million.

One of the chief sins is the racial basis of the hierarchy and exploitation of the Raj. If this story has any purpose aside from entertainment, then reminding people, if they need it, of that would be it. While completing this book I read Abir Mukherjee's first Sam Wyndham detective novel, *A Rising Man* (2016), which is set in 1920s Calcutta, because I was interested to see how another contemporary writer dealt with the racism of the era. I loved the book, though I was surprised at the strength of some of the racial words used, but it gave me confidence to follow suit and not to be afraid to reach for some of the language of the time.

I would like to thank my wife Ashley for supporting me and giving me the time this project needed away from our young boys to whom this book is dedicated. Much of this book was written on the London Underground, commuting to and from work, but the majority of it was completed in evenings and on weekends, and in the corners of family life when I might have been doing more useful things at home. This book also called for a field trip: in April 2019 I spent a long week in India, touring from Delhi through western Rajasthan to Bikaner, seeing the locations used in the story for myself. This trip was made possible by Jonny Bealby and the people at his firm Wild Frontiers and I cannot thank them all enough. On the ground in India, I would like especially to thank my guide in Bikaner, Vijay Singh, but also my wonderful driver for that trip, Amrit. Additional thanks must go to Martin Pugh who taught me the history of Britain in India as an undergraduate more than twenty years ago at Newcastle University. I would also like to thank Jess Whitlum-Cooper at my publisher Headline Accent, and my editor, Greg Rees, who has done superb work helping me craft the final version of this story. Finally, thanks have to go to Sir Ganga Singh himself. I hope this book contributes to reviving his memory in some small way. Sir Walter Lawrence, a prominent civil servant in India during the early part of this reign (he later served as Curzon's private secretary when he was Viceroy), paid a tribute to Ganga Singh at the elegant conclusion of Panikkar's biography in 1937. 'When years hence the story of Bikaner is written,' Lawrence declared, 'it will tell of a great and devoted ruler who allowed no distraction of ambition, pleasure, or sport to interfere with his noble effort to turn his desert state into a country of prosperous peace, ever advancing towards his ideal of congenial and compatible civilisation.' Few would disagree now, I feel.

Alec Marsh
March 2020